JUSTICE VALKYRIE REIKO

JUSTICE VALKYRIE REIKO

❖

TATE BUNCE

TABLE OF
CONTENTS

For Josephine
Edge
and Savanja.

EPISODE 01

ASSIGNMENT EARTH

WITH TEAR-STAINED CHEEKS, the priestess closed the dead child's eyes and covered his angelic face. She gently lowered the frail body toward the base of the altar where the other corpses were bundled in cloth scraps salvaged from the war. She bowed her head. "It's time to rest, little one," she whispered, forcing her overwhelming grief back down her throat.

The temple's double doors flew open, and another priestess clad in bloodstained robes rushed to the altar. "Misa, will the child live?"

"No." Her voice was barely audible. "He has succumbed to his injuries just like the others."

"Damn those demons!"

She stood. "Calm yourself, Ethia. We are still members of the Valkyr Sisterhood, and we must conduct ourselves as such. We are the calm in the center of the storm. The people of Shin Kirin are counting on our example."

"The people? Misa, the people are being taken from us! Our efforts are futile!"

"Faith, Sister!" she snapped.

Ethia clenched her teeth as she gazed at the young bodies stacked on older ones.

"When will it be safe for a burial?"

"Not for some time," she responded without removing her eyes from the dead. "The forces have pushed the demons further east. Rei and Naiomi have joined them in their efforts."

Misa gasped. "What? But I need them here."

"Those two were born fighters, and you know that. When the army pushed further east, they joined them. They said that they would act as spiritual guides while fighting alongside the soldiers."

"Like the Valkyries of legend. And what of the others?"

"Latoria, Vecia, and Contra joined me in assisting the injured. Unfortunately, their numbers have greatly increased."

"Yes, there is only so much we can do." Misa wiped a fresh tear from her face.

Ethia nodded at the corpses. "There are more out there, you know?"

"We are at war."

"Behind those doors, that's not a war. It's genocide!" she shouted. "Those demons won't stop until Volsogun—our *whole* planet—is a smoldering cinder."

"We must maintain our faith!"

"Until what, Misa? Until the Grand Matriarch finally makes her presence known or until there is no Volsogun left?!"

"We must maintain our faith!" she repeated.

"Your belief has always been the strongest. I admired that. I really did. But you see this?" Ethia raised her hands that were crusted with innocent blood. "They believed too."

More tears welled in Misa's eyes. "Return to your duties, Sister."

Ethia kept her further protests to herself and exited the temple, closing the doors behind her.

Misa turned to the stone statue of a woman that was illuminated by a bed of candles at its feet. The figure's arms lifted toward the heavens. "Please..." She fell to the base of the statue. "Please, remember us."

A white glow sheathed the statue, subtle at first but grew in intensity. Misa shielded her eyes as it brightened the entire temple. Daring to get a better look at the light's source, she pushed past her fear, raised her head, and noticed the statue looking down at her. The priestess gasped as the figure offered an affectionate smile and extended her hand.

The floating city of Shin Kirin, the celebrated home of the Justice Valkyries, hovered a mile and a half above Volsogun. Usually, life for the Valkyr Sisterhood was filled with teaching and training, but today was different.

Adorned in a radiant robe encircled by pinpoints of starlight, Grand Valkyrie Misa stood high on a platform before hundreds of women dressed in similar dazzling attire. With an air of nobility about her, she stretched out her arm and pointed at a majestic seven-bladed spear that hung on the marble wall behind her. The audience silenced as she spoke.

"The Oath Immortal. Two thousand years ago, the Abyssians invaded Volsogun and attempted to eradicate her people. Our efforts to fight against the demons proved futile. Our survival chances seemed hopeless. It was then that the Grand Matriarch heard our desperate prayers and came to Volsogun, gracing us with her presence. We were worthy. A pact—The Oath Immortal—was forged between the Grand Matriarch and the Valkyr Sisterhood and was symbolized by the seven-pointed spear, which represents the Grand Valkyrie and her six Ultra Valkyries. We are to preserve life, wherever it might be found, throughout the cosmos.

"Knowing this mission would be full of danger and hardships, the Grand Matriarch endowed the sisterhood with The Guiding Source's power. Only sisters of exceptional ability rise to this daunting challenge, and when they do, it is a reason to celebrate. One of our sisters has successfully met the challenge of the seven tests and has proven herself worthy of becoming a Valkyrie." In her hands, pinpoints of sparkling energy formed and shifted into an intricately designed wreath. "Come forth, Reiko."

The crowd parted as a petite young woman with shoulder-length raven hair and blue eyes made her way to the dais. Standing before the Grand Valkyrie, she bowed.

"Upon this ceremony's completion, you will become a part of the Valkyr Sisterhood's proud heritage of champions. It is with great pleasure that I welcome you into the ranks of the Valkyries. From this moment on, you shall be Justice Valkyrie Reiko." To a chorus of enthusiastic cheers, Grand Valkyrie Misa placed the wreath on Reiko's head.

The energy melted into streams of light that absorbed into the young woman. Her body illuminated a soft glow as euphoric energy washed over her. "I can feel the power flowing within me," she said. "This sensation... It's amazing!"

"Your body is fusing with The Guiding Source. The sensation you feel will soon pass." Misa grinned. "Now, go celebrate this joyous occasion with your sisters. Later this evening, your orientation of what it means to be a Valkyrie will begin. Listen well for your training starts tomorrow."

Reiko beamed. "Do you know of my first assignment? I know I have to complete my year-long Valkyrie training before I go, but may I ask where it will be?"

"Of course. It is a small Class Two planet located in the Sol quadrant called Terra. The inhabitants call it Earth."

Accentuated by the melting sun's fading rays, evening set upon the coastal metropolis of Driven. The Nishimura building stood among a collection of glass and steel towers within the city's center. It served as the home and position of power of Mr. Ryuhei Nishimura, an infamous business tycoon and industrialist. The public knew of his many successful enterprises, but few were aware of his darker endeavors as the leader of a notorious yakuza gang known as Tengu Raid.

Wearing a hakama and a grim expression, Mr. Nishimura stood in what he called his tranquil room, a beautiful area decorated with Japanese art and adorned with lush tapestries. Two tengu-masked henchmen in tailored suits stood at his side.

He watched with hard brown eyes as two more masked henchmen slid the room's doors open and entered, dragging a freshly beaten street punk. They halted before their master and dropped the bruised and bloodied punk between them.

With his remaining strength, the punk struggled to stand on his knees. He saw Nishimura's blurred face through his swollen eyes, but his attention was drawn to the sheathed katana gripped in Nishimura's left hand. Cold fear overshadowed his throbbing pain. He attempted to speak but could only produce a slight croak accompanied by fresh blood, which leaked from his swollen lips.

"As you are aware," Nishimura growled through his gritted teeth, "I have helmed the Tengu Raid for over two decades. Under my guidance, it has become the most feared organization Driven has ever known. A fact, of which, I am very proud."

Finding the punk's lack of focus insulting, one tengu-masked henchman grabbed him by his mohawk and jerked his head upward.

"I did not achieve my empire by cutting corners, taking foolish risks, or employing those who inform the police of our activities."

"Mr. Nishimura..." he choked. "Forgive me, please... I'm sorry."

Nishimura raised the sword before him. "This sacred blade, The Omni-Wing, has been in my family for generations." With a clean, metallic whisper, he freed the beautiful sword from its sheath. "It is a symbol of our power." He glared at his victim as he shifted his posture to an attack stance. "And our rage!"

The Omni-Wing sliced through the punk's neck, sweeping his head from his shoulders.

Nishimura watched in satisfaction as the victim's blood sizzled and dissolved into the blade. "The Omni-Wing accepts your apology. I do not."

He returned the blade to its sheath and handed it to one of his masked henchmen. "Return the blade to its resting place and rid this house of that wretched filth. I will be in my garden, meditating on the day's events. See to it that I am not disturbed."

When Mr. Nishimura was not concocting brilliant heists or drafting kidnapping plots, he could usually be found in the Zen garden on the twenty-fifth floor of his thirty-story building. He spent hours there in undisturbed silence, attempting to commune with ancestral spirits of whom he believed conspired to give him such a vast number of fortunes.

Amid his mind's calm corridors, a faint voice appeared. It muttered at first but then grew in intensity. Once the voice increased its volume enough, it oddly resembled his own. *Hear me, Nishimura. Hear my voice.*

"Who...are you?" he whispered. "An ancestor?"

Listen carefully, Nishimura. I am you from the future, speaking through a psychic link that I cannot maintain for long.

"I am listening."

Our situation is grave. We have lost everything, and our empire lies in ruins!

He gasped. "How can that be?! We have bested every competitor, eliminated every foe, and obtained a plethora of servants!"

All meaningless! The author of our pain comes from beyond the stars.

"The stars?" That claim seemed impossible to Nishimura.

One year from today, a being from another world will arrive and destroy everything we have built. You must prepare for her! She will be indistin-

guishable from any human. Have Dr. Denoda build a physiology scanner to reveal her true nature.

"How do I destroy her?"

The task will be difficult, so you must think radically. The voice grew fainter with each passing word. *Build an army. She must be destroyed!*

The yakuza boss' eyes opened as the voice dissolved. Rising from the garden's center, he held the gaze of a possessed man. "One year."

As Volsogun's sun rose, an enthusiastic Reiko navigated the stone streets of Shin Kirin. She hurried to the city's second tower, commonly regarded as the Tower of Ascent. As she entered, a tall woman, wearing turquoise body armor trimmed in gold, captured her attention with a wave. "Over here, Reiko."

She approached the woman with concern. "I'm not late, am I?"

"No, as a matter a fact, you're early. Like an hour early."

"That's a relief. I didn't want to be late. You're Super Valkyrie Kalkaya, right?"

"You got it. I'll be the one giving you a quick orientation while we make our way to the teleporter. Come on. Follow me."

"More orientation?" Reiko sighed. "I've spent the last year preparing for this day."

"That's the first lesson: there's always more to learn."

She took in her surroundings as she followed Kalkaya down a hall. "I've never been here before. The architecture is beautiful."

"You're quite a ball of nerves. Loosen up." Kalkaya glanced at her with a smile. "I'm sure the people of Terra aren't a bunch of notwhos."

"Oh, I'm not worried about that. I just don't want to screw anything up. You know, it's my first assignment and all."

"Why are you still in a robe? Haven't you chosen a uniform yet?"

"I couldn't make up my mind. I really like red and blue. And a cape. A cape would be neat."

"I can't help you there. Not a cape woman myself." Kalkaya paused and faced the new Justice Valkyrie. "You see this armor? I chose this when I was where you are now and stuck with it. This has been my armor of choice for three hundred years."

"It's magnificent." Reiko admired the intricate designs that she hadn't noticed were etched into the armor before.

"Remember that when you decide on a look, stick with it. That's how the universe will recognize you from every other Valkyrie."

"Do you think I can make Super Valkyrie in three hundred years?"

"It's all about dedication and service. Come on." Kalkaya continued down the corridor. "To tell you the truth, I'm thinking of requesting to be reassigned."

"To where?"

"Shin Kirin security. I've been off-world for far too long. I miss being home."

"Wow. I wonder if I'll ever be like that. You know, later, I mean."

"Maybe. Some Valkyries love it out there, living among the stars. I've had my fill."

"Where are you based now?"

"A nice, quiet world called Sornica."

"The trade hub?"

"That's the one. Because of all the trade that flows through there, they have a powerful security force, which means they don't have much use for a Super Valkyrie." As the two arrived at the end of the hall, Kalkaya opened a door. "I was on my way back, so I was asked to show you to the teleporter."

Reiko's eyes brightened as she entered an expansive room laden with multihued gleaming crystals. "This is the teleporter room?!" she exclaimed.

"Yes, it is. I'll make this quick. As you are aware, all our technology is based on a crystal interface, so it can draw power from The Guiding Source here on Shin Kirin. The crystals make sure your dimensional home, the servo-crystal, and your Valkyrie powers are all fueled by The Guiding Source."

"Right."

Kalkaya nodded to an alcove embedded in the crystal wall. "That is one of several teleporters here on Shin Kirin. When you're ready, it will send you to your dimensional home on Terra."

"So...that's it?" Reiko asked with a puzzled look. "That's your orientation?"

"Pretty much. You've had plenty of briefings during your training, and

I'm sure they already told you quite a bit about your assignment world, correct?"

"Well...yes."

"Your home has a terminal interface that can answer any other questions you may have. And if you need help around the house, just get your servo-crystal to do it. That's what it's there for."

"Oh, okay." She paused. "I just thought..."

Kalkaya offered a reassuring grin. "It will be okay. Get familiar with the planet and take some time to settle in. I spent three months learning about Sornica in my dimensional home before I revealed my presence to the public."

"How did they take it?"

"Not well. Establishing a rapport is paramount; I cannot stress that enough. I wish someone had told me that before I took the plunge. Just remember that communication with the people of your assigned world is just as important as your combat skills."

A beaming smile returned to Reiko's face. "I'll remember." She stepped into the teleporter and waved at the Super Valkyrie. "Thank you."

Kalkaya watched as Reiko faded within a cascade of gleaming light. "Sweet kid. I hope she does well."

With a melodic hum, Reiko materialized within the center of a swirling column of azure light. Once her teleportation was complete, the new Justice Valkyrie found herself within a vast room with walls composed of glistening crystals. On the far wall stood a glass pillar. At its peak, a translucent crystal shard about half a foot tall was docked.

She gasped as she took in her surroundings. "This place is breathtaking. Not to mention much larger than I imagined."

The crystal shard floated up from the pillar and glided toward her. "Welcome to your new home, Justice Valkyrie Reiko!" it stated in a chipper voice. "We are located three hundred feet above the surface of Terra, safely tucked away in your private dimensional home that cannot be detected by any native technology. You can reconstruct the interior to fit your aesthetic tastes at any time. Just say the word."

"I've heard you servo-crystals can be very accommodating." She smiled at her new assistant.

"We take pride in supporting our Valkyries. If you wish to take a tour of your new home, I can bring each room to you for a closer inspection."

"No, thank you. I'll walk." She takes a few steps forward. "Servo-crystal..."

"Yes, Reiko?"

"Since we'll be working together, it seems impersonal to refer to you as servo-crystal. Do you have a name?"

"Hmm... I suppose not. I've never thought about it."

"Let's see... What should I call you?" She gently poked the floating shard. "You have no distinctive features that will help."

"Well, I am rather transparent." The servo-crystal chuckled to itself. "Yes, that's a good one. I learned that one when I was still forming in the Under Caves."

"Maru."

"I'm sorry?"

"From this moment on, you shall be known as Maru."

"Splendid! Maru it is!" The servo-crystal spun in the air with a burst of excitement. "This means that I will have a name all throughout your future career. I'm Maru while you are a Justice Valkyrie, and I'll be Maru when you are a Super Valkyrie and then a Mega Valkyrie. And I will remain Maru when you reach the rank of Ultra Valkyrie. Perhaps one day, you will become the Grand Valkyrie, and I will still be Maru!"

"Grand Valkyrie? Me?" Her jaw dropped. "Slow down. I just arrived here, and I have to take care of a few things before I start the job."

"Such as?"

"For starters, I have to find where everything is in the house."

"A complete tour can be done in moments," Maru confirmed.

"And I still have to decide on a uniform."

"Oh, I see. Any thoughts?"

"A few. And they all involve capes." Reiko looked around the room. "Is there a mirror around here?"

"Say no more."

Her eyes widened as a portion of the wall near her shifted into a large reflective surface. "Wow. You have that much control over this place?"

"Of course! Via the crystal interface, servo-crystals basically are an extension of the house itself."

"That's neat." She turned from side to side as she examined herself before the mirror. "My uniform will have to be bright and flashy. I want to get people's attention, you know?"

"I suppose."

"That's right," she said to her reflection as she stood in a combat stance. "I'm Justice Valkyrie Reiko. Stop villain! I mean business, and you don't want this business because my business is knocking your head in. And business is good."

Maru drifted closer to her. "Who are you speaking to?"

"Come on, Maru. You're ruining the moment! I'm trying to find who I am as a Justice Valkyrie because I want my uniform to reflect that."

"Sorry. My apologies. Please, carry on."

"Who am I kidding? My business right now is to design my uniform, and that might take a while." She looked at her reflection and sighed. "So, in the meantime, Maru, tell me what you've learned about Earth."

Mr. Nishimura stood in quiet repose as he examined the city skyline, washed by the morning sun, through a window in his office, which was located twenty stories from the ground. He had been alone for hours, contemplating the strange woman from the stars who could possibly cement his demise. The time of her arrival was drawing near, and he had to be ready.

His office door thrusted open, breaking his concentration. A younger man dressed in bright clothing with spiked green hair and cumbersome white sunglasses entered.

Recognizing the intruder's reflection in the window, he continued to face the city. "Johnny Run-Time, did you forget how to knock?"

"Sorry, Mr. Nishimura." Johnny grinned. "You know how I love to make an entrance."

"Why are you here? I did not request a meeting."

"I come bearing good news, boss. I got guys all over the city, and they're equipped with Dr. Denoda's bioscanners. If any bipedal non-human pops up on the scene, we'll be ready."

"Are the battle robots online?"

Johnny moved next to Nishimura and joined him in viewing the city below. "Ops checks are good and ready to go. No matter where this alien appears in Driven, our rapid response team will deliver the battle drones within five minutes. After seeing their combat performance firsthand, I almost feel sorry for this chick."

"Anything else?" Nishimura asked with a disapproving glare.

"Nah, boss." With a nod, Johnny made his way to the door. "Later."

Nishimura returned to the skyline. His reflection in the bay window revealed a confident grin.

After spending hours solidifying the concept for her Valkyrie uniform, Reiko continued her creative streak by partnering with Maru to shift her home's architecture around. "There. Maru, what do you think?" She looked in satisfaction at the reconfigured interior. Her new design brought the teleporter and the crystal interface terminal closer to the main entrance.

"Simple yet elegant design with a certain flow about it. I am particularly fond of the lighting: bright but not intrusive with a hint of coloration. Warm and inviting, just like your personality."

"You're sweet."

"Now, you only have forty-four more rooms to go."

"Let's wait on those. For now, I really want to explore my new home away from home."

"Very well. I suppose that if you are to defend Earth, you should get some practical experience with it. Below us is a city called Driven, which has a population of roughly one million. It is situated on an island commonly referred to as the Big Island by the locals."

"Driven? Sounds used. All right then. I'll just fly down and see what it's like."

"Reiko, perhaps I can suggest an alternative."

"Something wrong?"

"Our data indicates that the general population of Driven has rarely seen a flying humanoid and that such event would be quite alarming to them. I'll transport you to a discreet location for the purposes of your investigation. Also, it would be appropriate that when you are more familiar with this planet and its people, you should formally introduce yourself as its new Justice Valkyrie."

"Then fly?"

"Yes. Then fly."

Reiko sighed. "You're right. I was advised to slowly integrate myself into the alien society. I guess my excitement is getting the better of me. It wouldn't be productive to scare the people I'm supposed to protect. Okay then. Just put me down."

"Ahem."

She turned. "What is it now, Maru?"

"Your attire. It does not fit the current cultural trend for a young woman in Driven."

"Are you kidding? My robe will terrify them, too?"

"No. But allow me to come up with something a bit more suitable for the climate and setting." Holographic images of various young women's clothing styles appeared around Reiko. "And, of course, you can choose a variety of colors and variations."

"It all looks pretty basic." With a wave of her hand, Reiko scrolled through a plethora of clothing types. "Let's just go with this." She ceased her search by choosing a casual red shirt, denim shorts, and comfortable trainers.

"As you wish."

Her robe dissipated, rearranged, and solidified into her new selection with a wave of multicolored light. She inspected her new attire in the mirror. "This isn't so bad, I guess."

"Excellent! Now, you can stroll around Driven undetected. Just call when you wish to return. And remember: no flying."

"Okay, okay." She rolled her eyes. "I got it. Just put me down, please."

"Have an engrossing observation!" Maru said cheerfully.

Reiko, sheathed in a shower of brilliant light, materialized in an abandoned alley. A moment after her arrival, she covered her nose. "Oh my! What is that?! The air is heavy here, and it *smells*. It smells like... I don't know what it smells like, but it stinks. I suppose I'll get used to it in time. Grand Valkyrie Misa did say that sacrifices would have to be made."

She stepped out of the alley and onto a sidewalk that lined a bustling intersection. Though comforted by the sun's midmorning rays and the open blue sky that hung above her, her senses were overwhelmed by the hectic pace of human and vehicle traffic.

"I've never seen such loosely structured chaos before," she muttered to herself. "This is strange...and interesting. Look at their faces." She watched the humans as they passed by her without notice. "This chaos is routine to them."

Further down the street from the baffled Reiko, Detective Akeda, clad in a suit, and his oversized, Hawaiian shirt-wearing partner, Detective Appulo, exited their unmarked police unit that was parked on the side of the street.

"Aw, man," Appulo said as he groaned. "Why does the captain always assign us the smallest car in the force?" He stood feet above the car at six foot four. "My legs cramp up every time I ride in this shoebox! It's so small that you'd think it winds up in the back like a kid's toy!" He winced in pain as he stretched out his arms and legs.

Ignoring his partner's complaint, Akeda said, "Hopefully, that witness at Zoltar's Pawn Shop is willing to talk. It would be nice to finally move this robbery case forward."

"Yeah, but what about my poor legs?"

"When we get back to the station, I'll ask the captain for another car."

"Don't bother, partner. I'm taking the bus." Detective Appulo's eyes widened as he fixed his gaze further down the row of shops. "Whoa! Hey, Akeda. You see what I see?!"

Akeda turned toward the storefronts. "No. What is it?"

"A ramen shop is over there! It must be new! Just lookin' at it makes me hungry! Come on, buddy. Let's check it out!"

He snorted. "You know I hate ramen."

With a wide grin, the jolly detective slapped his partner on the back. "That's okay. You can watch me eat!"

"We don't have time for that. We have to follow up on our lead."

"On an empty stomach?! The only thing I'm following up on is that ramen shop. Come on, Akeda! Let's go investigate it instead!"

Conceding to the will of Appulo's stomach, Akeda reluctantly followed his prominent partner.

The baffled Reiko walked further down the street, absorbing as much of her kinetic surroundings as possible. While observing the buildings and businesses within her vicinity, she noticed an unreadable script composed of jumbled words on every sign. "That can't be right," she muttered to herself. *Maru, are you there?* she asked through a telepathic link.

Yes, of course, Reiko, Maru's chipper voice responded. *How may I help?*

You should see this city. It's crazy down here with people going everywhere. I've never seen anything like it before.

Nothing at all like Shin Kirin, I take it.

You've got that right. There's something else, though. The written language down here is weird. I can't make sense of it.

I see. All Justice Valkyries are given the power to universally read, write, and speak all forms of language through The Guiding Source.

Yes, the universal translator, I know. Mine doesn't seem to be working.

Have you tried verbal communication with the inhabitants?

No, not yet. She looked around and saw a middle-aged man walking in her direction, toting plastic grocery bags. *Hold on. I'll test it out.* She beamed at the man as he walked by. "Hello."

"Hi," the man responded without breaking his stride.

Okay, Maru. Successful verbal communication established.

Perhaps you just need more time for The Guiding Source's energy to complete mental assimilation. Some powers take longer than others to activate.

Reiko continued further down the sidewalk. *I guess. You would think that all my powers would work correctly after a year. I hope it doesn't take much longer.*

If it does, just think of it as a window of opportunity to observe this brand-new world that you've been assigned to protect.

It's nice that we're both positive because I always like to... Her sentence trailed off as she stopped in her tracks.

Reiko? What's wrong?

Nothing. I'll talk to you later. She slowly approached a store window as she fixated on a poster that featured a cupcake cartoon character sporting the cheerful face of an adorable cat. "You. Are. So. Cute!" she shrieked. Her euphoria dissolved as she could not decipher the bold words bordering around her newfound love. "Whoever you are, I must have more of you!"

The store's main doors slid open, diverting her focus to a young girl exiting. "Excuse me." She smiled and pointed to the figure on the poster as the girl looked her way. "What is this adorable thing?"

The girl shrugged. "That's CupCake Kitty."

"Thank you," Reiko said as the girl continued on her way. "CupCake Kitty." She smiled at the poster. "You will be mine."

Perched on a rooftop, a Tengu Raid henchman in full body armor gazed over as a chime emitted from his bioscanner. "I don't believe it. This thing works after all." Peering through his high-tech binoculars, he examined the congested city block. He discovered his inhuman quarry with his scanner. He shook his head in disbelief as he activated his commlink. "Johnny, come in. It's me. Tyrone in Foxtrot sector. I have confirmation on the target. I repeat. I have confirmation on the target."

"Are you positive?!" Johnny's voice shared Tyrone's disbelief.

"Yeah, I'm positive! The bioscanner is flashing like a pinball machine, and it's screaming like my ex. It pegged a female as the signal's source."

"Tell me you got a visual."

"Affirmative. The target is about five foot tall, a brunette with Asian features. Honestly, she looks normal to me. You'd think alien invaders would have some sort of height requirement."

"All right, Tyrone. We've got to get serious with this. Call the others and tell them to meet up with you ASAP. The battle drones will arrive on-site in a few minutes, but don't wait for them. Boss man wants this chick dead, so as soon as you get your team together, start the fireworks. You copy?"

"Copy."

Reiko continued her journey through her new world as Johnny's armored attack squad filtered into the street. Upon spotting his quarry, one of the soldiers raised a rocket launcher and fired. The missile screamed over car roofs as it traveled to its intended target, and before she could react, the missile struck its mark.

With a burst of smoke and fire, her body shot through the air, smashing into the glass windows of a jewelry store. Brandishing their weapons in full view of the public, Tyrone's team assembled into an attack formation and closed in on their target. The panicked onlookers scattered from the armed aggressors and scrambled for safety.

Bolting out of the ramen shop with their guns drawn, Akeda and Appulo looked toward the source of the blast.

"What the hell is going on out there?! It sounds like a war zone!" Appulo wiped a trail of broth from his chin.

"Not sure, but I do see fire about half a block down from us!"

"You think it's a gas explosion?"

"It's hard to tell, but the crowd is fleeing. I'll call for the emergency crews."

Within the jewelry store, Reiko stirred, buried under rubble. With the aid of her enhanced strength, she tossed debris layers to the side until she could stand. She took a moment to compose herself. "Why?" she muttered.

She noticed a team of armed men creeping toward her position. Her fists clenched. "Maybe I should ask them, but...as a Justice Valkyrie!" In an instant, a sheath of light encased her body, which dissipated to reveal her red and blue uniform complete with a flowing red cape. She stepped out onto the sidewalk, crossed her arms, and scowled at her attackers. "Would anyone care to explain what just happened?"

One of the lead henchmen aimed his automatic rifle. "Fire!"

With a hammering cadence, a hail of gunfire decimated what remained of the building's interior but bounced off Reiko's body.

"Metal projectiles. Cute." She smirked and engaged her attackers by employing a flurry of well-placed punches at an inhuman speed. Due to her augmented strength, each blow sent her opponents flying out of the ruined building and crashing onto the street in agony. She smiled at the result of her combat prowess. "There. No more trouble from them."

"The trouble just started, bikini girl!" Detective Akeda barked from behind her as he ensnared her wrists with his handcuffs. "I'm Detective Akeda of the Driven Police Department. You and this rabble are all going down to the station with me!"

"And me too! I'm Detective Appulo," Appulo said from beside him. "I'm his partner!"

Distracted by the whirling blades overhead, Reiko spotted a large, twin-bladed helicopter approaching the scene from a distance. "I would love to go to your station, Detective Akeda, but now would not be a good time." She snapped the cuffs and peeled them off her wrists. She handed them back to the stunned detective. "You can have these back."

"Whoa! Did you see that?!" Appulo blurted. "She must work out!"

Akeda looked at the remains of his handcuffs in disbelief. "How did you do that?"

"We can discuss that later," she said. "Now, you two better get a safe distance away. I don't think the operator of that aircraft means well."

Both detectives turned their attention to the helicopter as it hovered in a fixed position over the street.

"What's that chopper doing?!" Appulo said.

The aircraft's side doors slid open. Three hulking metallic figures jumped from the chopper and landed among the collection of empty shell casings littered across the street. With efficient precision, they each surveyed the perimeter and focused on the Justice Valkyrie.

"Target identified!" one of them announced in a booming electronic voice. "Engage!"

Two of the battle robots drew their automatic rifles, which were attached to their backs, in perfect sync. At the same time, the third rushed toward its opponent with menacing, serrated blades that retracted from its forearms.

Determined to keep her attacker's attention, Reiko hovered into the air and flew toward her blade-wielding adversary with an astonishing burst of speed. She ripped its arms from its sockets and drove its own blades deep into its chest. In a blur, she punched the head off her second robotic aggressor and watched as its lifeless body collapsed onto the pavement in a shower of sparks. The remaining combatant skillfully attacked the heroine with its own set of retractable blades. She snapped the weapons with well-placed punches and followed those with a spinning kick through its abdomen, slicing it in two.

She clustered the remains of all three robots into a pile and lifted a vacant, bullet-riddled car over her head. She took to the air above and launched the car downward, triggering a fierce explosion upon impact.

Appulo stood still, bewildered. "Wow! Did you see that?! That was incredible!"

"Yeah, I saw it," Akeda confirmed as he cautiously stepped toward Reiko, who gently landed on the street. "Tell me something. Are you a friend or a foe?"

"Friend. My name is Reiko. I'm a Justice Valkyrie from the planet Volsogun, and I'm here to defend Earth from all threats, internal and external." She took his hand and shook it with a smile. "Pleased to meet you, Detective Akeda."

The detective adjusted his glasses. "If I had another pair of cuffs right now, you would be wearing them."

"This time, I wouldn't take them off."

He blushed. "Huh?"

"Akeda, your face is really red!" Appulo said as he wandered toward the robotic remains and surveyed the melting mound of slag. "Check out what's left of these robots! This is some pretty high-tech stuff. Well...it was some pretty high-tech stuff."

Akeda turned to his partner. "Secure the area as best you can!" He whipped around to where Reiko had stood to find no one. He looked up to the empty cloud-dotted sky. "Reiko."

Soaring over Driven, the heroine gushed. "Technologically primitive planet, check. Smelly air, check. Populace living in structured chaos, check. CupCake Kitty, check. One really cute guy, super check." She laughed. "I think I'm going to like this place called Earth."

Roughly a mile away from the battle-torn street, Johnny Run-Time sat in his mobile command center contained within a nondescript van. He sighed as he replayed the fight footage recorded by his robot soldiers before their violent demise. "Super strength, speed, and flight all nicely wrapped in a bikini." He chuckled as he shook his head. "Nishimura is in over his head. He doesn't know the first thing about Justice Valkyries. But fortunately, I do."

TIME OF VENGEANCE

REIKO FELT TERROR clutch at her heart. Laser bolts from her rifle burned multiple holes through the soldier who stood before her. Color drained from her face as his lifeless body collapsed onto the metal floor with a sickening thud.

"Reiko!" A voice echoed through the corridor. "Reiko, come on. He's dead!"

Her eyes did not move from the dead man until a hand clamped her shoulder. Pulled back to reality, she whipped around to meet the gaze of Tylaia, a fellow Valkyrie initiate.

"You okay?" she asked in a hurried tone.

Shaken, Reiko's voice barely tapped the air. "Yeah."

Halfway down the corridor, a door slid open. A youthful man with gray skin and unkept white hair poked his head out. "Hey, you two! In here! Quickly!"

"Come on." Tylaia took Reiko's hand and hurried through the door, which closed behind them.

"You killed him, didn't you?!" the Sovedin native barked. "We're not even inside Mount Vilrin yet, and you've already alerted the guards!"

"There shouldn't have been a patrol here in the first place!" Tylaia snapped back.

"You and I both know the intelligence my fellow separatists gathered was accurate. We all knew there was a chance the security patrol would vary its pattern."

She looked over toward her quiet partner. "He took her by surprise, and she did what she had to."

The explanation seemed futile to the fuming alien. "We were all relieved when we heard Volsogun was willing to support our cause, but we had no idea we would be given Valkyrie *initiates*!" He pointed at Reiko. "I can tell that one has no combat experience at all! Look at her! She's useless to us now!"

"Back off, Bazan!" Tylaia shouted. "Don't worry about us doing our part! She just needs a moment is all."

"We may not have that." He glared at them until a chime from his communicator diverted his focus. He pushed the respond button and moved away from the Valkyrie initiates.

While he spoke with his fellow separatists, Tylaia turned to her silent comrade. "Hey, are you okay?"

"I killed him..." Reiko whispered without lifting her eyes from the floor.

"This is a revolution. We knew that going in."

"Look at us." She nodded toward the sophisticated body armor that the two wore. "We're supposed to be here to help people. Not be soldiers."

"This is helping the people of Sovedin, Reiko. We're helping them fight for their independence."

Tears welled in her eyes. "I didn't know fighting in a war would be one of the trials."

"Neither did I." Tylaia placed a reassuring hand on her shoulder. "But think of it this way: if we survive, we pass."

Undetected by Earth technology, a large craft crept toward the unsuspecting planet through space. A humanoid with gray skin and cybernetic arms walked through the ship's sliding doors and into its dimly lit bridge. Long white hair surrounded the metallic mask which encompassed his face.

The figure walked toward a bald man with blue skin. He wore a regal tunic topped with an elaborately decorated cape that flowed from his shoulders. The masked man lowered himself to one knee and bowed before his master, who stared at the glowing blue planet through the bridge's expansive windows.

"Have you located your enemy on this planet below?" his master asked.

"I have," the masked man responded in a voice that resembled grinding stones.

"Does your heart still burn with rage at the very thought of her?"

"It does, my master."

"Go and fetch her then."

The masked man's metallic fists clenched. "I shall."

The red and blue clad Reiko basked in the sun's warm afternoon rays as she carelessly soared above Driven Bay. She flew into the clouds, performed an aerial loop, and dove downward. She found an excellent view of the sea below. She pivoted in the air and hovered over the bay's crystal waters to observe the ships and sailboats as they went about their routine.

I never knew I would enjoy flying around the city as much as I do, she said telepathically to Maru.

I can certainly tell, it responded from Reiko's dimensional home. *You spend a lot of time doing it.*

It's just that wonderful feeling of freedom, Maru. She put her gloved hands on her hips and took in a deep breath, tasting the sea air in her lungs. *Even the city's smell isn't as strong up here.*

Speaking of the city, don't you think you have scared the people of Driven enough with your consistent airborne antics? Ever since the robot attack a few days ago, they still have no idea what to make of you. You should hear the things they are saying.

The Justice Valkyrie folded her arms. *What are they saying?*

Well, according to the intelligence I have gathered, they keep mentioning something about a flying pinup girl.

Is that good?

At the moment, I am not sure. I've had quite a difficult time deciphering Earth languages.

How so?

For starters, the people of this planet have a multitude of languages. At my last count, it was over six thousand. I concede that it isn't unusual, but it will still take quite some time to get used to. Especially the evolving slang.

Mr. Nishimura, accompanied by an armed entourage, entered one of his private warehouses tucked away on the edge of the bay. His tech expert, Johnny Run-Time has labored for days to bring one of his visions to life.

He noted the sheer number of gutted computer terminals and other electronic components scattered around as a guard led him to where Johnny worked. Upon seeing the green-haired tech, he made no attempt to hide his disapproval. "I pushed back a meeting and canceled a conference call to be here, so I trust you have something impressive to show me."

Johnny faced his boss with his usual arrogant grin. "Hey, boss. What do you think?" He pointed to twin spire-like metal structures connected to a cumbersome computer terminal via a series of tangled cables.

The revelation of that bizarre structure produced no excitement in Nishimura's voice. "I'm confident you did not request my presence to show off one of your personal projects."

"Yes and no. Remember a few days ago when our battle drones took on the super hottie?"

"Within seconds, her combat skills exceeded my every expectation and turned your robots to scrap. A failed project that cost me handsomely."

"I know it looked bad, but—believe it or not—the robots did their job. They collected valuable combat data on her. We now know that most physical attacks are pointless. Guns, blades, etc. Forget it. And, as we saw firsthand, a well-placed missile will only slow her down."

"Have you discovered a more effective means of attack?"

"Indeed. I did, and you're looking at it."

Nishimura eyed the metal project again. "That pile of junk?"

"Check it out, boss! According to the data, every time she took a hit, her body released a strong energy signature. Every time she delivered some type of punishment, her body released a similar energy signature. Therefore, I am one hundred percent confident that our interstellar sweetheart is an energy-based life-form."

"Interesting."

"This beautiful hunk of junk here is my attempt at developing a dimensional field generator. In theory, this bad boy should create a negative energy space around her to negate her energy powers. Once she's trapped in the field, one bullet is all you'll need to drop her for good."

"An interesting approach."

"Yeah, I thought you'd like that." Johnny turned to his assistants.

"Okay, boys. Clear the area, and let's show the boss what this puppy can do."

Nishimura stood silent as Johnny flipped the control panel's power switch. With a loud wheeze, crackling energy leaped from the spires and joined together to form a large, revolving energy sphere. As it grew, the center turned black and ignited into a whirlpool of liquid fire.

Johnny's excitement turned sour as he read the instrumentation monitor. "What's it doing? It's not supposed to do that!"

With a flare of piercing light, a hole ripped within the spinning flames' circle, creating a tear within the dimensional maelstrom. A seven-foot demon-like creature with a crimson hide and serrated wings stepped through the portal and released a thunderous roar, showing off its knife-like teeth. Without hesitation, it lunged forth and ripped the field generator to pieces with its massive claws.

Nishimura's guards responded with a hail of gunfire, but their efforts proved useless against the creature's natural hide. With an echo of screams and a shower of blood, the beast cut through them like a chainsaw. The triumphant monster shrieked in rage as the last one flew upward, punching a hole through the shielded warehouse roof.

Nishimura watched with wide eyes as the creature disappeared into the blue sky above. "Johnny, would you care to explain what that was?" he asked in an icy tone.

Johnny stirred from the floor and touched the blood that had spattered over his hair. "Sorry, boss." He offered a weak smile. "I think my math was a bit off."

The winged creature tore through the skies and sneered at the activity it witnessed below. It descended and slammed onto a bustling city street, fracturing the pavement under it. Bystanders screamed and fled as the fearsome monster released another bloodcurdling roar, announcing its dreadful presence.

You should see all the water vessels on the sea, Maru. Reiko smiled. *They look like little—*

Uh-oh. Reiko! the apprehensive servo-crystal exclaimed. *A strange energy reading has just come within range of my sensors.*

How strange are we talking?

So strange that it has no business being on this planet! A powerful entity that burns with an otherworldly energy signature has just arrived in Driven. And it looks upset!

Reiko's carefree demeanor faded as she shifted her focus to the Driven skyline. *That doesn't sound good.* She shot through the sky and raced for the heart of the city. In moments, she witnessed a scene of utter chaos as the police struggled to maintain a safe perimeter while terrified citizens scrambled for safety from a rampaging beast.

That thing doesn't look like it's going to stop anytime soon! Maru said.

Then I'll get its attention! The Justice Valkyrie darted down toward the panicked streets and ripped a fire hydrant from the sidewalk as she flew by. Using her momentum, she smashed the beast's face with her improvised weapon, sending the monster skipping across the evacuated street.

The beast traveled a few yards until it caught itself by driving its steel-like claws into the road. It took to its feet with a fearsome cry only to be met by Reiko, who slammed the hydrant into its jaw again. Recovering from the blow faster this time, it responded to her next attack with a devastating punch of its own, sending her sailing over the street and crashing into the front of a savings and loan.

Maru's voice echoed in her head. *Reiko, are you okay?!*

She dislodged herself from a wall and returned to her feet. *Yeah, Maru.* She glanced toward where she last saw the creature. *It's confirmed. That thing is as strong as it looks.*

And ugly.

That too. Hearing a terrifying roar reverberate from neighboring structures, she stepped out of the damaged building.

The creature lifted a car overhead and launched it at her. She sprang into the air, caught the vehicle, and returned it safely to the street. The creature roared. It gripped another car and sent it sailing toward her. Again, she caught the vehicle in flight and placed it down. *This is getting out of hand.*

What do you intend to do?

The city could be torn to pieces if we keep this up. I'll try a nonviolent approach.

Are you sure about that? That thing looks like it's about eight-hundred pounds of violence.

Yes, I'm sure. Reiko glided a few yards from the monster and asserted a defensive posture. "Stop this rampage at once, creature!" she called out. "What is it you want?"

The creature paused and examined its small opponent. With an uncharacteristic smirk, it spoke in a deep, grinding voice. "Hows 'bout a date?"

Dumbfounded, Reiko dropped her clenched fists. "A what?"

"I am Devaston, Conqueror of the Ruined Beyond. Hows 'bout a date?"

"A date?" It took a moment for the unusual request to sink in. "No!"

She glanced over at the pedestrians huddled around the urban battle-field, hiding behind anything they could find. She realized that she had to get her deadly opponent out of the city as soon as possible. With a burst of speed, she drove her clenched fists into the creature's muscular abdomen and bolted toward the horizon. She cut through the cloud-littered sky, and when they were miles away from the city, she drew one fist back. "I—" She slammed her fist into Devaston's face, sending the creature tumbling in the air before her. "Said!" She delivered another devastating punch, forcing him toward a forest. "No!" Her final strike thrust her opponent deep into the forest's floor with a thunderous crash.

As the embedded creature clawed out of the newly formed crater, she landed and readied herself for battle.

"Izzata, maybe?" Devaston smiled, revealing a full array of jagged yellow teeth.

She folded her arms and turned her back to the inhuman suitor. "No."

"Aw, come on. Just one date, sweetums. We were made for each other! You, a beautiful alien to this world, and me, a horror from an abandoned dimension. That's a perfect combination!"

"No, Devaston," she said with more force. "Now stop terrorizing the good people of this planet with your drama!"

"It'll be great! I've got this whole thing planned. Check this out. We'll wreck a small civilization for starters."

"Go home."

"You wanna play it that way, tasty cakes?!" he spat. "Fine! Hows 'bout I burn this entire world to cinders just to show you how furious rejection can make me!"

"You wouldn't."

"Yeah?!" His voice thundered. "And why not?!"

"Because that would make me sad. If you want to impress me, you won't make me sad."

He paused. "I didn't... I just... GGGAAAHHH!" He held his head and stomped his heavy feet. "I can't win! I didn't mean it like that, schnookums. I ain't gonna make you sad! Promise!"

"Then go home and think about what you've done here today."

"Somebody kidnapped me from my dimension. Honest! I admit my anger may have gotten a little out of control."

"You were throwing vehicles!"

"You caught 'em."

Reiko placed one hand on her hip, and the other stabbed a finger toward the sky. "Home! Now!"

"Okay! Fine. You win!" His voice softened. "Can I at least get a smooch before I embark on my long journey, doll face?"

She looked up at the towering creature with a mischievous grin. "Very well. Close your eyes." As he followed her request, she drew back her fist and launched upward, smashing him under his square chin and sending him soaring into the air.

The dimensional monster shrugged as he flew up into space. "Wazzata maybe?"

She watched as Devaston's distant figure enveloped himself in a burning sphere of energy and vanished. The young heroine shook her head as she searched the endless blue for any trace of the monster. "Sicko." Her eyes trained on a faint object moving in the sky. "What's he doing up there?" She watched as a humanoid figure sailed toward Earth at an alarming speed. "That isn't Devaston. It looks...human." Concern gripped her as the figure streaked through the sky. "And he's coming straight for me!"

With his cybernetic fists pulsing with crimson energy, the masked man delivered a tremendous punch. Reiko slammed into the green earth. As she attempted to lift herself up to her feet, a series of vicious energy-charged strikes hit her. She tried to find an opening to trade blows with the mysterious opponent, but his rage-filled attacks overcame her. One final staggering strike sent her crashing to the ground, unconscious.

Arriving on the ship's command bridge, the masked man carried Reiko to a menacing X-shaped machine. Using its magnetically sealed clamps, he bound her wrists and ankles to the device.

Once she was secured, a regal figure drew closer to the bound heroine and smiled. "Excellent job, my servant."

The masked man bowed his head. "It is an honor to serve. Is she too damaged for your purposes?"

"No, no. You have done well. Any damage sustained to the specimen's exterior is of no concern."

Reiko's eyes fluttered as her body stirred. "What?" Her eyes opened, but her vision stayed blurred, limited by her dark surroundings. The steady hum of powered machinery surrounded her.

"You're finally awake, Justice Valkyrie."

Focusing on the voice near her, she witnessed a mysterious blue figure gradually become clearer. "Magdaglia!"

A smug grin crept on the man's face. "Interesting, isn't it? Although we have never met, you have no doubt of who I am. I find that quite flattering."

Anger gripped her. "Your reputation is well known. Not only are you the sworn enemy of the Valkyries, but you are despised by all of Volsogun as well, butcher!"

"Butcher? How vulgar! I simply employ methods of harvesting the bonded energy that flows through your fascinating sisterhood. The price that energy fetches is impressive, to say the least. Of course, I enjoy observing the extraction process, as you will soon discover."

She nodded at the masked man. "Who is your helper?"

"I carefully chose my loyal servant by considering the past you two share."

"Past? You must be as mad as you are evil. I don't recognize him."

"Of course not. He has endured extensive reconstruction since your last meeting. His name is Bazan."

Her mind drifted back to her initiate trial on the planet Sovedin. She, Tylaia, and a company of separatist rebels were to infiltrate a factory. Before they could make it to their target, they came under heavy fire. A bomb sheered the side of a cliff, sending Bazan tumbling into a channel of flowing lava. Reiko had grabbed his hand to save his life, but her grip waned under his and his equipment's weight. He slipped from her hand. His screams echoed in her mind.

"You lie!" Sadness and anger filtered into her voice. "Bazan died. I did what I could to save him."

"Obviously not enough. He told me how his fellow rebels perished because of careless Valkyrie trainees and how it was you who let him fall into the magma."

"No! It wasn't like that at all!"

"So you say. As you suffer, I want you to look deep into his eyes. See the delight he takes in your agony. If you look close enough, you will see that it will match my own."

"Do your worst, monster!" she spat through clenched teeth as she tested the strength of the clamps that held her.

"I intend to." He turned his attention to the extraction machine's control panel.

With a flip of a few switches, a bolt of energy that felt like a thousand cold needles stabbed through her body, forcing her to release an agonizing scream. The hellish extraction machine buzzed as it removed her bonded energy to fill its storage cells.

Carefully monitoring the machine's readings, Magdaglia grinned. "Well done, my dear!" he shouted over her screams. "The energy store is filling up nicely!"

Overwhelming pain coursed through her as her life essence drained. She slipped back toward unconsciousness, but before she drifted into oblivion, a burning sphere of energy materialized onto the bridge with an explosion of light. As the wisping fiery trails dissipated, Devaston's threatening figure revealed himself. The creature's gaze locked on Reiko.

"What is this intrusion?!" Magdaglia screamed. "Bazan, destroy that creature!"

"At once." The cybernetically enhanced Bazan sprang to attack the towering, winged brute.

With a single swipe of his massive hand, Devaston backhanded his masked opponent, sending him crashing into an array of terminals. "Move aside, No Face. I have to clarify somethin'." The dimensional horror stomped up to the Justice Valkyrie's side. "Hey, did you say yes before? I couldn't remember."

She weakly gazed at him and whispered, "Help me."

"That thing is hurtin' you?!" He followed the machine's connections to the control panel with his eyes.

"Stop!" Magdaglia moved in front of the hulking invader. "You'll ruin everything!"

"Out of my way, baldie. I've gotta save my schnookums!"

Devaston slapped Magdaglia aside. He drove his fist into the control panel, which was reduced to a twisted metal heap with a shower of sparks in an instant.

"No!" Magdaglia scrambled back to his feet. "My extractor! Bazan, kill that monster with haste!"

"Yes, master," Bazan said. He turned. "You!" His cyborg fists crackled with energy as he beckoned his enemy. "Show me your power!"

"You're already missing a face," Devaston said. "What else do you want to lose?"

He roared as he ran to engage his enemy. Magdaglia moved to a safe distance as the two combatants fought.

The fatigued Reiko noticed the fractured storage cells. She closed her eyes and concentrated. Taking in a deep breath of the ship's stale recycled air, she opened her crimson gloved hand and drew her stolen energy back into her weakened body. Her body drank deep of the precious power and consumed it within seconds. A familiar euphoric tingle spread through her. Focusing on her newfound strength, she tightened her fists and snapped the magnetic clasps that held her.

While the fight between Devaston and Bazan raged on, the sight of a partially hidden Magdaglia caught her eye. "Oh no you don't." With furious speed, she shot out of the extraction machine, slamming her fist into Magdaglia's face. He crashed against the flaming control terminals. "Despicable monster!"

"Keep away from me!" He spat dark blood as he struggled to return to his feet. "Stay away!"

Reiko, hovering, snatched him up by the neck and delivered another powerful punch, slamming him against the polished bridge floor. Her fist struck his face once again. Blood shot from his mouth.

"In a few moments, I will have fully recovered, and you will feel the full extent of what I can do!" she screamed. "So, answer me, butcher, while you still can speak. Is that truly Bazan?"

With fury in his eyes, a smile lifted across his bloodstained face. "Though my mission has failed, I take satisfaction in knowing that I can still cause you harm by leaving that question unanswered." With that, he pushed a button on the center of his belt, and in an explosion of light, he and the badly beaten Bazan teleported from sight.

"No!" she cried as she grasped the empty space of where her enemy once was.

An uninjured Devaston approached. "Hey. Where did No Face go?"

"Magdaglia teleported away and took his servant with him like a coward." She looked up and offered Devaston a kind smile. "Thank you for your help, Devaston. My name is Reiko."

"So, I did good?"

"Yes. You did good."

"So, hows 'bout a date?" He produced a wide fang-filled grin.

"Okay." She nodded. "Let's hang out and spend the day together, but that destruction business is completely out. Deal?"

"Yeah, okay." He scratched his head. "So, wazzata maybe?"

SPIDERS IN THE SKY

THE SIREN FROM Detective Akeda's unmarked police unit echoed through the humid night air. He and Appulo were in hot pursuit of two armed robbery suspects. They had intended to capture and arrest them earlier, but, unfortunately, the bust didn't go as planned. They slipped away and had now led the two detectives on a chase through Driven's back alleys, and it looked as though the pursuit wasn't going to end anytime soon.

"I can't believe these guys." Appulo sounded genuinely impressed. "They have the nerve to rob a bank in the heart of the financial district. They must have planned that heist for months."

"All the money in the world won't do them any good unless they get away with it," Akeda said.

"Look!" He pointed. "They're turning down that little alley!"

"I see them. They won't get far!" Akeda assured with a steel voice as he swerved his car into the narrow back street.

Within the perpetrator's vehicle, a nervous passenger locked and loaded his pistol while a determined driver focused on negotiating the tight brick corridor before them. "Come on, man! I don't want to get into a shoot-out with the cops! Can't you go any faster?!"

"Shut up and relax, will ya?!" the driver spat. "I know this part of town. There's a parking garage not far from here where we can ditch those cops. All we have to do is make it through this alley!"

A streak of red and blue flew toward the front of the bank robber's car. Reiko landed before the speeding vehicle, drew back her fist, and thrust it into the car's center. Her mighty punch's impact buckled the car's frame, sending both criminals crashing through the windshield and skipping across the pavement.

Akeda screeched his car to a halt, and the two detectives exited.

"That car is trashed!" Appulo said. Noting the smoking remains, he approached it with caution, hoping he wouldn't catch a glimpse of mangled corpses.

As Akeda stepped closer, he noticed the beaming young heroine illuminated by his car's headlights. She lifted both criminals' limp bodies into the air before her.

"Now we know why," he said. "They just met Reiko."

"Good evening, detectives," she said in a cheerful voice.

"Whoa!" Appulo turned to his partner. "How did she get here so fast? We were right behind them!"

Akeda sighed. "Reiko, you can put them down now."

"I'm just trying to help." She gently laid the battered criminals onto the pavement.

"Wow!" Appulo surveyed the devastation sustained by the destroyed getaway car. "Hey, Akeda. She must've punched the car to stop it! You should see the knuckle prints she left on the engine block! She snaps handcuffs like snack chips. Now this?! I gotta find out her workout routine!"

"Knuckle prints. Great. Reiko, you are aware that there are people in the city who are dedicated to stopping guys like these, right? They're called the police, and I'm one of them."

"I know Driven has a wonderful crime-fighting force," she said, "but I'm sure they wouldn't mind if I occasionally assisted them in capturing notwhos like these."

He shrugged. "What's a notwho?"

"It is a term from my world that means a disgraceful individual."

"I've never heard of that one before." Appulo chuckled. "I'll be sure to use it on the new cadets."

"Uh, Reiko..." Akeda adjusted his glasses. "Before I call this in, I wanted to talk to you about something."

The grinning heroine leaned toward the detective. "Yes, Detective Akeda?"

"You realize that the people of this city—and even the whole world—have no idea what to make of you, right?"

She nodded. "I realize."

"My boss, Captain Tower, wanted to speak with you but has no way to contact you. Nobody seems to."

"Communicate with the people of Earth?" She pondered the concept.

"I guess I should have done something about that sooner like I was advised to. Sorry about that. I would love to meet your Tower."

"Captain Tower. Well, at least that's a start." He produced a business card from his suit jacket pocket. "Take this."

"What is it?" She could not believe her good fortune as she gripped the card with both gloved hands.

"It's my business card. The police station's address is on it. If you can, let's meet at nine tomorrow morning on the station's roof. It will draw less attention from the public if we meet up there."

"I'll be there." She gushed. "I promise. Goodbye, Detective Appulo." She waved.

Appulo, still inspecting the vehicle's damage, glanced up. "See you later. Keep working on that right hook."

"I will." She gave him a grin. "Goodbye, Detective Akeda."

"I'll see you tomorrow."

The elated heroine, who attempted to hide her giddy smile, shot into the night sky and flew to her dimensional home.

Within the crystal interior of her hidden abode, Reiko beamed as she triumphantly held Akeda's business card before her.

Maru, hovering from its docking pedestal, turned and drifted toward her. "Welcome home, Reiko. How were the sights and smells of Driven today?"

"He gave me something, Maru! He gave me something!" Reiko pushed her new treasure toward the servo-crystal. "He gave me a card!" Seeming in a different world, she pressed the card to her nose and inhaled.

"Calm yourself, Reiko. You're supposed to be a Justice Valkyrie representing Volsogun and—"

"It smells like him too!"

"Oh my! This is disgraceful behavior! I'm sure you remember your briefing about developing certain affections for planet natives. It never works out. Many Valkyries have fallen into that trap, and they always end with a broken heart or worse."

Reiko transformed her red and blue uniform into a flowing robe with a showering cascade of light. She moved down the hall and toward her room with Maru trailing behind.

There, she stretched across the plush surface of her crystal-encrusted bed. "He won't break my heart," she muttered. "Maru, I would like to be alone if you don't mind."

"As you wish." The servo-crystal floated out of her bedroom. "Goodnight."

"Goodnight." Her mind drifted to happier places as she smiled at her new trophy.

At the appointed time, Reiko coasted through Driven's azure sky and landed on the police station's roof in front of Detective Akeda and a tall, dark-skinned man with broad shoulders, a neatly trimmed mustache, and a stern gaze. She decided that it would be a good first impression if she addressed them in her best professional tone. "Good morning, gentlemen."

Akeda stepped forward. "Captain, this is Reiko. Reiko, this is Captain Tower."

"Good to meet you, sir," she said with a cordial bow.

"You are a difficult person to get a hold of, Ms. Reiko," Tower said.

"Sorry about that. I'm kind of new at this. Defending Earth is my first assignment."

"Assignment? May I ask who gave you this great responsibility?"

"I am a Justice Valkyrie from the planet of Volsogun. After rigorous training, we Valkyries are assigned to defend inhabited worlds. Earth is considered a Class Two planet, so it's a perfect starter world for a novice like myself."

"You're...an alien rookie?"

"I... Well, yes. Does that alarm you?"

"I guess it makes sense considering you can fly. The alien part, I mean." Tower tilted his head. "Excuse me for asking, but how old are you? Eighteen? Nineteen?"

"Age is not really recognized among Valkyries. As long as I can remember, I have appeared just as you see me now."

"I see." Though not satisfied by the answer, he let it go.

"Sir," Akeda interjected. "I think we should get to the matter at hand."

Tower nodded. "There is an issue we would like to ask your assistance with if you're up to it."

"Absolutely," she responded with a warm smile.

"We are dealing with a case that involves a missing plane. A cargo jet to be precise."

Akeda reached into his jacket, produced a small package of documents, and handed them to her.

"Can you read English?" Tower inquired.

"Yes. We Valkyries are gifted with universal translating energy."

"Sounds convenient."

"I must admit that English slang is difficult to keep up with though."

"That won't ever change." Akeda nodded. "That packet you're holding contains the jet's information, the transcript of our last contact, and the flight pattern. While in flight, the jet dropped off the radar. It vanished over the city two days ago. According to its flight pattern, if the jet had crashed, it would have done so within the city limits. The captain wants to offer any assistance he can."

"The situation sounds bizarre," she said. "I expect you already have a plan of action."

"Yes, we do," the captain stated. "Your part is simple. Go to the airport and retrace the jet's flight pattern to the point where it vanished."

"What do you expect me to find up there that your radar could not?"

"At this point, we have no idea, but there has to be something. A four-hundred-and-fifty-ton jet does not simply vanish into thin air."

She dug a picture of the aircraft out of the package. "Oh, yes. This thing is big. What of the pilots? I assume it had pilots."

"Yes," Akeda said. "Two. Their conversation with the control tower sounded like business as usual. Then it broke off." He shrugged.

She gave a quick scan of his documents, stuffed it back into its package, and handed it back to the detective. "Okay. It all seems simple enough."

"Remember, Ms. Reiko, nobody knows what to make of you," Tower warned. "This is a good opportunity to prove to Driven and the rest of the world that you are a trustworthy ally."

"Yes, sir. I won't let you down," she assured. "Detective Akeda, may I have a word in private?"

"Sure," he agreed with a tinge of apparent apprehension. "Excuse us." He followed her to the side of the roof that was farthest from the captain.

She opened her hand to expose a small translucent crystal in her palm. She offered it to the perplexed detective.

"What's this?"

"This crystal will allow you to contact me through a telepathic link. When you wish to use it, just hold the crystal and speak to me in your mind. I'll hear you."

He accepted the shard and held it up to the sunlight. "Wouldn't it be easier if you just gave me your number?"

"I don't own a phone. Besides, there's no room for a phone in my uniform. See?" She lifted her cape and turned around before the detective, who averted his eyes.

"Good point." His bright red face did not leave the tops of his shoes.

"Goodbye, Detective Akeda," she said with an affectionate tone. "I hope to see you soon."

"Uh... Goodbye, Reiko." He still did not lift his eyes. "Good luck."

She bolted upward and vanished into the sky above.

Looking up at the distant fading heroine, Akeda slid the crystal into his pocket.

Captain Tower approached him. "Akeda, is there something between you and Ms. Reiko that I should know about?"

"No, sir," he responded while still watching the sky. "Nothing at all."

With the wind manipulating her scarlet cape, Reiko arrived at Driven City Airport. She hovered in the air while assessing the ill-fated cargo jet's path. "Okay," she said to herself. "The airport is below me, and the jet took off from that eastern runway over there." She narrated her assessment with a pointing finger. "So that means I need to head upward and go west."

With that, she soared up toward a canopy of downy clouds and continued her flight until she arrived at a collection of clouds that resembled towering mountains. She paused and admired the breathtaking scenery around her. "It's so gorgeous up here. Tranquil."

She turned her head toward a glint of light that caught her eye. "That's strange. Clouds don't shine like that." As she got closer, she noticed the light reflect off a large metallic object in the clouds. She gasped. "By the six Ultra Valkyries, that's the cargo jet! How odd..."

As she floated closer, she noticed large silk strands suspended it in the air. In absolute silence, large, translucent spiders, who shared the same colors as their environment, crawled from the adjacent gaseous layers.

"What are these creatures?!"

The monsters launched their webs, ensnaring her with their sticky projectiles. Even with her incredible strength, she found herself failing to break free from the thick strands. She attempted to fly upward, but the webs tangled her further. The more she struggled, the stronger the bonds became until motion was no longer an option. One of the spiders gathered up their fresh prey and spun her in a circle until the webs wrapped her in a tight bundle. Once she was secured, the creature held its prey before its mouth and extended its enormous fangs, which dripped with fresh saliva.

"That's enough," a lazy, aristocratic voice rang out. "We don't want to be rude to our guest after all, now do we?"

The spider dropped the bound heroine on a blanket of clouds and returned to hide within the vaporous folds. The other spiders followed suit. With a wave of a stranger's glowing hand, Reiko's web prison slashed open and folded outward. She lifted her head and widened her eyes at her rescuer's odd appearance: a cat with piercing emerald eyes stood like a man dressed in a finely crafted suit. His right paw gripped a walking cane with a golden tiger's head at the top. "As you can no doubt tell," the creature said with a grin, "everything is not as it seems."

The weakened Valkyrie struggled to stand before the sharp-dressed cat with her aching muscles. "Apparently so. Why is a cat walking among the clouds?"

"You, young lady, are speaking with one of the legends of the ages," he said with a smooth voice. "But you may refer to me as the Gentleman Cat."

"I'm Reiko. You keep strange company for a well-mannered cat."

"Oh, the spiders? Yes, that is a bit of a problem that we both now share, and that is why I wished to spare your life."

"And I thought you were just being a gentleman," she responded cheekily.

"Oh, you're quite a charmer. That might excuse your provocative attire. Though the situation in which we find ourselves may seem dire, I'm sure we can assist one another. You see, like you, I too am a prisoner of the spiders."

"Then how could you command them?"

"Benefits of a fragile arrangement," he stated with a purr. "Some time ago, I summoned them from the Elemental Plane of Air itself to make their home here among this realm's clouds."

"For what purpose?"

"An arrangement. The spiders would capture aircrafts in flight while I get whatever treasures are contained within."

"That doesn't sound like much of an arrangement. You get all the benefits."

"Not at all. I get the treasure, and they get to dine on any live prey they find onboard."

"That's horrid!" Reiko said with panic in her voice. "Are the pilots of that tangled cargo jet still alive?"

"For the moment. They have been most useful in offering information concerning future flights."

"That's...some relief, I suppose. But something isn't right if you're a prisoner like me. What went wrong with your arrangement?"

"It was the spider queen, you see. When she first arrived in this realm with her followers, she was much more cooperative with my scheme. But recently, she has become...difficult."

"She finally realized you were using them, didn't she?"

"Barbaric arachnid!" the cat spat. "Now, I am to remain her prisoner, so I can maintain the portal with my magic."

"Magic is your source of power?"

"Give an ear. Generations ago, I was a beggar child on the streets of Cairo," the cat explained with a sly grin. "I stole a decorative lamp from a curious shop, and much to my surprise later that night, mystical smoke billowed from the lamp. Within the smoke, a catlike creature that resembled a man formed. Before my eyes, I witnessed a legendary djinn. He offered to grant me a wish, and being the cunning young man I was, I responded that I wished to be like him." The Gentleman Cat looked toward the infinite sky. "For over a thousand years, I have enjoyed almost limitless power."

"Almost limitless? What limits you?"

"Unfortunately, the djinn who granted me my powers was more cunning than I. Along with his appearance and magic, he also gave me a home like his: a majestic castle that stands in an oasis far beyond humans' reaching fingers."

"A home away from others? Sounds ideal for a cat."

"If it were complete. You see, the castle is an abstract three-dimensional blueprint formed by magic. The more I steal, the more the castle fills in. It will become tangible once I steal enough, and I will finally possess it in all its glory."

"You've been at this for over a thousand years, and you haven't finished your dream home?"

"For every floor or wing I complete, the castle expands and becomes even more majestic."

"An unattainable treasure." She smiled at the cat's ironic predicament. "You're being punished. The djinn trapped you, using your own greed."

"He did nothing of the kind!" Rage filled the cat's voice once more. "I will complete the castle! It will be mine! Mine! I deserve it!"

"You certainly do."

The Gentleman Cat took a moment to compose himself. His voice returned to its usual silkiness. "Here's what I'm offering. You help me get the spider queen through the portal, and I'll close it off forever. Sustaining its connection to this realm has drained most of my magic, so I can't do it by myself."

"And in return for my help?"

"You get your precious pilots, and the spiders will be gone from this world. As for myself, I get my freedom from that troublesome queen, and I leave with the jet and all it contains."

"You plan on stealing a whole jet?"

"Of course not, you simple child. I'll be acquiring its treasure. You see, the more the treasure is worth, the more the castle fills in."

"Doesn't seem like there are too many options. Okay. It's a deal, kitty cat."

"Would you kindly refrain from referring to me as that? It's the Gentleman Cat, if you please."

Reiko removed the remaining strands of webbing that stuck to her cape. "Before we do anything, I want to check on the pilots. I'll be right back."

"Compassionate hearts make me nauseous." The cat rolled his eyes and sighed. "Make it quick."

Watching her unpredictable surroundings, she made a brief flight to the jet's door and entered. Among the rows of passenger seats, she saw the two captive pilots secured in a thick coat of webbing. "Are you two okay?"

One turned his neck in the direction of her voice. "I'm Captain Ralph Cullen and... Wait a minute. Aren't you that flying pinup girl who fought those mechanical soldiers in downtown Driven?"

She ignored him. "I'm Justice Valkyrie Reiko, and I'm going to get you two safely home, but first, I have to deal with a spider problem."

"The spiders..." The copilot sputtered. "It's like they came out of nowhere. When they showed up, the jet's instruments just went dead. We couldn't contact anyone!"

"The jet...lost power? I had suspected it was the handiwork of the kitty's magic."

Cullen gasped. "Kitty magic?! Look, I don't care how you do it. Just get us out of here. Please!"

"I promise." She smiled. "Just...stick around." With a muted giggle, she soared from the aircraft and landed on the clouds near the impatient cat. "They're shaken but okay."

"I'm so relieved." The Gentleman Cat made no attempt to hide his sarcasm.

"For being a gentleman, you really could work on your manners. Kitty."

"While you wasted time with those humans, your movements did not go unnoticed. I certainly hope your strength has returned."

She scanned the clouds and noticed several elemental spiders crawling from the thick, gaseous perimeter. Her eyes fixed on another creature further in the distance. The queen's fierce-looking appearance overshadowed the spiders in size.

"You knew they would attack as soon as I checked on the pilots, didn't you?"

"They can feel the slightest movements within the clouds like a common spider does with its own web."

"Okay. I can do this," she said in an attempt to hide her insecurity. "I just have to make sure their silk doesn't touch me, and I'll be fine. I suppose you'll watch the fight from here."

"This is a comfortable distance, I think. The portal is further behind the spider queen. Large shining hole in the fabric of reality. You can't miss it. Drive her into it, and her subjects will blindly follow. They're loyal like that."

"All right, kitty. Here I go!" She bolted for the jet's left wing and tore off its outer engine. Skillfully dodging sprays of webbing, she moved close to her spider opponents and batted them out of her path, using the jet engine.

The Air Spider Queen launched herself into the air to take Reiko by surprise. However, utilizing her superior speed, she smashed the queen with such force that the engine shattered against the queen's exoskeleton, sending its casing and blades scattering through the air. She denied the queen any combat advantage as she unleashed a barrage of staggering punches. With a final mighty strike, she sent the queen sailing toward the elemental portal's glowing entrance. Before she fell through, she drove all eight of her legs into the portal's vaporous edge.

Reiko landed on a bed of clouds and steadied herself. "Oh no!" She watched the subordinate spiders rush to their queen's aid. "With them in the way, I can't move her. Well, I never thought I would have to use this so soon, but there isn't another way." She closed her eyes, steadied her breath, and stretched her arms out before her. She channeled her energy into her hands until they burned with power. Her eyes opened. "Valkyrie Flare!" A crackling beam fired from her hands and into the spider queen. The energy projectile's impact burned away the surrounding clouds and blasted the creature back through the portal. The other spiders dove into the opening to tend to their injured queen in an instant.

The Gentleman Cat grinned as he casually made his way to her. "Not bad, I suppose. Still, a bit brutish for my taste. Also, you damaged my treasure. That wasn't a part of the bargain."

"Close the portal, kitty!" she huffed with bated breath, shaken from such an enormous output of power.

"Easily." With a wave of his paw, a gleaming aura surrounded the portal, shrinking it.

Faster than a blink, she snatched the mischievous cat by his collar and lifted him into the air. "This isn't a part of the bargain either!"

"What do you think you're doing?!" he shrieked with wide eyes. "How dare you handle me in this brutish manner!"

"The djinn punished you for being greedy; I'm punishing you for starting this trouble. You're a bad kitty!" With that, she tossed the Gentleman Cat through the elemental portal a moment before it sealed and faded from existence. "Don't worry." She smirked. "I'm sure you'll find your way back."

Through an opening in the cloud floor, she saw patches of the world illuminated by filtered golden rays. The planet below looked so calm, peaceful.

"There is so much wonder and beauty to preserve. Captain Tower is right. I have to take my responsibilities seriously for this planet and its people." She took in a deep breath and exhaled. "Okay, Earth. I'm ready now. It's time you meet your new protector."

MEMORIES CAUSE PAIN

I *sn't CupCake Kitty just adorable, Maru?* Reiko telepathically exclaimed as she levitated in front of a highway billboard. An announcement of the new CupCake Kitty television series in bold, child-friendly colors splashed across its surface.

Charming, Maru responded dryly.

She has a cute little friend with her. He's a duck called Daffy Quacky! You should see him. He has a plump little chunky belly!

Quite. I hate to interfere with the admiration of an obsessed CupCake Kitty fan, but don't you have more pressing matters to attend to this morning?

Yes, but I'm such a nervous wreck. I needed to see something cute to curb my anxiety.

You will do fine. Just think of how much trouble Captain Tower went through to coordinate with the city's leaders to get you this press conference. This is exactly what you need to announce your presence to your assignment world.

Reiko sighed. *Yes, you're right. Protecting the people of Earth should be my sole focus. Okay. I'm on my way to the city hall.*

Very good.

After I stare at this picture a bit longer. I can't help myself, Maru! I've been captured by CupCake Kitty's cuteness.

A cloaked spaceship hovered over the heart of Driven. Its lone cyborg pilot, Memories Cause Pain, stood by a holographic map of the city. Washed by his ship's dim lighting, MCP poured over the map to familiarize himself with the urban terrain below. Once satisfied, he initiated a bioscan. He suspected the results: his quarry moved within the city's confines. He collected his rifle that equaled almost half his towering height and moved to the ship's teleportation pad.

"The quarry isn't far. Computer, load the teleportation sequence."

At his command, MCP dematerialized into a flash of radiant light.

From the comfort of his office, Mr. Nishimura held a grave expression as he watched the live press conference conducted on the city hall's steps. The mayor welcomed Justice Valkyrie Reiko to Driven and to the world. Anger swelled up inside him. The admiring crowd roared and clapped for their new alien guardian. His fists tightened.

Johnny Run-Time strolled into the room and plopped himself onto a leather couch. "I can't believe you're watching that garbage, boss. If you're going to rot your brain by watching TV, there are better shows."

"They are falling for her feckless charms. How could they be so foolish?"

"Two reasons. One: she's the media's new darling, and she's really easy on the eyes. That body of hers is smoking hot."

His statement earned a stern glare from his displeased boss.

"And, of course, she's got to die and all that."

"Now that she exists in the public eye, her demise will require more subtlety."

"You will be pleased to know that all the evidence concerning the robot soldiers magically disappeared, and the inquiries about the flying demon have all been hushed up. It's a good thing you own half the politicians and cops in this city. See, that's a testament of a solid investment."

"Since her purpose in this world is to destroy everything that I have built, she may rally the city against me," Nishimura said. "This situation begs a new strategy."

"I have some ideas... Been working on some angles."

"Then continue." His hateful glare pierced Reiko's TV image. "Your blood will be mine."

As the day crept toward the evening, Detective Akeda traveled along a congested downtown street and toward a quaint coffee shop complete with a scenic patio. An attractive blonde woman dressed in business attire sat on the terrace. She waved at him in hopes of capturing his attention.

Returning a brief wave back, he smiled and joined her at the table. "I hope I didn't keep you waiting long."

"No, it's fine. How have you been?"

"It seems like it's been forever since we've seen each other, but to answer your question, busy. The arrival of our new alien guardian has taken the city by storm."

"I bet it's total chaos at city hall."

"At the moment, the mayor and the commissioner have no idea how to handle the situation, so they're in panic mode. The press isn't helping matters either, and modern media is no better than tabloid trash."

"I can see why everybody is up in arms. Of all the aliens out there in the universe, we had to get a girl in a bikini."

"Yeah." He nodded. "I was surprised when you said you wanted to meet here. Our anniversary isn't for another three months."

"I wanted to tell you in person that I accepted the firm's job offer."

"Congratulations, Lillian. You've been dreaming about that job for a long time. It's going to be quite a change for us."

"Yes, it will." Her warm smile dissolved. "The original position they offered was filled, so they offered me a better one, and I accepted."

"Sounds perfect. Why the long face?"

"It's in New York."

It took a moment for her words to sink in. "New York? You mean...you're leaving Driven?"

"This is something I've always wanted, and this is my opportunity to start over in a new job and a new environment. This isn't easy for me to say, but I want to start over...alone."

Akeda looked down at her left hand. "You're not wearing your engagement ring." His heart sank. "Is there someone else?"

"It's not like that, Daniel," she said with empty words. "I just feel like I have to start over, you know? Without Driven. Without..."

"Me."

"Please tell me you understand."

From the sidewalk, a man in a tailored suit approached her. "Are you ready, babe? Let's not be late for the meeting; you know how the boss gets. Oh, and don't worry about booking your flight. I had my secretary arrange everything."

Lillian's tone turned sharp. "Chad, could you wait for me in the car, please? I'll only be a moment."

"Don't bother," Akeda said in a dark voice. He stood. "Goodbye, Lillian. I hope you find what you're looking for."

Her face softened. "Daniel. I thought it would give us both closure to end where we first met." She stood and offered her engagement ring to the detective, who slowly took it from her hand. "I'm sorry. It took me a long time to realize it, but our relationship just wasn't what I wanted."

With a brief glance, he left the patio. "That was him? The cop?" he heard Chad say as he left. "You said you ended it weeks ago."

"Let's go," she said.

Akeda stuffed the ring into his pocket and wandered down the street in hopes of coming to terms with his chaotic emotions. He turned down an alleyway to escape the intrusive crowd and persistent street noise. Once he was hidden from the street's view, he paused his trek and leaned against a building wall. He drew in a deep breath and rubbed the fresh tears from his eyes.

Movement shuffled above him. He adjusted his glasses and looked up. A creature—that looked like a bizarre mix between a lizard and spider— crept down the wall toward him. Without hesitation, he bolted further into the alley. The creature moved swiftly along the building walls until it could pounce on its evading prey. The beast sprang toward the detective, who rolled out of the way. Standing on one knee, he drew his pistol and emptied the clip into the creature's face and torso. The attack only succeeded in enraging the weird assailant as it released a furious shriek.

Akeda reached into his pocket and grasped the crystal Reiko gave him not long ago. "Reiko, I hope you can find my location on this thing!" he shouted. "I'm being attacked by a monster! I need assistance now!"

The beast hurled itself at him again but was shot by a powerful energy blast. It slammed against an alley wall and crumpled to the pavement. Its six legs folded inward.

He turned. His eyes widened as he realized the blast came from a tall figure dressed in black metallic armor. He noted the massive rifle that the figure carried. "Who are you, and what's going on here?!"

"Out of the way!" the intruder barked.

The monster lifted itself and sprayed a jet of green liquid toward the cyborg, who, with surprising speed, dodged the attack. The stream hit Akeda, and within moments, his skin turned bright red as his consciousness slipped away.

From a distance, the approaching Reiko witnessed the detective collapse. "Oh no..." She accelerated and sent a fist into the tall figure, embedding him into the side of a building.

Taking advantage of the confusion, the monster hurled itself toward Reiko. She punched the beast and sent it into the sky. She darted above it and, with one drawn-back fist, hammed it into the pavement below. A hideous crunch echoed throughout the alley as the monster's bones snapped on impact. Landing near the monster's corpse, she noticed that her other opponent had returned to his feet with his rifle ready. Ignoring the cyborg, she rushed to Akeda's side.

"It's okay. I'm here." She cradled him in her arms.

"Uhhh..." he groaned with labored breathing.

One of her hands balled into a fist. She turned toward the cyborg. "What did you do to him?!"

The cyborg inspected the damage inflicted upon the monster's lifeless body. "Nothing. He was hit by the xygrel's venom."

"Xygrel venom will kill him in a matter of minutes. This world has no medical facility to treat a venom that potent. Do you have anything that could save him?"

"Yes," the cyborg said with an electronic hiss. "But why should I?"

"I am a Justice Valkyrie from Volsogun, and I am holding you personally responsible if this man dies. Now hurry!"

"Move away from him." The cyborg launched four metallic disks from his right armguard. The thin projectiles placed themselves on each side of the detective. Once all disks were in place, they emitted a series of connecting beams that formed a radiant barrier.

Reiko's eyes widened. "A portable stasis field?"

"His vital signs will remain stable, and the venom will stay at a standstill. Power will drain from the units in three Terran days. I intended on using it on the xygrel."

"You were hunting that thing?"

"That's what I do. I'm a bounty hunter known as Memories Cause Pain."

"I've heard of you. You're the second most notorious hunter in the known systems. You're also supposed to be as wicked as those you hunt."

"The human is stable. Satisfied?"

"Akeda is far from safe. That stasis field only bought him three more days. As long as the poison remains in his system, he will die." She momentarily closed her eyes and established contact with Maru. *Maru, check and see if there are any medical crafts or stations within the Sol quadrant.*

Very well. Give me a moment... There is...a Turexian medi-craft, the Tor-Dal-Zah, is in stationary orbit near Mars.

She sighed. *Great! Thank you.*

You sound concerned. What's wrong?

I'll talk to you later. The heroine canceled her telepathic communication and returned her attention to the bounty hunter. "I assume you have a ship."

"Why?"

"There's a Turexian medi-craft near Earth. We can take him there."

"Don't you have your own transport?"

"We Justice Valkyries generate an energy field around ourselves that allow us to travel throughout the cosmos without the aid of a craft, but that ability does not extend to passengers. Now please. Let's hurry."

The reluctant bounty hunter activated his ship's internal remote control and teleported them and himself into the craft. Once inside, he took to the flight controls and set a course for the Turexian ship.

Reiko noticed a holding cell, complete with manacles, situated behind the pilot's seat.

"This ship's interior is ghastly as it is depressing. Suits you, actually."

Ignoring her commentary, he piloted his cloaked spacecraft over the city. "We'll make this quick. I'm going to activate the hyperdrive." With that, his ship burst through the clouds and shot into space.

MCP's ship docked on the *Tor-Dal-Zah*, a massive vessel that extended about a mile with towing spires rising from its center. Once MCP and Reiko disembarked the ship, four Turexians garbed in clean, white vestments approached. The bald, slender aliens greeted their guests with cordial bows.

One of them stepped forward and spoke in a soothing voice. "Greetings, travelers. I am Morvandes, a species relations specialist. Welcome to the *Tor-Dal-Zah*. Please remember that this vessel is protected under the Terran Magnera Agreement. Violence of any kind will be considered a violation of intergalactic law."

"Of course," Reiko responded with a sweet smile. "Thank you for your hospitality. I am Justice Valkyrie Reiko, and this is—"

"Just get on with it," MCP said, glaring at her.

Disregarding his rudeness, she returned her attention to her alien hosts. "We have brought a human who desperately requires medical treatment."

"What is the nature of his ailment?" Morvandes asked.

Her tone turned grave. "He has been poisoned with xygrel venom."

"Very well. The human will be transported to the medical bay at once." The Turexian turned to his fellows and gave commands to aid the afflicted human.

Reiko watched as a summoned medical staff moved with robotic precision as they collected Akeda from MCP's ship and placed him on a hovering medical table. "Thank you for your help, MCP. I'll stay here with Akeda until he's better. When he recovers, I'll borrow one of their remote vessels to return him to Earth. I suppose you'll be on your way."

"There's something I have to do before I leave. When you're through with the human, I need to speak with you. Meet me back at my ship."

"Okay." She nodded. "I'll be there as soon as I can."

She followed the team of Turexians into a large, sophisticated room with a series of tall exo-suits lining the walls. A few members of the staff prepped one of the suits for use.

"Wow!" She gasped. "I've heard of those healing suits. They're supposed to be the height of your race's medical technology, aren't they?"

"You have heard correctly, Justice Valkyrie," a Turexian doctor confirmed with a grin. "Once a patient is sealed within its airtight frame, the mobile treatment unit can heal a vast array of ailments and conditions."

"I hope xygrel venom is among those medical treatments."

"Of course. We Turexians are one of the few healers in the galaxy with the capability of dealing with such a strong toxin."

The medical team disabled Akeda's stasis field. They placed him upright into the prepared exo-suit and sealed it closed.

"How long does the treatment normally take?" she asked.

"Twenty-four standard hours are usually required to fully purge the venom." The doctor shrugged. "Since the patient is human, I estimate about twenty-eight. Some species require a longer time to recover than others."

"Of course. Will he remain unconscious during the procedure?"

"Yes. It is standard practice for patients to remain unaware of their time within a treatment unit. It eliminates the possibility of a patient becoming fearful or hostile during the process."

"Understandable. Akeda isn't very aware of other sentient life-forms other than his own people and...me. It would be best if I were present when he recovers."

The doctor nodded. "As you wish. Justice Valkyrie, will there be anything else?"

"No, doctor. You have been most helpful. I cannot thank you enough." She bowed and made her way back to the docking bay. While in transit, she reestablished her mental link with Maru. *I'm currently on the Turexian medi-craft. You should see this place. It's impressive. The Turexians certainly live up to their reputation.*

Are you injured? Maru asked.

No, I had to bring Detective Akeda here. He was poisoned by a xygrel. He'll be here for the next day or so.

I see. Wait. No, I don't. Did you say a xygrel? What was a xygrel doing on Earth?

That's a good question. Sometimes, they travel on asteroids. Maybe that's how?

Hideous beasts. All of them. I trust it isn't running around in Driven.

No. It's as dead as disco, Reiko said.

Dead as what?

It's a term I read on a sign while flying through downtown. I suppose it's a common Earth phrase.

Disco. I shall have to look that up. I'll see you when you return.

Okay. Bye. Reiko returned to the landing bay and saw MCP standing by his ship with his arms crossed. "Akeda is going to survive," she chirped. "Thank you again for your help."

MCP pointed his right arm at her and fired a clamp from his arm-guard. It secured itself around her neck. A sensation of weakness overcame her as she dropped to her knees. He removed a pair of metal bands from his belt and secured them to her wrists.

She gasped. "What did you do to me?"

"It's a power dampener calibrated for energy-based life-forms like yourself. You are now no stronger than a standard humanoid."

"Why...?"

He produced a chain and magnetically attached it to the collar. He jerked her upward. "When you terminated the xygrel, you cost me big! While you wasted time with the Turexians, I arranged another sale, and this time, I will deliver my quarry without fail."

"Deliver me... Where?" She struggled to remove the clasp fastened around her neck in vain.

"The slave mines of Menteraz."

Hours later, MCP's ship broke through the turbulent atmosphere that surrounded the tropical planet of Menteraz. Reiko sat on a bench in the cage behind him. Manacles fastened her arms above her while a blindfold obstructed her vision.

Once the ship was cleared to land, it settled on a platform near a tall pyramid-like temple. A party of eight armed soldiers led by two military officers dressed in blood-red uniforms with service hats and polished knee-high boots excited the temple as if on cue. The group approached MCP as he stepped out of the ship, pulling Reiko in tow by the chain. Colonel Rask and Captain Torber paused upon seeing the caped heroine.

The colonel gave the cyborg a disapproving look. "When Captain Torber informed me that you wished to alter our arrangement, I became concerned. I hired you to capture a xygrel for experimentation, and you bring me a girl instead? If I wanted more slaves to work in the mines, I would take them from the local population."

"This is a once in a lifetime purchase, Colonel." MCP's tone remained no less businesslike. "She's a Justice Valkyrie. Your people can verify her nature."

"You captured a Justice Valkyrie?" he asked with a smirk.

"She is subdued with a power inhibitor. Thirty million. Agree, or I find another buyer."

"I see." Rask moved closer to Reiko to get a better look. "She certainly wears their ostentatious uniform." He circled the bound heroine and noticed her wrists tightly fastened behind her. "Agreed. You will have your money upon confirmation of her identity." He turned to his subordinate. "Captain Torber, take the girl to your office and affirm her biological status. I will join you shortly."

The youthful, fair-haired captain nodded. "Very well, sir."

MCP handed Reiko's chain to the captain, who led her into the pyramid-shaped temple.

"You have done an invaluable service for our cause, MCP," Rask said as he watched the captain and the captive disappear within the temple. "But I believe you can offer us more."

With a tip of the colonel's finger, all eight red-clad soldiers opened fire on the bounty hunter. A multitude of devastating energy blasts bombarded MCP. MCP did not cease fighting until he collapsed onto the landing platform.

Rask knelt by his stunned opponent. "The electromagnetic bolts should confuse your famous armor long enough for you to be secured." He rose and turned to his soldiers. "Collect the prisoner and follow me."

The soldiers combined their strength to lift MCP and followed their colonel.

After leading his prisoner through a network of stone corridors, Captain Torber entered his sizable office that once served as a ceremonial chamber. He positioned Reiko in the center of the room and released the chain. "Stand there and do not move."

She noted that his authoritative voice did not hold the underlying harshness as his superior.

He collected a small readout device from his desk and held it near her heart. Within seconds, it completed a full bioscan of the Valkyrie's anatomy. "Extraordinary... Your biological readings are quite exceptional. You truly are a Volsogun Valkyrie."

Some distance away, MCP tightened a hand into a fist as Rask's soldiers dragged him into an improvised detention unit located on the temple's ground floor.

The colonel watched as they employed a series of large metal chains to restrain the bounty hunter to a stone wall. "Excellent." He nodded as they finished. "I want two guards no less than fifteen feet from the prisoner at all times. Another two will stand guard outside his cell. See to it."

Rask's soldiers moved into their positions.

MCP's armor's internal systems began rebooting quietly. "You should kill me now while you have the chance," he hissed.

"General Gore wishes to expand our noble army to the Seta quadrant," Rask explained. "To gain a foothold there, I secured a deal with the Haznivites. I don't know what you did to make them hate you so much, but they are more than willing to support our war effort in exchange for your blood. This isn't personal. This is business. A man in your trade should appreciate that."

"When the time comes, I'll crush your neck under my boot."

"Wag your tongue well, bounty hunter," the colonel spat through gritted teeth. "Don't think I won't deliver you with your limbs removed! As long as you remain in my custody, you will do well to be silent!"

Reiko remained still in the center of Torber's office as he viewed an informational update from his office's terminal.

"Interesting," he said. "It seems that the colonel has arrested MCP. I wonder what for."

"May I make a request?" she asked in a dull voice.

"Like what?"

"Could you remove the blindfold?"

"I suppose it won't do any harm." He stepped toward her, unfastened the covering, and stared at her.

His prolonged observation made her stomach turn. "Why are you looking at me like that?"

"Your eyes," he blurted. "I've never seen that shade of blue before."

She examined his uniform and his office. The flags and tapestries' symbols revealed the detestable identity of her crimson-clad captors. "You're a member of the Blood Dire Army!" She erupted with anger. "What are you butchers doing here on Menteraz?!"

Torber raised his eyebrows at her. "This planet possesses a wealth of mineral resources. Our mining operation aids the war effort." He paused. "And we are not butchers."

"I doubt the populace of Menteraz willingly gave up their minerals or one of their ancestral temples for your war effort. Your operation is nothing more than an invasion that takes what it wants and enslaves the indigenous people to get it."

"It's not necessary for you to approve of our methods or policies. Orders must be followed."

"Do you agree with your orders?"

"Orders must be followed," the captain repeated robotically.

"You don't. I can see it in your eyes. You disapprove of this operation on Menteraz, and it disturbs you."

He averted his eyes from her piercing gaze. "It doesn't matter what I think. What matters is that your nature has been confirmed as the colonel requested."

"How many slaves work in your mines?"

"Why does that matter?" he asked, refusing to look at her.

"How many children work in your mines?"

He shifted his view toward the lush jungle landscape outside the temple window. "Too many."

Colonel Rask appeared in the office doorway. He crossed his right arm in front of his chest and clicked his heels in one fluid motion. "For the blood that was spilled!"

Torber faced his superior and responded in kind. "For the blood that was spilled!"

Rask approached Reiko and gripped her face with his gloved hand. "Is this specimen genuine?"

"Yes, sir. I have confirmed her nature. She is as the bounty hunter claimed."

"A rare prize indeed." He turned his focus to Torber. "What is the status of the mineral shipment?"

"On schedule," the captain reported. "The cargo freighter is currently at sixty percent capacity, and it will be at a hundred percent capacity in six hours. Only one minor problem, though. We had to use the freighter on platform three instead of platform two."

"Reason?"

"Some of the slaves discovered how to nullify their shock collars and took the opportunity to sabotage the freighter's navigational computer. Maintenance is currently resolving the issue. Fortunately, we have the adequate parts to do so."

"And what of the slaves?"

"Detained."

Anger seeped into his voice. "Examples must be made, Captain. It is the only way others will learn the futility of disobedience." He clenched his fist.

"Leave them alone!" Reiko shouted. "Haven't you done enough damage to this planet and its people?"

Rage engulfed the colonel. "When you address me, alien, you will do so with tact! I will not tolerate a soul-sucking vampire like yourself to speak out of turn!"

"Vampire?" She tilted her head. "What do you mean?"

"It is documented that you Valkyries drain others of their bioenergy to sustain yourselves."

Torber looked at her. "Is that true?"

"Of course not!" she said, mortified. "That's utter nonsense. We Valkyries have existed for two thousand years. Many false rumors about us and our abilities have taken root. If I were you, I would be more concerned about the disturbing truth of your army."

"I do not expect an enemy to appreciate our glorious military efforts!" Rask barked.

"Appreciate?!" Her mouth dropped. "Your murderous deeds are impossible to appreciate!"

"So"—a smug grin crept along the colonel's face—"you are aware of our rise to power."

"I know the good people of Greshin Minor rose against Kuldak Lurez, the tyrant who controlled half of the planet. The revolution led by the newly formed Red Dire Army was costly but successful. Lurez was defeated, and his oppressive government was crushed. That's when your leader, General Gore of the Bloodstained Hands, took Greshin Major and Minor for himself. The Red Dire Army changed its name to the Blood Dire Army, and it became the very thing it was created to oppose!"

"Ten years ago, the general decided to move beyond the boundaries of Greshin and wished to offer his gifts of peace and order to the rest of the galaxy."

"Peace and order?" Reiko laughed. "Is that what you call turning people into living statues?"

"Ah, yes. The Process of Immortalization. It is an interesting tool of psychological warfare conceived by the general's brilliant mind. Why kill your opponents when you can leave them trapped in a sheathe of metal like statues until they die? It is one of the many reasons why rival governments are quick to surrender when our glorious army enters the fray."

"Why does your general want to inflict more atrocities across the cosmos?"

"You can ask him yourself."

"Myself?"

"When the cargo freighter is loaded to full capacity, I will take you back to Greshin Major with me. You will be presented to General Gore as a trophy of war. Living proof that not even the great Valkyries of Volsogun can stand against the might of the Blood Dire Army."

"Colonel, if I may?" Torber interjected.

"Proceed."

"I was hoping to keep the prisoner here under my command. There is a wealth of knowledge we can obtain about her people and Volsogun itself. This is quite a unique opportunity to gather intelligence, and I doubt we will ever get this chance again."

As Rask turned to address his subordinate, Reiko shot out her foot and kicked the colonel, sending him tumbling over the captain's desk. Torber stood idle, frozen, as she ran out of the office and down the corridor. She turned a corner and attracted the attention of a patrolling soldier.

Using the element of surprise, she darted toward him and leaped upward, executing a flying kick. Her boot connected with the soldier's exposed face, sending him into the stone floor.

With his sidearm in hand, Colonel Rask sprinted down the hall and closed in on Reiko. "Valkyrie!" he shrieked.

She whipped around and faced him as he fired a laser bolt that dropped her on impact.

"Did you kill her?!" Torber cried as he approached her limp body.

The colonel holstered his pistol, gripped the captain by his uniform, and slammed him against the wall. "Take a good look at her, Captain!" he shouted as he struck Torber across the face. "That is the face of the enemy! Before you were placed under my command, I heard you were soft, but now I see it for myself! I will make you a respectable officer, worthy of the uniform you wear! You will summon a patrol! You will collect the girl! Then you will give the order to immortalize her!"

"What...?"

"Yes, you, Captain. When the alien is a statue decorating my office, I just might forgive you for your cowardice! See to it!"

The captain glanced toward the floor. "Yes, sir."

Rask released his grip and stomped down the stone corridor. As he turned down the next hall, he heard the captain call for a patrol.

Many quadrants away on Earth, Maru drifted back and forth within the dimensional home. "Why hasn't Reiko arrived yet? She should have returned by now. Although, they could still be on the Turexian medi-craft..." It paused for a moment. "I could get into a lot of trouble for this, but I think I'll take a little peek. Since Turexian technology employs a crystal interface, I should have no trouble at all connecting."

Utilizing its innate telepathic abilities, the servo-crystal linked itself with the medical spaceship's network. It only took a few moments. "There we are. Now, diving into the ship's security system." It viewed multiple areas of the craft via its internal security monitors. The venture came up empty. "That's odd... Let's go back into the ship's memory a bit."

In seconds, it gained access to the ship's security records. "Oh look. They placed the detective in one of those medical suits. Those are quite impressive. Who's the large fellow...? Memories Cause Pain, according to our records. A bounty hunter." It watched and listened in horror as MCP launched a clamp around Reiko's neck. "Oh no! He captured Reiko! And plans to take her to the slave mines of Menteraz?! That doesn't make sense. Menteraz is a peaceful Class Two; there are no slave mines. Unless...someone created slave mines. But that would mean Menteraz is under threat by some sort of oppressive villainy. This is not good! I must do something!"

The servo-crystal watched the screen as it displayed Reiko being taken away. "I must rescue my Justice Valkyrie!"

Leading the patrol, Captain Torber had them carry the unconscious Reiko into a large industrial chamber found deep within the temple. They placed her inside a sizable glass tube with a machine at its base at the center of the room. The captain's heart sank as he looked at her slumped figure. As she stirred, he motioned for one of his soldiers to command the Immortalizer control panel.

Her eyes gradually opened and looked around. She rose to her feet, using the tube as support. "What is happening, Captain?" she asked Torber when they locked eyes. "What is this place?"

"The colonel has ordered you to be immortalized."

"You must stop this madness! Minerals are no reason to enslave a peaceful culture! Your colonel has no compassion, but you do. You can stop them and save Menteraz!"

Torn between duty and the Valkyrie's words, the captain looked at Reiko with soft eyes and placed his hand on the glass shielding. "I'm sorry," he whispered as his eyes sank to the floor. He turned to the soldier operating the control panel and nodded.

She closed her eyes as a rush of metal liquid splashed down the tube and cascaded across her skin. The silver substance was then bombarded with energy, which froze it in place. A heavy fog clouded the tube. The control panel beeped, indicating that the process was complete.

"Open it."

One soldier activated a lever, which drew the tube upward. A blanket of fog rolled across the floor, revealing a statue-like form of Reiko encased in a gleaming metallic sheath. Torber stood before her. A mixture of guilt and rage filled his chest as he gently touched her frozen face.

A familiar booming voice from the intercom system broke his moment of silence. "Captain, I was informed that the Immortalizer has been activated. Is the task complete?"

"Yes, sir," the somber captain responded. "The Justice Valkyrie has been immortalized."

Maru focused its will and infiltrated the Turexian medi-craft's crystal network. From there, its consciousness infiltrated the mobile medi-suit occupied by Akeda.

"Contact has been established, and all systems are online," it said to itself. "But how do I get it to work?" After a brief search through the medi-suit's schematics, it found the answer. "Oh, I see. Let's go mobile."

The Turexians furrowed their eyebrows as the medi-suit raised from its docking station and stood.

"That is very odd," one doctor said. "The unconscious patient should have no knowledge of the suit's operation."

"Please, do not be alarmed!" Maru's voice boomed through the medi-suit's external voice modulator. "Hold on. Is that me?" It realized that its voice, projected through the suit, sounded deeper, quite the opposite of its usual high-pitched tone. "Oh, that sounds very authoritative. I like that!"

One Turexian doctor, bolder than the rest, stepped forward. "Whoever you are, could you explain why you have taken control of our patient?"

"Excuse my actions, good healers! My name is Maru, and I am on official Justice Valkyrie business! I must find the location of a bounty hunter who calls himself Memories Cause Pain. He recently left this magnificent craft. Ah! Wait a moment. I can simply access this vessel's particle scanner to follow his ship's engine trail. Perfect! Now, my good people, let's talk about weapon attachments for this most ingenious battlefield medi-suit."

Colonel Rask peered out his office's window and at Menteraz's lush green jungles and vibrant blue sky. Behind him, in the center of his office, Reiko's statue stood on a thin, metal platform fitted with a small control panel.

"This world and her people," Rask whispered, "have no idea how fortunate they are to play a part of the general's New Age of Expansion."

A knock sounded on his office's door, ending his moment of reflection.

"Enter," he said sharply as he turned away from the view.

Captain Torber entered, offered a hesitant glance at the frozen Justice Valkyrie, and then addressed his superior. "I have the report you requested, sir." He handed Rask a disk containing charts and pertinent data. "The mineral shipment's load will be complete, and the cargo transport will be ready to launch in three hours."

The colonel accepted the disk and tossed it onto his desk. "Excellent, Captain."

"Will there be anything else, sir?"

"Yes. I was thinking about something you said earlier, and you are correct. There is much we can learn from this Valkyrie. So, when General Gore finishes his interrogation, I will ask permission to have her dissected at the research laboratory." Rask watched the captain's calm demeanor turn. He continued with an arrogant smirk. "And before the procedure begins, I will be sure to mention to the general that it was your idea. I want him to know of your undying devotion to our noble cause."

Torber, with a blend of sorrow and dedication cast on his face, turned away from the colonel. "Thank you, sir," he said with an eerie calmness to him. "Will that be all?"

"Yes. You may go."

MCP stayed as still as possible with his eyes closed as he listened in on his guards' conversations.

"When do they plan to transport the prisoner off-world?" one of them asked his partner.

The other shrugged. "They never said. The colonel says to watch him, so we watch."

"Yeah, but for how long?"

"Until the colonel says otherwise. I'm just glad this guy is such a model prisoner, nice and quiet. It's for the better. I've heard stories."

The first soldier let his partner's words hang in the air for a moment. "It is weird, isn't it? This bounty hunter is supposed to have some great reputation, and we took him down in no time."

"Better than him fighting back. Like I said, I've heard stories."

The soldier chuckled. "Stories of what? Of him getting beatdown? All that hardware is for show."

"Stay focused," the second soldier warned. "If the colonel comes in, and you're not focused on the job, you'll have something to be scared about. You know how he loves his surprise inspections."

"I wouldn't worry about that. He's got that Valkyrie to deal with. Hey, Memories Cause Pain, you awake?"

"What are you doing?" his partner asked in a lowered voice. "Let the cyborg sleep."

MCP's dark eyes opened.

The first soldier took half a step back. "That's better," he said with shaking confidence. "You better look at me when I'm addressing you."

The second soldier grabbed his partner. "What are you doing?"

Ignoring the question, the first soldier continued. "I heard you have quite the reputation for violence, but after seeing you in action, I'm not so sure." He stepped closer to the bound hunter. "You know, I'll go so far as to say I'm disappointed with what I saw."

"That's too bad," MCP responded with an electronic rasp, "because I'm the last thing you'll ever see."

Out on the platform, via MCP's mental control, his ship's engines fired on and lifted the craft into the air while aiming its exterior guns at the soldiers assigned to guard the landing platform. The ship's cannons fired a spray of automatic lasers, killing all in the vicinity. MCP then blasted both cargo freighters, sending the Blood Dire Army's precious crystals flying like bullets in all directions. The ship then unloaded a hail of lasers onto the temple, blasting the walls to rubble and cutting an untold number of soldiers to pieces. The attack ruptured several power stores, which exploded in a spectacular chain reaction throughout the structure. Within seconds, a majority of the ancient temple's interior was reduced to smoldering rubble.

Lifting himself from charred stones and debris, MCP took a quick survey of the satisfying destruction. As he walked out of the temple's remains, he commanded his ship to land and power down.

Rask coughed. Blood and dust laid heavy in his mouth. Using the twisted frame of his office's interior lighting, he hoisted himself up from a pile of stone blocks and damaged furniture. He got onto his feet and coughed, checking himself for injuries. Satisfied that he had no broken bones, he took a moment to collect himself. His eyes were drawn to the immortalized Reiko, who was still contained within her metallic prison.

"MCP!" he growled as he drew his pistol and maneuvered through a large hole punched through his office. It opened into what remained of the main corridor. Through a cloud of dust, he spotted a small group of soldiers attempting to find survivors. "Over here! To me!"

"What is going on, sir? What hit us?!" one bloodied soldier asked. "Was it the natives?"

"No, it was MCP! It has to be! Shoot him on sight! I want him dead! If you find others, have them join you! Off you go!"

They left to fulfill their orders as another coughing fit gripped Rask. While doubled over, he noticed Torber's injured figure stumbling his way to the colonel's ruined office.

MCP effortlessly threw large pieces of the temple wall out of his path as he strode outside toward his ship. At his command, the craft launched a weapons container that unfolded while in the air and attached itself onto portions of his armor. The new weaponry included shoulder cannons, guided missiles, and forearm rotary guns.

"There he is!" a soldier shouted through the dust-filled air.

MCP's sensors confirmed it was a group of eight. He whipped around and fired his forearm rotary guns, littering the ill-fated soldiers' bodies with searing holes.

In Rask's damaged office, Torber removed the debris from the base of Reiko's prison, finding the immortalization unit's control panel. He punched a series of buttons to prompt the reversal process. "I need your help," he whispered. "I can't save these people on my own."

Reiko's still figure ignited into a bright light, dissolving the metallic prison. Once free, her body flopped forward, only for the captain to catch her. Her brittle power-dampening collar crumbled to a multitude of pieces and fell onto the rubble below.

Torber threw her arm around his neck. "I know you're disoriented. That's a common side effect. It will pass. We must get to the collar control terminal and shut it down. Then the natives will be free." Carrying her, he exited the office and did his best to navigate the building through a series of damaged corridors until he reached his destination.

In a room congested with various computer terminals and independent generators to keep them running, he leaned her against the wall for support. "There it is." He pointed to a particular terminal and kneeled before it. He inputted his credentials and gained access. "This should only take a moment. Afterward, we'll seize a ship to—"

"Traitor!" Rask shouted, entering the room. Without hesitation, he fired, shooting Torber in the back.

"No!" Reiko cried.

With a brief yelp, the captain completed the command to deactivate the shock collars. Smiling, he stumbled to his feet and faced the armed colonel.

"You fool!" Rask shrieked. "What have you done?!"

Torber offered a gentle smile. "They're free."

With another blast from his pistol, Rask shot Torber in the heart. The captain's body collapsed onto the stone tile floor.

Rask stepped toward the corpse and looked down at his former subordinate with a sneer. "Weak fool! Your attempt to undermine our noble efforts have failed. I can put the collars back online." He turned his anger toward Reiko, who still held onto the wall. "You!" He aimed his sidearm at her head. "You took advantage of Torber's weakness! Filled his head with your alien lies!"

"Underneath, Torber had a noble heart and freed the people of Menteraz from a tyrant like you," she said.

"I'm afraid I will have to disappoint the general by delivering your corpse instead. For the blood that was spilled!"

Before he could discharge his weapon, the stone wall near them exploded, tossing them both onto the floor. A metal cord shot from the cloud of smoke and wrapped itself around Rask's neck. It yanked the colonel's body up and reeled him toward the hole in the wall.

MCP, standing near the hole, grabbed the stunned colonel by his torn collar. "I made you a promise." He threw Rask at his feet, placed his metal boot on his neck, and applied weight.

Reiko closed her eyes as a sickening snap echoed around the room. "Murderer!" she cried as she lifted herself from the rubble-littered floor.

He fired another power dampener collar toward her, who slapped it out of the air.

"You'll find that my fists will cause you more pain than your memories." Feeling her power restored, she shot forward and delivered a mighty punch, sending him flying through three standing temple walls. He ended up rolling on platform three next to the burning remains of the cargo freighter.

As he returned to his feet, another figure screamed through the sky and struck him with its shoulder, driving MCP into the smoldering remains of the destroyed ship.

Reiko flew out of the temple and saw the new robotic combatant face off against MCP. She took a step forward to aid the newcomer, but sounds of echoing laser fire caught her attention. She turned. A few of the freed natives engaged in a firefight against some remaining soldiers. She flew into the air and came crashing down with her fist slamming in front of the Blood Dire soldiers. The impact created a violent shockwave that sent them flying through the air.

She turned to the Menteraz natives' fearful faces. "It's okay. I'm Justice Valkyrie Reiko, and I'm here to help. You guys wait here while I see if any other enemies are hiding out. I shouldn't be long." With that, she once again took to the skies.

MCP tore his way out of the freighter's airframe only to be struck by several missiles, which destroyed his new weapon attachments. Fire rolled off his armor as he rushed toward his mysterious adversary and held it in his grasp. One good look inside the medi-suit's viewing window disclosed his enemy's identity. "You're the poisoned human! That's impossible. You're unconscious!"

"You are correct, scourge," a voice boomed from the suit. "I'm in control!"

"And you are?"

"Maru! That Justice Valkyrie you're trying to harm...she gave me that name!" It delivered a fearsome punch that staggered MCP.

"Then take it to your grave!"

He steadied himself and opened fire with his forearm cannons at point-blank range. Maru commanded the suit to respond in kind. Both released a barrage of laser shots into the other.

Reiko pulled the medi-suit and MCP apart and tossed them on opposite sides of the platform. "Enough!" she shouted at the two. "There has been enough killing today!" She stepped toward MCP, who gathered himself enough to stand. "Leave while you still can. If we ever meet again, I won't be so lenient."

"Watch your back, Valkyrie," he growled as he entered his ship. Within seconds, he turned it toward the open sky and flew away.

Closing her eyes, she sighed. "Good riddance." She then turned her attention to the medi-suit, which had stepped closer to her. She noticed a familiar face in the suit's viewing window. "Detective Akeda?!" she shrieked.

"Um... Not exactly."

"Then who are you?"

"Detective Akeda and the suit were sort of a package deal. An acquisition, really."

She thought about it for a moment. Once she made the connection, she placed her hands on her hips. "You wouldn't happen to be someone I know, would you?"

"Perhaps, in a manner of speaking." The medi-suit stirred its foot across the platform's metal grating.

Reiko's voice took a more serious tone. "You wouldn't happen to be someone I live with, would you?"

The suit shrugged. "I know how this looks, but I can explain."

"Maru! How could you?!"

"It's not as bad as it seems."

"Not as bad?! You stole a Turexian medi-suit!"

"*Borrowed.*"

Her temper rose. "You stole Detective Akeda!"

"He hasn't noticed a thing."

"That's no excuse!" She stabbed her finger into the suit's chest. "You violated the Terran Magnera Agreement! Do you know how much trouble we're in now?! I'll be surprised if Grand Valkyrie Misa doesn't revoke my Valkyrie status and remove my source power! Servo-crystals aren't supposed to do reckless things like this! Do you have anything to say for yourself?!"

"He snores."

Reiko did a double take. "What?"

"The detective. He snores."

She took in a deep breath, shook her head, and chuckled. "You came all this way to help me, didn't you?"

"I am your servo-crystal, after all."

"No, you're not." She patted the suit's chest plate. "You're Maru. My Maru. I'm sorry I got angry with you. I can't believe I've made so many naïve mistakes. Sometimes, I wish I was as strong and as intelligent as Ultra Valkyrie Rei."

"Be thankful you're not. Then you might end up as jaded as she."

"I guess that's what happens after you fight countless battles for years. I mean, she is the last surviving Ultra Valkyrie, and you have to be tough to be the last one standing."

"You shouldn't be so hard on yourself, Reiko. Remember that even the

Ultra Valkyries had to start somewhere, and I'm sure they made their fair share of mistakes along the way."

"Thanks for trying to make me feel better." Cheers drew her attention to the temple ruins. "Well, I've still got a job to do. The people of Menteraz will need some help cleaning things up."

"Um... May I offer further assistance?"

"You're already here, so I suppose. But this is the last time. In the future, if I get myself into trouble, I'll have to get myself out, okay?"

The medi-suit nodded. "Promise."

"All right, Maru. Let's help these good people clean up this mess. After that, it's back to the Turexian ship and then comes the hard part.

"Hard part?"

"I'll have to return to Volsogun and explain the borrowed medi-suit. Then...let's just hope I don't get fired."

EPISODE 05

PLANET OF THE
VAMPIRE BRAIN

Tossed by a flurry of wind, Reiko's crimson cape wildly flapped as she descended and landed in front of the Driven Community Hospital. She stepped through the main sliding glass doors and approached the nurse seated behind the reception desk.

The nurse froze as Reiko met her with a kind smile.

"Hello. I'm looking for a patient who is staying here. Can you help me find him?"

The nurse remained silent.

"His name is Detective Akeda. A few days ago, he was poisoned by a xygrel and had to be taken to a Turexian medi-craft because they are the only ones in the Sol quadrant who can purge the venom. It was actually amazing because they had to put him in a mobile medi-suit. First time I had ever seen one too! But anyway, I got kidnapped by a cyborg bounty hunter who is supposed to be the second-best in the known systems. Imagine that. A bunch of other stuff happened, and some intergalactic laws kind of got broken. Anyway, the medi-suit cured the venom, but he didn't take it too well when he woke up on a Turexian ship. Thankfully, the doctors were wonderful, and they sent us back to Earth in one of their transport pods. Detective Akeda said that after he talked to his boss, he would check himself into a hospital. This hospital. So, I'm here to visit him, and I don't know what room he's in."

After an awkward silence, the nurse spoke. "Okay. One moment." She navigated to her computer. "He's on the third floor. Room 313. You can take an elevator there." She pointed to a series of elevators located behind the desk.

"Thank you." Reiko gave her another grin as she headed for the elevators.

Several people in the lobby took pictures of her with their phones as she passed by.

A clown, holding a modest collection of multicolored balloons, held open the elevator door for Reiko as she entered behind him. A huge tooth-filled smile graced his lips. "What floor?"

"What floor is Room 313 on?"

"Three," he said as he pushed the button. "I didn't know you girls did hospitals."

"We go where we are needed." She looked up at the colorful bizarre figure wearing a polka-dot tie.

"I'm sure you do. Who's the lucky guy?"

"A detective."

"Well, I'm sure you'll be amazing," he said with a starry gaze. "You got a number, a card, or something because I would love to see you again?"

"A card?" She had no idea what to make of the request.

"Here." His free hand fumbled in his oversized pockets. "Take mine. Call me, and we'll set something up, okay?" He stuffed a business card into the heroine's gloved hand as the elevator bell rang, and the door slid open.

She stepped off the elevator and held the card up. "Thank you." She watched the doors shut on the giddy clown. "Jimbo Limbo," she read. She gave it a quick sniff. "Gross. Akeda's card was much better." She set the card within the leaves of a potted plant next to the elevator and then made her way down the hall in search of Akeda's room. "This place is bigger on the inside," she muttered as she walked further down the blue halls. "Finally." She drew in a deep breath and knocked on the door.

"Come in," a familiar voice responded from within.

Trying her best to contain her nervous excitement, she opened the door and entered.

Akeda's eyes widened as he sat up in his bed and turned down the television's volume. "Reiko, what are you doing here?"

"I came to see how you are doing," she said with a smile playing along her lips. "So, how are you doing?"

"Still trying to accept everything I've been through these past few days. As long as I don't run into any other hostile aliens for a while, I think I'll be fine."

"Good. Good." She grabbed a chair from the corner of the room and placed it beside his bed. She sat.

"How did things work out with your superiors?"

"Not so good. The moment I returned to Volsogun, the Grand Valkyrie reprimanded me because of what she called 'my naïve recklessness.' I'm under probation for the next ten years. I also had to offer an official apology to the Turexian people and the Unified Council of Terran Magnera. Fortunately, both were gracious to accept."

"That sounds pretty heavy, but I suppose it could have been worse."

"Yes, it could have. Captain Tower was right," she said in a soft voice. She looked down. "I am just an alien rookie."

"Oh, come on. Don't be so hard on yourself. We've all made mistakes on the job. I mean, you had your big press conference, right? At least a good portion of the people on Earth know who you are now."

"I didn't realize how spread out the people of this planet are. It's not like that on Volsogun. Anyway, enough about that. I don't understand why you want to be here. The Turexians said you were fully healed."

"I'm just here for observational purposes," he admitted. "I'm not saying those alien healers aren't good at what they do. I just want a second opinion. You know, from Earth doctors."

"I suppose." She shrugged. A strange object, wrapped in colored plastic and resting on the bedside table, caught her eye. She pointed. "What's that?"

"A gift basket." He lifted the basket and handed it to her. "Detective Appulo showed up earlier, and he brought this by. He claimed he picked it out, but I know better. His wife did."

"How do you know that?"

"He admitted years ago that he's terrible at picking presents, and that's why his wife does all the gift shopping for their kids' birthdays."

She peeled back the decorative plastic and examined the basket's contents. "What is this stuff?"

"A gift basket is like a collection of fruit or candy that you give to wish someone well." He grinned. "I keep forgetting that you have no idea how we do things here on Earth."

She held a bar enveloped in colorful wrapping and smelled its sweet scent. "Oh my goodness. This smells good. What is it?"

"It's a chocolate bar." He took the bar from her, peeled it open, and handed it back. "Try it. I'm not really a sweets guy, but you might like it."

After another cautionary sniff, she took a bite. She paused in awe as the sweetness captured her taste buds. "Chocolate changes everything!" She took another bite. "This is amazing!"

"I take it they don't have chocolate in your home world."

She shook her head. "After we Valkyries are endowed with The Guiding Source, its power provides us with all the energy we need to sustain ourselves. Eating becomes a luxury, not a necessity."

"So, The Guiding Source... That's what gives you your powers?"

She nodded as she consumed the last section of the chocolate bar. "So good," she whispered.

Akeda tried again. "The Guiding Source?"

"Oh, yeah. I mean, yes. If a member of our sisterhood is seen to have the potential to become a Justice Valkyrie, she must pass a series of trials to prove herself worthy of The Guiding Source's power. Once it is given, the source's energy bonds with the Valkyrie, giving her powerful abilities."

"Oh. I thought you Valkyries were born with your powers."

"No. The power has to be earned." She turned back to the gift basket's contents. "What other delicious secrets does this item contain?"

A knock on the hospital room door pounded.

"Come in," Akeda said.

A nurse entered, wearing a concerned expression. "Excuse me, detective. But can I borrow your friend?"

"Sure."

Reiko stood. "Are you going to be okay?"

"Yes." The detective nodded. "Don't worry about me. Right now, I just want to do something normal. Like watch TV. I'll see you later."

She followed the nurse into the hall. "What can I help you with?"

"I'm sorry to bother you, but the hospital administration asked me to get you. There's a situation outside that requires your attention."

"Lead the way."

She followed the nurse to the lobby. As soon as the elevator doors opened, she noticed a mob of people from all walks of life congregated outside the hospital's main doors. Some cheered and called out when they saw her.

"What's this?" she asked the nurse.

"We were hoping you could tell us. This flash mob formed about ten minutes ago, and their numbers keep growing. A few are holding signs up with your name on them, so we're all assuming they're here for you."

"Here for me? Why?"

"That's the price of being a celebrity, honey. Could you at least try to get them away from the building, please? We would rather not have to call the police."

She shrugged. "Sure."

She stepped through the sliding doors to a roar of cheers. In seconds, the herd encircled her. A variety of voices formed a wall around her, demanding pictures and autographs. Some even wore T-shirts that had her likeness. As she tried to make sense of the situation, the crowd swelled.

"I can't believe it. You're really here!" one cried. "I'm actually talking to you!"

"I love you!" another voice screamed. "Will you marry me?!"

She stepped back, attempting to maintain some distance from them. "It's nice to meet you, but what's all this about?"

"Can you take me to your planet?" one asked.

"Look how short you are," one noted. "You're so adorable!"

One middle-aged man with a receding hairline pushed his way to her with a wide tooth-filled smile. "Don't be alarmed. I'm Richard Blando, and I'm the founder of your biggest fan club. We call ourselves the Reikonoids!" He threw his arm around her shoulder and took a selfie.

As she brushed the man's arm off, a younger man in his twenties thrust a crude picture toward her. "This is a drawing I did of us flying by the moon. Can you autograph this for me?"

"Autograph? What's that?"

"You don't know what an autograph is? You're so precious! An autograph is like when you sign something with your name."

"I recently learned how to speak native languages, but I'm not skilled at writing them." She took a closer look at the crude drawing. "Is this supposed to be me?"

"Yeah. We're flying by the moon. Romantic, right?"

"The only thing I'm wearing is my cape."

He grinned. "Yeah, I know. Just like in my fan fiction."

She gave the picture back. "Don't be vulgar!"

"Are you in love?" a voice echoed. "Do you have a boyfriend?"

She was taken aback. "Um..."

"Just scribble something!" the young man exclaimed. "That'll be cool!"

One girl grabbed the lower portion of Reiko's cape and moved the fabric between her fingers. "This is really smooth. What's it made of? Did you get the material here or somewhere else?"

Questions kept bombarding her.

"Where do you live?"

"What do you think of Earth?"

"Are you staying here long?"

"What's it like to fly? Can you take me flying with you?"

The surrounding admirers pushed closer toward her. Various hands touched her.

"Hey!" she shouted as she whipped around. "Could everyone please give me some space?"

Reiko, Maru's voice echoed in her head. *I just received a distress signal!*

Thank goodness! She turned to the crowd. "Excuse me, Reikonoids, but I'm needed elsewhere!" Without delay, she zipped into the sky and flew several blocks away from the admiring mob. She found a vacant rooftop and touched down with a long sigh. *Maru, you should have seen them!*

Who?

The Reikonoids! My...fans.

You mean admirers? You have admirers?

Apparently so.

You don't sound too pleased.

It was just too much. She closed her eyes and shook her head. *They were everywhere! Swarming me and talking all at once. Several of them couldn't keep their hands off me. For a minute there, I couldn't breathe. It's hard to describe, but I didn't like it.*

How did they find you?

I visited Detective Akeda at the hospital to see how he was doing, and they just showed up out of nowhere.

Were you in uniform or in Earth attire?

Ah. Reiko winched. *I kind of forgot about that.*

Oh, dear. Let's hope your admirers did not find out about Detective Akeda, or they might mob him as well.

I didn't think of that either, she stated with foreboding dread. *Oh, Maru. I just keep screwing everything up.*

I wish I had time to console you, but a mission has come to light.

A mission? Right. You said something about a distress signal?

Indeed. I picked up a faint distress signal that I believe originated from the Zeserous quadrant.

That far? It's a miracle it traveled as far as it did. It must've been sent by hyperspace relay.

Agreed. My guess is that the message has been looping for quite some time.

Then it's safe to assume that plenty of people have picked it up. The person who sent the signal could've already been rescued.

You are still obligated to investigate, I'm afraid.

Why? That long of a journey would remove me too far from my assigned planet.

The person who sent the signal is a Volsogun Valkyrie.

What? A Valkyrie? Why didn't you tell me sooner? Reiko ascended into the atmosphere. *I'll use the closest wormhole to get there.*

The message itself was quite vague, Maru admitted, *but she did mention a planet called Crondorone, so I assume that is her location.*

If I recall correctly, Zeserous doesn't have much in it, so Crondorone shouldn't be too hard to find.

Be careful. Once you travel through the wormhole, our psychic link will cut off, and we can't communicate.

Understood. Show me a map of the quadrant before I get to the wormhole.

While she sailed past the moon, Maru showed her a holographic map of Zeserous. *Thank you, Maru. I'm headed for the wormhole now.*

Reiko blasted to light speed and shot into the wormhole's swirling vortex. In a matter of minutes, she exited the funnel of celestial energy and slowed her flight as she appeared in an unfamiliar patch of space. She traveled for some distance until she recognized the small, rock-encrusted planet known as Crondorone from Maru's map. She coasted over its jagged surface, unimpressed by the planet's naturally formed features. "Not very inviting, are you?"

Flying further, something grabbed her interest. Pieces of several spacecraft littered a particular area of the minor planet's rocky surface. She landed next to the ship graveyard for a closer look and picked up a piece of what looked like the remains of a ship's wing. Bite marks tore through the wing's atmospheric shielding.

A rustling sound from under a pile of ship remains broke her concentration. As she dropped the wing's damaged portion, a creature resembling a five-foot-long winged insect with a metallic exoskeleton emerged from under the rubble. Three more surfaced behind the first. Their wings buzzed as they launched themselves toward her.

She flew upward and met the lead insect with a staggering punch that sent it crashing into a ship's chewed airframe. She then flew backward as the other three took turns using their jagged mandibles to rip her to pieces. She struck one, but the attack opened an opportunity for another to clamp its jaw across her leg. She gripped the creature's jaw with a sharp cry of pain and struggled to pry it apart.

A volley of laser bolts streaked across the thin atmosphere, striking the beast holding her leg and killing it. The remaining two insectoids cautiously flew away. Reiko took to the ground and ripped the dead insect's mandible from her leg.

"This way!" a voice shouted to her. "In here! Before more show up!"

She noticed a squat figure in a space suit beckoning her from near the mouth of a cave. She flew to the location and followed the figure into the structure. As they crossed the cave's lip, the figure activated a small box that projected a holographic image. The image masterfully camouflaged the cave's entrance, making it look like just another slab of natural rock.

"How can you breathe out there?" the figure inquired. "Where's your suit?"

"I don't need one," she said as she rubbed her sore leg. Taking a good look at her host, she identified him as a native of Ochonda, a planet whose natives resemble azure toads of short stature.

"Humph." The Ochondan scoffed with a grave voice as he holstered his rifle onto his back. "Must be nice."

"I'm a Justice Valkyrie from Volsogun. My name is Reiko."

"I'm Commander Tromus of The Unquiet Deep, a wanderer class cruiser." He pointed to his suited crew members. "That's Winven, Pornal, Drovak, and Daullis."

"Pleased to meet all of you." She bowed. "What brought you so far away from Ochonda?"

"Sales, of course. We were delivering half a ton of Mevnos spice to Outer Fralen when we picked up a distress beacon that originated from this cursed rock. When we got close enough to land, those creatures came out of nowhere and attacked my ship. Before we could give a proper response, they had already eaten a wing and forced us down. We grabbed what supplies we could and bailed out. Luckily, we found this hole, and we've been here ever since."

"How long ago was that?"

"About five days. Maybe six."

"I also received a distress call," she admitted, "but it was on a telepathic wavelength. Have you had an opportunity to investigate the origin of the signal?"

"Are you joking?" Tromus laughed. "Those things will tear you to pieces. We've been hiding in this cave the whole time, and as far as we know, it's the only safe place on this rock." He walked away toward the back of the cave.

"I ventured out briefly about a day ago," Drovak interjected. "I did see a metal structure with a door a good way east of here."

"I see," she said. "Then that is where I will begin my search."

"Listen." He stepped closer to her and lowered his voice. "Tromus won't mention it because he's too proud, but our suits are running low on air. We'll be finished in a couple of days, and I've heard that you Valkyries help those in need."

"You have heard correctly."

"Then, please help us."

"I won't let you down. I promise," she said with a reassuring smile. "Commander Tromus?"

"Yeah." He approached her as she walked toward the cave's hidden entrance.

"Just stay put, and I'll get to the bottom of this, okay?"

"Sure." He huffed. "Don't get killed out there."

"I won't."

"And if you happen to find a cruiser to get us home, that would be wonderful."

"I'll keep my eyes open," she said as she stepped out of the cave. She surveyed the terrain and found no trace of the insect creatures. Relieved, she took to the sparse air and flew east. It didn't take long before she spotted a metal building partially embedded into a cliff.

Landing near its door, she heard a whirring sound originating from the surrounding rock. A series of laser turrets sprung upward and targeted her.

"A defense grid?" Reiko crossed her arms as a volley of lasers shot her. Taking advantage of a momentary pause in the attack, she sped to each turret and smashed them to pieces with her fists. She surveyed her handiwork, shrugged, and approached the metal door. Since she saw no visible control panel to negotiate with, she drove her hands into the door and ripped it from its place. She tossed it on top of the rest of the metallic remains that littered the area.

The interior had a typical bunker design with the stale scent of recycled air. An electric cable strung along the wall. Going lower into the earth, she followed the cable down a few corridors until it ended at a junction box next to a door. Several other thick cables joined the same box. "So, this is where the power goes," she muttered as she pressed a green button on the door's control panel.

The door slid open, and she entered a large room lined with a series of humming computer terminals. A laser shot rang out, and a tingling sensation coursed through her body.

She couldn't help but giggle. "That tickles."

"Oh... I... Uh..." A green humanoid in a silver jumpsuit next to a nearby terminal dropped his sidearm. "I shot you... I... Don't harm me!"

She smiled. "I'm not here to harm you. I'm Reiko, a Justice Valkyrie. What's your name?"

"Kero. Kero Killrazen." His voice shook, and he put his hands open before him. "I apologize for shooting you. I'm afraid caution has become second nature to me."

She placed her hands on her hips. "More like paranoia. Is there a particular reason for this behavior?"

"On my world, I was once a renowned scientist and researcher. Have you heard of Dev-Sravan?"

"Who hasn't? It amazes me that your people redesigned your home world and now make custom-built worlds for others. That must be expensive."

"Unbelievably so. As you know, complex innovations also breed complex dilemmas. Our world designs brought rise to an astounding number of unwanted byproducts, such as various metals, plastics, and chemical wastes."

"Price of progress, I guess. I would think that your people would already have measures in place to deal with such things. After all, Dev-Sravan has been planetscaping for centuries."

"Yes, but over the last hundred years or so, the populace has objected to the old methods of disposal. They said that it would harm the planet if we buried the waste or launched it elsewhere into space. Therefore, the governing lords gave me the task of coming up with a solution. It was truly an honor." The soft-spoken alien smiled. "My team and I worked for over a year to come up with a suitable resolution, but nothing was satisfactory. It was then that a colleague of mine suggested we use Orinium."

"That stuff's like metallic acid. You rarely hear of anybody using Orinium for anything, and besides, I've heard finding it is next to impossible."

"That is correct." He nodded. "Although it is rare to find Orinium on any known worlds, we did find some on a small asteroid drifting on the edge of the Verolon quadrant."

"That asteroid didn't have enough Orinium to solve your pollution problem, did it?"

"No, of course not, but we formulated ways to synthesize it. It was then that I made a most fascinating discovery, and it wasn't about the metal itself but what was on it: millions of microscopic insects feeding off the Orinium."

"Insects?"

"Yes. It didn't require much imagination to take our research in a whole new direction. I knew what must be done."

"If those bugs could eat Orinium, they could eat just about anything in existence."

"Precisely." Kero's face brightened. "It only took three years to genetically alter and cultivate the first batch."

"Then something must have gone very wrong. If everything worked out for you and your team, you wouldn't be here on this lonely rock."

"Yes, that's true. They didn't appreciate my solution. My vision."

"When I arrived on Crondorone, I met your monsters. They're insatiable. How many did they kill on Dev-Sravan?"

"They said that I caused it all!" Rage overcame Kero's calm nature. "They said that I was responsible, and they exiled me! It's all a gross miscarriage of justice! I just needed more time to..." His voice trailed off as a puzzled look grew along his face. "Why are you here?"

"I responded to a psychic distress signal sent from this planet. I'm guessing they're another victim stranded somewhere on this planet because of your creatures."

"I admit, while I furthered my research, some of the insectoids escaped."

Reiko gasped. "Hold on! You're still working on those things?!"

"Yes." He nodded. "This desolate facility is my lab. Ever since my exile, I have worked diligently to evolve the insectoids to be less aggressive and more controllable. Come. I'll show you."

She followed him down the corridor. "This is fascinating and all." She stopped in her tracks. "But the show and tell can wait. I have to find who sent that distress signal."

"Please. It will only take a moment." With a kind smile, he continued down the passage. "This way."

"Very well." She followed. "But only for a moment."

Kero and Reiko entered a room that was shrouded in darkness.

"Allow me to get the power on," he said. He stepped away from her, and in a moment, light flooded the expansive metal chamber.

Horror gripped the heroine as she saw hundreds of insectoids kept in neatly rowed cages. "Kero, I'm not going to ask why they haven't chewed through their cages, but why are you keeping hundreds of these things here?" Receiving no reply, she turned to see the door closed and locked. "What?"

The cages' doors all scraped open at once and provided a bitter response.

"I did it again, didn't I?" she murmured as she readied herself for combat against the swarm of buzzing insectoids. "I walked right into a trap."

Back in the terminal room, Kero sat in a plush chair and watched the spectacular battle unfold between the Valkyrie and the countless mutated insects on a holographic screen. "Try as you might," he murmured.

A woman's voice penetrated his mind via telepathic wavelength. *Is she here?*

Yes, dearest, but I think we can do better, so I fed her to the experiments.

Is she a Valkyrie?

Yes, but—

Bring her to me at once, Kero! The booming voice's intensity dropped him to his knees and forced a trickle of blood from his nose.

Okay. Yes, dearest. As you wish.

Using the terminal as support, he lifted himself onto his feet and manually turned on the novonex gas flow inside the insectoid chamber. All combatants slowed their fighting, and in mere seconds, they dropped unconscious as the powerful sedative flooded the room.

They're all sleeping. I'll bring her to you shortly.

Thank you for your loving devotion, my dearest.

Inside the Ochondan cave, Commander Tromus paced, finding it impossible to come to terms with his growing aggravation.

"You're going to rub away the footpads on your suit, Commander," Winven said, attempting to ease the tension.

He paused his pacing. "My what?"

"Your footpads. On your suit."

All Winven received was a blank stare "You weren't paying attention, were you?"

"Right." Tromus checked his rifle's ammunition. "I'm going out."

"Are you mad?" Daullis spat. "Those creatures will kill you! There's no way you can outrun them!"

"What's mad is doing nothing while our air runs out!"

Drovak kept his voice calm. "Let's give that Valkyrie some time. She promised she would help us."

"And what are we supposed to do in the meantime? Wait to die?" Tromus barked. "I'm going out there, and I'm going to find that structure you saw."

Drovak sighed as he readied his rifle. "Then I'm going with you. If nothing else, two guns are better than one."

"Right." He turned toward the other two group members. "You two keep alert. We'll need cover fire if those things chase us back here."

Pornal nodded. "You got it, Commander. Just come back in one piece, ya hear?"

He turned to Drovak. "You got enough rounds?"

"Yeah." Drovak made a quick check. "Full capacity. I'm good."

"All right then. Let's head out."

Reiko's eyes moved rapidly under her eyelids.

A gentle voice drifted through the air. "Awake, Sister. I wish for us to speak."

"Sister?" she muttered in a drowsy voice as her consciousness returned.

"Yes, of course. We are all sisters, are we not? A new era for the both of us is on the horizon. Awake. Let us speak about that glorious future."

Reiko attempted to lift her hand to scratch her nose, but it wouldn't move. Her eyes opened. She gasped. Magnetic clamps restrained her limbs to a vertical metal table. "What is this?"

"You'll only hurt yourself if you struggle," Kero said as he stepped toward her.

"You! You little notwho!" she fumed. "You betrayed me!"

"Calm yourself, Sister," the gentle voice said. "He was working on my behalf."

"So, who are you?" A shaft of light that originated from the ceiling illuminated her and her table. But the rest of the room remained in darkness. "Why are you hiding?"

"You're right, Sister," the smooth-spoken voice articulated. "I shouldn't hide. I'm only making our conversation more difficult to conduct. My love, turn the lights on."

Kero's voice spoke from within the darkness. "Yes, my dearest."

Reiko closed her eyes as the room burst with light. When she opened them, she screamed. In front of her, a machine contained a partial decaying shell of a woman's body floating in a green-tinted bubbling solution. Another transparent capsule containing a brain with various nodes connected sat on top of that machine. Metallic tentacles that waved at the whim of erratic brain impulses were affixed to the body container's sides.

"By the Grand Matriarch!" Reiko exclaimed with her mouth wide open.

"I am Super Valkyrie Solesta," the gentle voice said. "And it was I who sent the signal."

She averted her eyes. "What happened to you?"

"The Valkyries betrayed me! My own sisters!" Solesta shrieked. "They thought they knew best!"

"What are you talking about?" she asked as she glared at the pathetic creature. "The Valkyr Sisterhood has always had everyone's best interest at heart."

"That's Misa talking! You must be a new Justice Valkyrie, I'll wager."

"Yes. I'm Justice Valkyrie Reiko, assigned to Terra in the Sol quadrant."

"An assigned planet?" Solesta paused. "Yes...I remember my first planet. I was so young and ambitious. Like you. It was a small Class Two called Xendvis IV. So quiet and peaceful and beautiful." Solesta's voice took on a dreamlike quality. "I earned the people's trust, and they loved me. They built statues of me and even dedicated one day out of their harvest year to honor me."

"That doesn't sound like the proper way to—"

"The children made a crown of their rarest flowers and rested it on my head as I sat upon a throne, which was carved into the trunk of a feydorlin tree. Only three exist on the planet, you know. Such adoration. I protected my precious flock, and in return, they gave me tribute."

"That's wrong!" Reiko recoiled. "That's not how a Valkyrie should be to those she protects. We do not defend for the sake of our egos. We do it as a selfless act of service."

"Save me Misa's rhetoric, Sister. I've heard it all before."

"She was right to say so, and you should have listened!"

"The day came when Misa reassigned me to some damn rock hanging on the edge of an asteroid belt. Only simple mammals lived there. How dare she insult me!"

"What happened?"

"I refused."

"Refused?" Reiko's jaw dropped. "You can't refuse a direct order from the Grand Valkyrie."

"She made that abundantly clear."

"How?"

"She sent Ultra Valkyrie Naiomi to use her powers of persuasion."

"Powers of persuasion? What do you mean?"

"Look at me!" the floating brain screamed through its voice modulator. "Is my condition not enough?! Naiomi said that I wasn't deemed worthy, so she placed my battered body into a life support capsule and sent me adrift through the void. Years ago, Kero, my dearest, found me shortly after his exile, and he brought me here, so we could both start anew."

"Ultra Valkyrie Naiomi has been dead for almost two hundred years now. Drifting in space for such a long time must've driven you mad."

"Oh, little Reiko." Solesta laughed. "Make no illusions. I'm positively insane!"

Tromus and Drovak crept across the rocky terrain, employing the mangled space vessel remains as cover when possible. Once they spotted the partially buried building, the two lowered themselves behind a cumbersome collection of stones.

Drovak pointed. "There it is."

"I see it." Tromus noted the destroyed turrets scattered across the surface. "The defense system is compromised, and the door is ripped off its hinges. I bet the Valkyrie found this place too."

"I wonder why that building requires so much security."

"I don't know, but a setup like that must have cost a nice bit of coin. The actuators in those turrets alone must have cost thousands. Look how they came up from the ground."

Drovak nodded. "Good camouflage."

"I bet they did that because those creatures would have eaten them if they saw them."

"Sounds plausible."

"Plausible?" Tromus huffed. "That observation was genius."

"Yes, Commander."

"All right. It looks pretty clear. Let's go. But keep a lookout. If one of those flying things spots us, we're done for."

Reiko glared at Solesta and Kero from her bounds.

"Release her, dearest," Solesta told her alien love.

"I don't think that would be wise." He wrung his hands. "She isn't to be trusted."

"I said to release her!" she snapped. "After all, my dearest, she is a guest."

"A guest. Of course." He trotted over to the table's control panel and punched a few buttons, opening the magnetic clamps that held Reiko down.

She stepped away from the table and confronted the life support system that contained Solesta's remains. "Thank you. Now, you have some explaining to do."

"Of course," Solesta said. "When she burned off parts of my body, Naiomi promised that she wouldn't kill me. I make you the same promise."

"What are you talking about?"

"Your body is so young and strong. I want it. I wish to reconstitute myself. To be whole again. My psychic signal could only be received by a citizen of Shin Kirin. You were the only one who responded to my call, so you have been chosen to return me to my former glory."

"You want to take over my body?" She crossed her arms. "And just how do you plan to do that?"

"You will give it to me voluntarily," Solesta admitted.

"You're right. You are insane."

"Kero, dear. Would you please show her the breeding tanks?"

"Yes, love." He activated the room's holographic monitor. The picture showed thousands of liquid-filled tanks containing growing insectoids. "The ones you faced were those grown to maturity."

"There are three inhabited planets nearby with a hundred billion souls each." Solesta's velvety voice could not veil its threatening nature. "Once the swarm is released, they will move from planet to planet, eating everything in their path. They will also breed, creating more to spread across the quadrant and beyond. If you attempt to harm me or leave this room, I will have no choice but to release them. Even with your power and might, you cannot stop them all."

Reiko bit her lip, attempting to hide her horror. "You wouldn't."

"I am giving you an opportunity to display that selfless nature you and Misa so righteously speak of."

"Have you forgotten what it means to be a Valkyrie? This is blackmail!"

"No, Sister. This is saving lives. You are saving their lives and mine."

"You had your chance as a Valkyrie. You made your choice!"

"Now, you make yours."

Frozen with uncertainty, Reiko stood silent.

But then an alarm pierced through the engulfing silence.

Kero scrambled and searched for the disturbance's source. "Corridor eight!" he exclaimed with a panic-stricken voice. "The sensor picked up movement, dearest. Someone's here."

"Then deal with them! I don't have time for more guests."

He nodded. "Yes, my dearest." He left, going down the corridor.

"So, what do you say, Reiko?" Solesta asked. "Give me your answer. Now!"

Reiko hesitated. "Okay. Just don't release those creatures!"

"See," she purred. "It's not hard to be a hero, is it?" The metallic tendrils stretched from Solesta's sides and wrapped themselves around Reiko. "Now, Sister. Come to me."

"Do you think we should take our helmets off, Commander?" Drovak whispered as he crept through the empty corridor.

"Nah. We'll leave them on. The door was ripped off, remember? Besides, we may have to make a hasty retreat if things go awry."

"What do you suppose this place is?"

"Not sure. Awfully quiet, though. I don't like that."

"It's got plenty of power running through it," Drovak noted. "I can hear it humming."

"Hold up." Tromus readied his rifle as a green-skinned humanoid stepped into view near a corridor junction. "Up ahead."

"I see him." He pointed his rifle.

"Hey there!" Tromus called. "We're stranded on this planet and could use some help. Do you got a communication—"

Laser bolts—fired from Kero's pistol—cut the commander's statements short.

Drovak opened the nearest door he could find. "In here!"

The two Ochondans piled in.

"Close it!" Tromus shouted.

Drovak searched the pad of buttons by the door and punched several until it slid shut.

"Okay. They're hostile," Tromus seethed.

"Good thing that one was a bad shot."

"Let's find some cover before the ones who know how to aim show up."

"Right." Drovak turned to further examine the room. Thousands of insectoid larvae were stored in transparent containers. On the far wall, laboratory equipment and a series of sophisticated machinery stood. Terror gripped his soul. "Commander?"

"What?" Tromus turned. He froze.

"This is a breeding lab."

"By the Great One Beyond the Stars..."

As Reiko moved closer to Solesta, the container's front portion opened. All she could do was close her eyes.

"I can feel The Guiding Source within you," Solesta said. "I had forgotten what that felt like."

"No," she whispered as her energy ripped from her. Her quiet word grew into an agonizing scream.

A black streak ripped across Crondorone's hollow atmosphere. Noticing the disturbance, the three remaining insectoid creatures lifted themselves to attack in hopes of an easy meal. The clad figure—dressed in sleek black armor with long, silver-white hair sticking out from the back of her helmet—paused momentarily and watched as the new threats approached. Unimpressed, she raised her hands and fired searing bolts that decimated her new foes into a black cloud of ash.

"Yes!" Solesta cheered as Reiko's power coursed through her tattered flesh. "I will be whole again!"

The black-armored figure punched through the ceiling and landed between Reiko and Solesta. Her hand formed a laser blade that sliced through the tendrils that had wrapped themselves around the unconscious Reiko.

"What?!" Broken from the intoxicating power, Solesta realized the source of her renewal had been removed.

The black-armored figure collected Reiko, flew outside to the planet's surface, and laid her on a bed of rocks. She then turned her attention back to the building and flew toward the two Ochondans, ripping through each wall in her path.

"What the—" Tromus shouted when she stood by his side.

"Come," she said. "I'll get you two to safety." With that, she grabbed them both, soared out of the building, and dropped them off near Reiko.

Drovak kneeled beside her. "Is she gonna be okay?"

"She doesn't deserve to be," the dark figure responded coldly. "You two wait here. I'll be back."

"Hold on." Tromus' eyes searched the sky. "It's not safe out here. Murderous insect creatures fly around all over the place."

"Not anymore." The black-armored figure bolted through the sky and returned once again to Solesta's chamber.

"You!" Solesta shrieked. "You defied me! Give me back my new body!"

The black-armored figure casually drew closer to her.

"I can feel...power. From you. Tell me who you are."

"Rei."

"Ultra Valkyrie Rei. The killer of killers." Fear drowned Solesta's voice. "Did Misa send you to kill me?"

"No. You attempted to kill a Valkyrie to prolong your worthless existence. I won't allow that."

"I pity you. You're no better than a puppet dangling from Misa's strings!"

Rei raised her glowing fist that crackled with burning energy. "If it's any comfort, Naiomi said she regretted not terminating you. Sometimes, I get tired of the battles...the killing. Then I see a pathetic sack of flesh like you, and just like that, I'm fine with it again."

"We Valkyries are all killers in the end."

A grin formed on Rei's black lips. "There is much you never knew about us, Solesta. And you never will."

With a short laser burst and the echo of a fading scream, Solesta burned into a swirling cloud of cinders.

Rei navigated back to the breeding room and incinerated all the creatures contained within. She then overloaded a power junction box, which caused an explosive chain reaction throughout each room. Standing amid the devastation, she noticed a ship docked in a small underground hanger below her feet.

Reiko gasped and raised her upper body forward. "What's going on?" she asked with a woozy voice.

Drovak shrugged. "No idea. But at least it stopped."

The black-armored figure coasted from the thick layer of smoke and landed beside the confused aliens. Her voice was sharp and businesslike. "Are you Ochondans stranded here?"

Tromus spoke up. "Well, uh, yeah. We wanted to—"

"How many of you are there?"

"Five."

"There's a beta class cruiser in a hidden hanger underneath the compound. It will be a tight fit, but you should manage."

"I'll grab the rest of my men, and we'll be off." Tromus nodded. "What's your name? I want to thank you properly."

"Ultra Valkyrie Rei."

"Well, thanks for helping us out, Rei. If you ever find yourself on Ochonda, look me up. The name's Tromus War'nr. My brother owns a shop that sells armor. He might even have some to fit your humanoid shape. I'll let him know to give you a discount for helping us out."

"I'll keep that in mind."

"And, uh, thank you for trying to help us," Drovak said as he helped Reiko to her feet. "Hope things work out."

"They will," Rei answered them.

"Oh, yeah," Tromus said. "There's a room housing thousands of creatures that—"

"They're dead."

"Right." He nodded as he turned for the cave. "Come on, Drovak."

Reiko, who had still not fully recovered, watched the two disappear over the rocks.

"Snap out of it!" Rei growled.

"Ultra Valkyrie Rei." Reiko's eyes widened. "It's an honor to meet you."

She folded her arms. "What were you doing here?!"

"I followed a psychic distress signal that originated from a Valkyrie."

"You did not verify the signal, and you abandoned your assigned planet! Furthermore, you did not survey the perimeter or read the energy signatures of this structure to identify it as a laboratory. You put two Ochondan lives in danger, and worst of all, you almost got yourself killed by a rogue Valkyrie."

"You're right..." Reiko looked down at the ground under her boots. "I'm sorry."

"No! You don't apologize!" Rei shouted. "You get better! The Grand Valkyrie granted you great power because you proved yourself worthy, and she trusted you! Is this how you repay that trust?!"

Absent of a response, she didn't move.

"I will not save you again. Do you understand? Go back to your assigned planet!" Rei stepped away and burst upward toward the stars at the speed of light.

Reiko still didn't move. After a while, she drew in a deep breath and released a long sigh. "I finally met Ultra Valkyrie Rei. She's certainly as abrasive as everyone said she would be." She covered her mouth with her hand. "Oh no. Maybe I'm still being evaluated. This incident isn't going to look good at all. I can't believe how badly I screwed this up. I bet Rei thinks I'm a total notwho now. If she had her way, my career would be as dead as disco."

She floated from the ground and hovered in the fragile air. "At least I can make sure the Ochondans get away safely. At least."

Stirring within the destroyed laboratory's charred rubble, Kero slid out from under a scorched metal beam. He winced. Persistent throbbing pulsated through his broken left leg. He slid a few more feet until he could reach a fragment of Solesta's life support chamber. What had been a fragment of brain matter melted onto the concave surface.

Tears welled in his eyes. He held the fragment close to his lips and kissed it. "Dearest," he choked. "Valkyries of Volsogun..." His teeth clenched as tears slid down his face. "I'll kill you all. I swear it!"

MERMAID MACHINE GUN

NISHIMURA WANTED TO kill Reiko. That was all he thought about, and yet seeing her in action made him pause. Her violence moved like the wind in an open sky with no regrets. He admired her skill. But he hated her more.

"Sir, we've arrived," his driver announced as the luxury car pulled in front of Stratnum Applied Research Laboratories, which served as nothing more than one of his front companies. Dr. Denoda, a brilliant research scientist whose primary duty was to explore new ways to kill Reiko, ran this one.

As his driver opened his door, Nishimura stepped out and drew in a deep breath of evening air. He exhaled. "Have you tasted the air this evening?" he asked his driver.

"No, sir. I haven't."

"Do it."

The driver inhaled and slowly exhaled.

"Well?"

"Tastes like Driven, sir."

Nishimura's mouth curved into a grin. "Exactly. And it will not change until I say so."

He entered one of the restricted labs.

"Hey, boss! What a nice surprise," the garish-clothed Johnny greeted.

Dr. Denoda followed behind Johnny. "Mr. Nishimura, it's a pleasure to see you. If I knew you were coming, I would have put together a formal presentation of your new alien fighting assets. Please, sir. Come this way."

Nishimura followed Dr. Denoda, who he always found unusually tall and muscular for a scientist, and Johnny into a plexiglass chamber. A robot that appeared more human than previous ones mimicked the same precise combat style as the Valkyrie. He knew that style well. After reviewing her techniques for hours, he had committed them to memory.

"Is this new unit to replace the battlebots?" he asked.

Dr. Denoda nodded. "Yes, sir. Based on the combat data provided, we've determined that our battlebots lost because they carried too much weight. Speed played a factor in their demise. Not only will these new models be lighter and faster, but they can also use hundreds of weapons and martial arts skills. Including hers."

Nishimura watched the robots with a void of emotion. "How soon will they be ready?"

Two men in suits walked beside the yakuza boss and stood idle.

"Tonight," Dr. Denoda said with a confident grin.

Nishimura took a closer look at the two unfamiliar figures that stood beside him and smiled. "Impressive. Only up close can I spot small discrepancies in their skin texture. Their eye movements are striking, almost identical to a human's."

"I know, right?" Johnny chuckled. "Dr. Denoda has outdone himself on these bad boys. I think we should call them infiltrators, disguise-o-bots, or alien butt kickers."

"They're animots," Dr. Denoda said in a dry voice. "They're a form of android."

"Excellent job, Dr. Denoda," Nishimura said. "I would like to see them in the field as soon as possible."

"Thank you, sir."

"And after the alien's death is secured, I also would like to see these animots used in a more infiltration capacity."

"Of course."

He nodded with an approving grunt. "Although your technological applications have their place, I feel a more traditional approach is needed as well. Johnny."

"Yeah, boss?"

With a wave of Nishimura's finger, one of his men stepped forward, holding a leather suitcase. "I have arranged to make a purchase this evening. Make sure it goes smoothly."

Johnny took the case. "Can do, boss. So, what are you buying?"

"A piece of tragic history."

In his best suit, Akeda entered the Driven Convention Center's spacious Sapphire Room. His muscles tensed as crowds of smartly dressed couples flooded the floor. He wanted to turn around, but he *did* buy a ticket, and the cause was a good one: to improve a children's burned wing at Driven Community Hospital. He told himself that it was only a benefit dinner. Eat and leave. He took another look at the plethora of couples. Whether genuine or not, they seemed happy together. Lillian and their relationship crossed his mind. He asked himself, as he often did nowadays, if he truly loved her. He must have. It wouldn't hurt this bad if he didn't.

"Hey, buddy!" Appulo threw his beefy arm around his partner's neck. "When did you get here?"

"Just arrived." He smiled when he saw Leilani, Appulo's charming, heavy-set wife, approach. "It's been a long time, Leilani. How have you been?"

"Keeping this one fed and on his toes." She beamed in her bright formal dress. Her black, wavy hair shined as it cascaded over her shoulders. "It's about time your partner took me out."

"You look stunning."

"Thank you. You always are a sweetheart, Daniel." She paused. "Kainoa said you spent some time in the hospital. You doing okay?"

"Oh, yeah. I was just under observation for a couple of days. Nothing big."

"Where's Lillian? Is she here?"

Her name stabbed deep through him. He tried his best not to show it. "No, she isn't. We're not together anymore."

"I'm so sorry, Daniel," Leilani said. "I know how much you loved that girl."

"So that's why you've been dragging your feet lately," his partner said. "I thought you were sick. I'm really sorry about that, pal."

"Thanks." Akeda's painful emotions welled up within him. "You two have a good time." With a weak smile, he walked away.

He moved through the crowd of unfamiliar faces until he saw a blonde woman from behind. Sadness gripped him once again. He needed to get out. Some night air would do him good. He exited the Sapphire Room, found the elevators, and took one to the tenth floor's outdoor patio. Comforted by the quiet, he leaned his hands against the railing and took in the busy illuminated streets below.

"You look nice tonight, detective," a familiar voice said.

Akeda raised his head and saw Reiko floating before him. "Where did you come from?"

"The sea. I pulled a stranded boat to shore. It was more like a yacht. That was what they called it at least. After I finished there, I was flying home, but I saw you."

"You pulled a boat to shore? How strong are you anyway?"

She shrugged with a grin. "Strong enough to pull a yacht. Excuse me for saying so, but you look sad. Is something wrong?"

He shook his head. "I don't want to burden you with my problems. You have enough of your own."

"Me? Problems? Like what?"

"Weight of the world, for starters. And the Reikonoids come to mind."

"Oh, yeah. Them," she muttered. After a moment of awkward silence, she perched on the railing beside him. "I don't understand why those people hold me in such high regard. I'm only doing my duty."

"You're a celebrity now. It comes with the territory."

"I thought celebrities sing songs, play sports, or do entertaining things."

"They do, but you seem to be a whole new category."

"That's...unnerving."

"To say the least."

Johnny Run-Time and two of Nishimura's suited henchmen stepped onto a cargo ship that was tied at the harbor near the industrial district. He smiled and raised the suitcase in his hand as several shady characters approached him. "Which way to your boss, gentlemen, cause I'm ready to do some business?"

"This way," one responded.

They led Johnny's group into the ship's inner cabin.

Inside, Johnny saw five armed characters huddled around a table with a metal container placed upon it. One of the individuals caught his attention. "Well, I'll be. Fingers Jackson, how have you been, man?" He greeted his acquaintance with a hardy handshake.

"Run-Time, if I had known I was dealin' with you, I would have rolled out the red carpet." Jackson laughed. "I heard you've made quite a name for yourself in Driven."

"Well, what can I say? I'm people who know people. You should stick around town. I might be able to hook you up. We could use a good smuggler."

"No thanks, brother. Not my style. I gotta keep on the move, you know? There are too many out there in the world who require my services."

"I hear ya. Well, let's get this party started." He placed the suitcase on the table and opened it, allowing its contents to radiate. "Two million in gold, as agreed."

"And here's your prize." Jackson nodded to one of his men, who opened the bulky container exposing an odd-shaped stone about the size of a paper towel roll. It was flat on one end and hexagonal on the other. Strange, unfamiliar markings littered its surface.

Outside the room and obscured by shadows, a young woman with long blue hair crouched and watched the proceedings in awe. Once the curious object was exposed, she could feel a latent power emanating from it.

"Straight and to the point. Just the way I like it." Johnny chuckled. He turned to his henchmen. "Okay, boys. Let's grab the goods and make our way home. Thank you very much, Jackson. It's been cosmic."

Behind the spying woman's ear, she felt the cold steel of a gun barrel.

"Don't even blink," a burly voice behind her growled. "Now on your feet, and don't do anything stupid!"

As she stood, a second man produced a zip tie and bound her wrists behind her.

The two henchmen marched the woman into the room. "I found this one snooping around, boss."

Jackson widened his eyes at her, who was clad only in a bikini and an elaborately carved necklace. He then looked toward Johnny, who appeared equally as baffled. "Is there something you want to tell me?"

"All I know is that this chick is hot," Johnny said. "Who is she?"

Jackson pointed to a few of his men. "Make sure she is alone." As they filtered out of the room, he turned his attention to the woman. "You got a name?"

Defiantly, she looked away.

Johnny smiled at the captive. "Planning on going for a swim? I bet you were planning on swiping my pretty little rock and diving overboard with it."

"Tell you what," Jackson said with a nod, "since I'm in such a good mood after making a lot of money, I'm gonna let you go for that swim. Let's take this outside."

The henchmen pulled her onto the deck outside and walked to the side of the boat.

"Even though it's a calm night, you better be careful." Jackson pulled a pistol from the back of his pants. "More sharks swim in the water than on this boat." With that, he fired a round that tore a strip of flesh from her left arm.

A sharp cry of pain escaped her lips.

He shoved her off the boat's side and watched her tumble in the air before splashing into the dark waters below. "Keep your eyes peeled. If she pokes her head out of the water, blast her."

The henchmen readied their weapons and watched for any disturbance on the water's surface.

The dark water felt like a mother's embrace. The woman voluntarily sank further as she drank large gulps of the ocean. With each breath, her strength grew, allowing her to snap the restrains around her hands. Her arm's bleeding wound sealed itself shut. Now free, she extended her arms outward and pressed her legs together, forming them into a fishtail with gorgeous azure scales.

She dove deeper to gather momentum, pivoted, and shot upward, breaking through the water's surface and sailing into the air. Curving her body, she drove into Jackson, knocking him onto the ship's metal floor. She shifted back to her legs, stood on her feet, and touched her necklace with a shimmer of ethereal light. Two automatic rifles of an alien design formed in her hands. She opened fire.

The henchmen fortunate enough scattered across the ship's surface for cover. Those who weren't fell into a pool of their own blood.

"You still haven't said why you're so down," Reiko said, pressing Akeda further. "You look too nice this evening to be unhappy."

"Oh, that." He looked down at his suit. "I'm attending a charity dinner for the hospital. But I came up here to be away from people. Alone."

"Not anymore."

He sighed. "Fine. I was in a serious relationship, and I had planned to spend the rest of my life with her. You know, the big house, the white picket fence, kids, etc. She decided that her career was more important than me, so she ended our relationship."

"I'm sorry."

"Thanks."

"I'm no expert on romantic relationships. I mean, I've never been in one. I wish there was something more I can say."

"There's nothing to say."

"It's strange to think of, but even with all my power, I can't heal a broken heart."

"It's not your burden to heal broken hearts, but thanks for the sentiment."

With a compassionate smile, she placed her hand over his. Both stayed silent as they looked at each other, lost at what else to say.

An explosion ripped through the night.

Her expression grew dark. "That didn't sound right."

"It's a good thing you didn't go home yet."

"I have to find out where it came from."

"Okay. Be careful."

With an affirming smile, she leaped upward and bolted through the dark sky.

As soon as the woman could close the distance between her and the remaining henchmen, her rifles morphed into swords that she used with deadly precision. She took note of Johnny Run-Time attempting to sneak off the ship with the metal box.

Before she could pursue him, a bullet shot through her hair, barely missing her head by centimeters. She spun around.

Fingers Jackson stood armed and ready for a fight. "What are you? Huh?"

"Angry." She deflected a shot from his gun with one of her blades and used her other blade to slice off his hand that held the weapon. She then plunged both blades into his chest. To the smuggler's gurgled screams, she watched as his body slid from her blades and collapsed onto the metal floor.

Not sparing a moment, she ran straight for Johnny. "Stop!" Her blades shifted back into rifles. "Drop the case!"

"Sure, babe." Johnny, smiling, let the case fall to the floor and raised his hands. "Let's not get too twitchy with those fancy firearms. Okay?"

She grabbed the dropped case and hoisted it overboard.

"You're really gonna upset my boss, and that's never a good thing."

She pointed one rifle at him. "I wouldn't worry too much about that. You've got bigger problems."

"Enough!" Reiko landed beside the woman and slapped the rifle toward the sky as it fired.

Johnny grabbed the suitcase filled with gold and fled into the night.

"I almost had him!" Enraged, she spun her foot to kick Reiko in the face.

Reiko caught her ankle and threw her into a metal container, denting its side. She winced as a stabbing pain shot through her right arm. The rifle that fell from her hand dissipated into a stream of energy and returned to her necklace.

Reiko walked over toward her. "What happened here?"

With a final glance, she cradled her injured arm, ran for the side of the boat, and jumped into the night air. She shifted into her mermaid form and disappeared under the dark waves.

Abe Medalious, or Porthole as his old shipmates called him, sat in an antique leather chair at a carved oak table. He poured over his latest hobby: building a model ship within a bottle. It was tedious, but with classical music in the air and brandy in his glass, he was ready to ride the uncertain waters. The sea was in his blood, his whole life. Which was why he retired at a lighthouse on Driven's coast.

The wooden front door flung open. A blue-haired woman, holding a metal case in her arm, stumbled through the doorway and collapsed onto the floor.

"What tha blazes?" Abe shot up from his chair and rushed to her side. "Keanid, what the hell happened to you?"

She gasped. "Help me into the tank."

He scooped her up in his arms and made a break for the backroom, which contained a large tank filled with seawater. "Good God, girl. You're a real mess. What have you gotten yourself into this time?"

"I think she broke my arm." Keanid gritted her teeth.

"Who?"

"That alien girl in the news. The one who flies around in a red cape and wears a bikini."

"You're one to talk. You ran into her?"

"Not exactly. She ran into me."

"Okay." He lifted Keanid over the tank's edge and set her in slowly. "Gently now."

"Ow!" She whined. "Ow!"

"I'm going as easy as I can. Just relax. You'll feel better when you're submerged."

Once in the healing water, she drank deep and slowly relaxed.

"What possessed you to pick a fight with her?" he asked.

Her head lifted above the water. "Never mind her. Could you get the case I came in with?"

"All right. You sit back and heal up, and I'll be back in a sec. You still have a butt chewing coming your way, and don't think you're getting out of it!"

"I know, Dad. Sorry."

"Sorry?" He exited the room. "You'll be sorry," he grumbled as he walked into the living room. "Mermaids fighting aliens. Great." He gathered the case, stomped back into the tank room, and placed it by the tank. "In all my years, I never thought that..." His words trailed away as he opened the case and examined the unique object within. "Holy mackerel. Would you look at that? The symbols on that thing is similar to your necklace."

She nodded. "It's almost the same design as well."

"Yeah, but this piece is too big to be jewelry. It looks like some kind of rock or stone. You mind telling me how you got your hands on this?"

She rolled her shoulder and stretched out her arm. "You know that smuggler who deals in so-called relics I was telling you about?"

"That Jackson guy, right?"

"Yeah. Well, my surveillance paid off."

"Surveillance? Is that what you've been doing these past few months? Spying on people?"

"Yes. What did you think I was doing?"

"Oh, I don't know." He threw his hands into the air. "Maybe going out and having a good time. You know, living the life of a normal young lady."

"Normal? When was I ever that? I don't have time for that kind of stuff. I have to get to the bottom of this. That object could explain a lot about my past and who my mother was."

"You are so damn hardheaded," he muttered. "You know that, don't you?"

"Kind of. My dad keeps telling me."

He sighed. "Okay. So, this relic dealer, why don't you ask him where he got it?"

"Can't. He's sort of dead."

"Damn it, Keanid!" he exploded.

She sank under the water's surface.

"No! You get up here, so you can hear me yelling at you!"

"I didn't have a choice," she said as her head popped out of the water. "He and his henchmen had every intention of taking me out. There was also a guy there who I never saw before. He had green hair and stupid-looking glasses."

"What's so important about him?"

"He was buying this artifact for his boss with two million in gold."

"Gold? He was paying in *gold*?"

"Yeah, but we might have other problems. He sort of saw what I am. And he got away."

"Good Lord." He stroked his bushy, gray-shot beard. "We do have problems."

From his office window, Nishimura gazed at downtown Driven's lit streets. He was lost in thought, dwelling on his new animot soldiers.

After a soft knock, Johnny entered.

"Something went wrong," he stated as he saw Johnny's reflection in the window.

"What makes you say that, boss?"

"You knocked." He turned and faced Johnny.

"I managed to recover your gold." Johnny smiled as he lifted the suitcase, which sported blood spatter flecks about its leather surface.

"Well?"

He placed the suitcase down on his desk, slid his bulky white glasses to his forehead, and rubbed his eyes. "I don't know how to tell you this, so I'm just gonna come out and say it. We've got more than an alien problem."

The following morning, Detective Akeda wandered on the cargo ship's deck as the forensic team toiled to piece together the previous night's events.

A thin individual in a suit and crumpled tie entered the crime scene and headed to the detective. "How are you doing, Detective Akeda? I'm

Detective Dasko," he said, shaking his hand. "The captain told me that I'm temporarily replacing Detective Appulo while he's on vacation."

"Good to meet you, Dasko. You made detective not long ago, didn't you?"

"Six months and counting. The captain said that I can learn a lot from a veteran like yourself." He placed his hands on his hips and surveyed the scene. "So, what do you think caused the bloodbath here? Drugs, arms, human trafficking?" He smiled. "Domestic dispute?"

"I showed up an hour ago, and I can already tell this case has a lot of moving parts."

"How many stiffs?"

"Victims," Akeda corrected.

"How many victims?"

"Ten so far. One of the deceased is none other than Fingers Jackson himself."

"I've heard of him. Smuggler extraordinaire. He was supposed to be one of the smart ones."

"That's the odd thing. He's known for dealing in stolen merchandise, but we haven't found any product or money so far. I'm guessing not all parties are present."

"Someone got away, huh? Sounds reasonable. I'm going to take a look around, if that's cool."

"Knock yourself out. But before you do, what do you make of this?" Akeda produced a medium-sized plastic bag that held a decent-sized fish scale. The morning sun reflected off its gleaming surface, creating a brilliant azure light.

"That's one big fish. Pretty too. I've never seen that type of scale. Do you think Jackson lowered his standards and started dealing in seafood?"

"Exotic fish? Possibly. I'll take it over to the lab and see what they make of it."

"Gotcha. I'll continue detecting."

Akeda left the ship and walked to his car. He removed the telepathic crystal from his pocket and held onto it. *Got a minute?* he thought.

Of course, Reiko said in his head. *I'll be there in a second.*

He took a step back. *I heard... You never said this thing has two-way communication.*

It can. I just have to concentrate harder for it to function.

Okay, I guess? I'll see you soon. He slipped the shard back into its place and sighed. "Mental communication? Superhero on demand?" He shook his head. "What have I got myself into?"

In moments, Reiko glided down and landed in front of him. "I was here last night," she said matter-of-factly, looking around. "This was where that explosion originated from."

"That's what I wanted to talk to you about." He opened the passenger door. "Get in."

"Ooo. I've never been in an Earth vehicle before." She sat in the passenger seat, glanced around the interior, and inhaled. "It smells like you."

Akeda entered and sat. "What?"

"Nothing." She focused on the car's radio. "What does this do?" She pressed its buttons.

He found the rapid change in music annoying. "Do you mind?" He set the radio back on his favorite jazz station.

She listened for a bit. "What kind of music is that?"

"Contemporary jazz. I find it relaxing. What kind of music do you listen to?"

"Ildeklatik, but this planet doesn't have the proper minerals to play it."

"Ildeka... What?"

"Ildeklatik."

"What's it sound like?"

"Oh, I can't do it. It sounds real ethereal. Soothing. Peaceful."

"Right." He started the car. "Could you fill me in on what happened on that ship last night?"

"Hold on." She flicked the AC vents up and down. "After we spoke last night, I flew here, and I found a young woman fighting armed aggressors. She had blue hair, and she could change her form."

"Change her form to what?"

"Her lower half turned into a glossy fishtail."

"What?" Akeda spat. "You're telling me you saw a mermaid?"

"Is that what they're called?"

He removed the bagged fish scale from his inside jacket pocket. "I found this at the scene."

"That's hers. That deep blue is such a gorgeous color."

"Blue hair and a blue tail. It just gets stranger by the day." He returned the bag and got out his phone.

"What are you doing now?" she asked as she tested her seat belt.

"Making a call."

"Those phone devices. Everyone I've seen has one. Are they issued to the public by some governing body?"

"No. It doesn't work like that."

Dasko's voice rang through the phone's speaker. "Hey, detective. Long time no see. What's up?"

"A source just informed me that one of the suspects from last night's fiasco was a young woman with blue hair." Akeda glanced over to find Reiko rifling through the car's glove compartment.

"Well, that describes just about a quarter of the young women in Driven. Could you be more specific?"

"Sorry. That's all I have for now. Just keep an eye out. Bye."

"Later." The new detective put away his phone and strolled to the side of the ship. "Young lady, blue hair. Yeah."

To his unbelieving eyes, he saw a woman, a comfortable distance from the boat, dressed in a light-colored jacket and shorts. She sat on a motorcycle, monitoring the police activity. Long blue hair poured out of the back of her helmet. Noticing him watching her, she started her bike and sped off.

"Oh no, you don't," he said as he hastily headed to his car.

"Here we are," Akeda said as his car turned into the end of the forensic lab's parking lot.

"What is this place?" Reiko asked.

"A crime lab. It's basically a comprehensive science lab that we use to gather evidence concerning crimes."

"Oh."

"I'll have them look at this scale, and maybe they can shed some light on our mysterious mermaid. I've got a funny feeling they'll refer me to a marine biologist."

"Are they rare?"

"What? Mermaids or marine biologists?"

"The fishy girl."

"You could say that. They're not supposed to exist."

"I see. Most perplexing."

"Certainly. Let's go."

"Disengage," Reiko said as she pressed the release button on her seat belt. She left the vehicle and joined Akeda as he exited the driver's side. "Is that the building you need to go to?" She pointed at a multi-story structure located a good hike from where they were.

"Yeah. I parked out here, so you can take off without your admirers showing up."

"That was very thoughtful." She smiled. "I'm sure I'll see you soon."

"I have that feeling as well. Goodbye for now."

"Bye, Detective Akeda," she said before she blasted up into the blue sky.

"She's growing on me," he muttered as he watched her vanish into a haze of distant clouds. "And there I go overanalyzing again."

Keanid rode her bike onto a bustling boardwalk with an accompanying pier that stretched out to the sea. Being immersed in the large crowd and colorful storefronts always gave her comfort. Made her feel human. She removed her helmet and put a hand through her hair. "Are you there?" she asked.

"Yeah, I'm here," Abe responded from his living room table. "I can't stand having this damn high-tech thingy shoved in my ear."

"Sorry, but they're supposed to be the best nonintrusive communicators on the market. Waterproof too."

"Yeah, yeah. Still feels like I've got someone's finger jammed in my ear. So, what's the word?"

"The ship was crawling with cops, so I couldn't look around." She locked her helmet to her bike and dismounted.

"I told you that was going to happen. They won't leave the area until they get some solid answers."

She drew in the sea breeze as she mixed in within the morning crowd. "I guess I'll just slip in there tonight."

"No point. Anything of interest will be gone by then."

"Then what can I do?!" she blurted as frustration overcame her. "I have to find out who that idiot with the green hair was."

"Say, that's a nice bike," a man in a suit said as he approached her.

"Thanks," Keanid casually answered. "Nice suit. Aren't you a little overdressed for the beach?"

"Not really." He flashed his badge. "I'm Detective Joe Dasko. Do you mind if I ask you a few questions?"

"I... Why?" she stammered.

"I'm investigating a situation that happened at the docks last night. One of our witnesses said that a person of interest, who looks a lot like you, might know something. So, is that true? You got something you want to tell me?"

Her mind raced. "Uh..."

Her eyes moved away from the youthful detective and focused on two individuals garbed in trench coats and sunglasses. When the two got close, they produced submachine guns from under their bulky coats. She grabbed Dasko and shoved him to the boardwalk's floor as the two individuals sprayed the crowd and nearby stores with a hail of gunfire.

"Everybody get down!" Dasko whipped around with his pistol ready and returned fire.

As the two emotionless assailants reloaded their weapons, Keanid touched her necklace, manifesting her rifles. The panic screams from the fleeing crowd filled her with rage. She opened fire.

Combining their efforts, Dasko and Keanid dropped the two attackers. He reloaded his gun while cautiously approaching the still bodies. Sparks flashed from their joints. Their rubbery faces resembled a strange amalgamation of a human and a doll.

He gasped. "What are these things?"

"Come on. We've got to go!" Keanid grabbed his arm. "More of them are coming!"

"I have to protect the public, okay? I'm not going anywhere!" He turned to face four more of the same-looking individuals as they approached. "Stop where you are and show me your hands!"

One of the animots removed a small missile launcher from under its coat and aimed at Keanid. The projectile shot across the air as she tackled Dasko. It struck an ice cream store behind them, blowing up the building into a violent plume of smoke and flames. The blast sent them both flying further down the boardwalk.

An animot soldier grabbed the dazed Keanid by her hair and yanked her to her feet. She spun her arm upward, breaking the android's grip. She then followed that with a series of quick punches and a strong kick, knocking the opponent back. With some space between them, she drew in a deep breath and released a piercing siren scream. The sonic attack overloaded the robot's sensory functions, causing it to stand idle and shut down. Its lifeless body collapsed to the ground.

"What...did you just do to him?!" Dasko asked.

"We've got to go!"

"You wanna tell me why they're targeting you?!"

Another missile took flight toward them. Speechless, the two could do nothing but wait for the inevitable impact.

With a burst of speed, Reiko snatched the projectile out of the air and launched it back at the animot who fired it, destroying the robot and another that stood beside it.

"You've got to be kidding me." Dasko gasped. "It's her."

She hovered in the air and glanced at the two. She and Keanid made eye contact, and with a nod, she flew to engage with the remaining animots.

From above the stores, three more animots, flying with personal jet-packs, came into view. They opened fire on Keanid and Dasko with their automatic weapons.

"These guys can fly now?" the exasperated detective blurted.

She grabbed his arm once again and pulled him along. "To the pier!"

"If we go there, they'll box us in!"

"Just trust me!"

She rushed to the pier as quickly as she could. One of the airborne animots launched a missile at them. The thunderous explosion threw the two flailing into the air with a shower of debris.

Keanid opened the lighthouse's door and dragged in the soaked, unconscious Dasko behind her. She used the last of her strength to slide him through the door. She huffed. "Dad?" she called out. "A little help here."

"What are you playing at this time?" Abe walked over and stopped when he saw the unconscious young man pooling water on the floor. "Who the hell is that?"

"The catch of the day," she said as she struggled to get her breath back.

"Don't get smart with me, young lady! First, you bring home a mysterious rock and now this?!"

"Could you help me? He's heavier than he looks."

"How could he be? He's skin and bones."

"Please, Dad. I'm really not in the mood."

"With the way you've been acting as of late, you could have fooled me," he said as he hoisted Dasko off the floor and moved him to a living room chair. "So, what's this kid's story?"

She stroked the detective's wet hair out of his eyes. "He's a cop."

"And you brought him here?"

"I didn't have a choice. I swear!" She folded her arms. "You're not going to believe this, but robots that looked like people were trying to kill us."

"We're fighting robots now? Aliens weren't enough?"

"I know it sounds crazy, but it's true. Speaking of aliens, fly girl showed up to help."

"Your party pal from last night? This just gets better and better." He groaned as he grabbed the remote and turned on the big-screen TV. Each local channel offered its take on the boardwalk attack and highlighted their new Valkyrie's heroic efforts. Abe turned off the TV and stabbed Keanid with an angry glare.

She looked at the floor. "I'm sorry, Dad. I let you down."

He opened his arms and collected his adopted daughter in a comforting embrace.

"I feel like I'm so close to understanding the truth about myself, and the world is trying to stop me." Her voice wavered as she fought back frustrated tears.

"No matter what's happening, we'll face it together, kiddo. You know that."

Dasko let out a sharp series of coughs.

"Showtime," he mumbled. "Put your game face on."

"Right." Keanid pulled a chair from the table and sat by her guest.

The detective wiped his eyes and took in his surroundings. "It's you." He smiled as he saw Keanid. "Where are we?"

"You're in my home. You're safe. I'm Keanid, and this is my dad, Abe."

"Abraham 'Porthole' Medalious," Abe said with a vigorous shake.

"Joe Dasko."

"So, you're a cop, huh?"

Dasko sat up, looking at his soaked clothes. "Detective. This suit is done for. Great. Does anybody want to fill me in on what the hell is going on?"

Keanid collected the strange stone relic and handed it to the baffled detective. "I think everything has to do with this."

"What is it? Some kind of antique? Well, actually, uh..." He gave her an insecure grin. "I don't mean to impose or anything, but you guys got a towel or something?"

"Yeah." Abe stepped away. "Give me a sec."

"I'm guessing this piece costs a pretty penny." Dasko ran his fingers along the odd inscriptions embedded in the object's surface.

"Maybe. I don't really care. I suspect it serves another function."

"Like what?"

"I'm not sure yet."

"You had some guns earlier, and you used them like a pro. Where did you get those?"

"My necklace." She held it up. "Believe it or not, it's magical."

Returning with a couple of towels in hand, Abe cleared his throat and glared at his daughter. "Here you go."

"Thanks." Dasko accepted the towels and wiped his face. "Magical, you say?"

"It belonged to my mother." She nodded at the object. "I think my heritage is linked to this relic. Its architecture looks similar to my necklace."

"Yeah, I can see that. It's possible they were made by the same culture. Which heritage do you think it is?"

"I'm a mermaid."

"Oh, boy!" Abe tossed his arms up into the air.

"Mermaid." Dasko grinned. "I thought mermaids wore seashell bras."

She raised her eyebrow. "You're about to find yourself back in the ocean."

The roof exploded above their heads in a furious display, blanketing the three in a heap of brick and debris.

As Nishimura stared across the city from his office window, his phone vibrated. Johnny's number displayed. With some reluctance, the yakuza boss answered. "Yes?"

"Good news, boss," Johnny reported. "Through the miracle of modern science and awesome ingenuity, we've captured the relic and blue hair."

"Blue hair?"

"You know, the freaky fish girl I was telling you about."

"Is she alive?"

"Well, yeah. But she doesn't have to be."

"Keep her alive. She cannot answer my questions if she's dead."

"You're the boss. Where do you want em?"

"Take both to our oceanic lab."

"Cosmic! I finally get to see that place! We'll take a chopper over. See you soon."

Abe coughed as dust entered his lungs. With what little room he had, he attempted to rub the soot from his eyes. A considerable amount of weight pressed down on his body, making it difficult to breathe. He drew in what breath he could and shouted. "Keanid!"

Oddly enough, the crushing weight lifted and disappeared altogether.

"Wha..." He groaned as a small pair of hands lifted him to his feet. After a good wipe over his eyes, he noticed the short alien girl with the glaring red cape standing in front of him.

"It's all right, mister." She smiled. "You're going to be okay. An ambulance is on its way. So are the police."

"It's you..."

"Reiko."

"Yeah."

"Here." She lifted a wooden chair and placed it behind him.

He sat, fighting through a dizzy fog that clouded his mind. "Keanid...

Is Keanid here? She's got long blue hair and an attitude. She's my little girl. Have you seen her?"

"I only found you and the other guy." She pointed toward an unconscious Dasko. "No one else is here."

"Asleep again? That kid sleeps more than he works." Abe coughed. "But if she isn't here, they've got her. You've got to get her back!"

"Calm down. While battling the androids, I noticed a few flying in this direction. I caught up with them as soon as I could. I don't know why they would want to attack you."

"It's that relic Keanid picked up. It's got to be."

"Relic?"

"It doesn't matter. Listen." He dug into his pants pocket, produced a turquoise stone, and stuffed it into her gloved hand. "Take this. It's a scrying stone that can locate her necklace. Please! You gotta find my daughter!"

Sirens approached from a distance.

"I will," she said. "I promise." Without hesitation, she exploded up into the endless sky.

Keanid's eyes opened. She found herself bound to a surgical table with thick leather straps in a metal room. At least her necklace still draped across her neck. But she noticed electric nodes, placed through tears in her clothing, were attached to both sides of her head and her chest. She pulled against the straps but to no avail.

The man with the green hair entered the room and stood by the table. "You sure are a feisty one. The boss is right behind me, so let me give you some advice if you want to remain pretty: don't make him angry."

The lab door slid open once more. Two more of those robots that looked like people entered with two determined-looking men.

"You will answer my questions," said the one who should be the boss in a monotone voice. "Failure to comply will result in exquisite pain. What exactly are you?"

She looked at the ceiling and remained silent.

"Excellent." The boss nodded.

The man who entered with him turned a lever protruding from a control panel. Electricity shot through her body, making her heart and lungs feel as if they were on fire. After she released an agonizing scream, the pain stopped.

"I'm...I'm a mermaid," she panted.

"Told ya, boss," the fool with the green hair said. "Saw it myself. The freakiest thing I've ever seen. Well, maybe the seventh freakiest."

"You claim to be a mermaid," the boss continued. "Is that why you stole the key?"

"Key? Is that what it's supposed to be?"

He nodded again. She screamed as the searing pain flowed through her. The electricity pulsed a few seconds longer than the first before it stopped.

"I am conducting this interview, not you," the boss declared.

Tears streamed down the side of her face. "I don't know what the relic is!"

"I believe her, boss." The fool rubbed his chin. "It's tough to fake that doe-eyed look. I don't think she knows what's going on."

"Perhaps," the boss admitted. "The key was crafted by an ancient race of aquatic humanoids called Kryodons. It has taken years of research and a small fortune to learn that their underwater temple is a mile from here. Legend has it that their elite warrior—Blood Water—rests within the temple. As we speak, I have animots using the key to release him. Once freed, he will cause havoc upon the surface. I will make sure of it."

"Even if all that is true, that alien girl will stop him. She's stronger than she looks."

"I intend for them to meet. Blood Water will kill the Valkyrie, and I will watch."

Deep under the ocean's dark waves, two of Nishimura's animots floated outside the massive doors of a partially embedded stone temple. One took the relic, inserted it into an appropriately sized slot, and turned. A hatch, roughly ten feet in circumference, opened, allowing a rush of seawater to flood the interior. As the water entered, one of the animots dropped a few explosive charges into the current, so they would enter the structure. After an explosion went off inside the temple, the animots returned to the surface.

Echoing through the temple's corridors, a furious cry for vengeance went unheard.

In the oceanic lab, an alarm chimed, accompanied by flashing red lights. Johnny moved to a terminal and viewed the security footage. "Guess what, boss? Your favorite flying heroine is on her way."

"Like clockwork," he said. "Fire the missiles."

"You got it."

They watched as missiles, over the waves, raced toward Reiko. She soared to each one and punched them, so they detonated in the air before they reached the shore. She grabbed the last one and threw it back at the lab, resulting in an explosion.

"She's knocking at the door," Nishimura said to his subjects. "Let's take our positions."

Johnny shrugged. "What about the mermaid?"

"Mermaid? All I see is a scared girl. She is irrelevant."

Moments after they exited the room, Reiko's hands pierced the metal wall and ripped a hole open. She stepped in.

"Get me out of this thing!" Keanid shrieked. She pulled at the leather straps.

"Your father is worried," she said as she snapped the straps.

"Is he okay?" Keanid slid off the table and yanked the electrical nodes from her body.

"Yes. He and the guy in the suit should be at a hospital by now. Who did this to you?"

"I don't know, but they can wait. We've got bigger problems right now. Come on!" She led Reiko back through the hole and stood on the building's edge. The gentle salty breeze was a welcoming sensation.

"It's a beautiful view," Reiko admitted. "But what are we looking at?"

"Hold on." She looked toward the flowing waves.

In moments, the water rumbled and formed into a tidal wave. An armored, muscular figure stood at its crest with scaly skin and large protruding fins that resembled razor-sharp swords. The figure grasped a trident with his clawed hands. The waves moved like they obeyed his commands.

Reiko's eyes widened. "Who is that?"

"His name is Blood Water." Keanid removed the remains of her ruined clothes, standing only in a bikini. "Ever heard of the Kryodons?"

"Of course. They're a reclusive aquatic race."

"They're aliens?"

"They don't originate on this planet if that's what you mean." She pointed. "He doesn't look like a Kryodon."

"We can figure that out later. We've got to stop him from wiping out Driven."

"Is he capable?"

"I'd rather not take the chance."

"Right. I'll go above, and you go below."

"Sounds like a plan. My name is Keanid, by the way. Keanid Medalious."

"Reiko."

"Okay, Reiko. Let's do this." With that, Keanid launched herself from the side of the lab and plummeted ten stories until she broke the sea's welcoming waves.

From the sky, Reiko soared toward Blood Water, who lifted his trident. Large spears, formed from the water, launched from the wave beneath him and struck several buildings close to the beach. Their impact's devastation looked as if the structures were hit by concrete.

She gasped. "He's changing the water's density! How can he do that?!"

In the comfort of a military-grade helicopter, Mr. Nishimura, Johnny, and Dr. Denoda watched conflict unfold.

"You did it, boss." Johnny cackled. "Fish face is angry. Ha! Look at that dude go!"

Mr. Nishimura ignored him. "Dr. Denoda, are you monitoring this?"

"Yes, sir," Dr. Denoda said as he typed on his laptop. "So far, the Kryodon's capabilities are off the charts. His ability to manipulate water is nothing less than breathtaking."

"Keep monitoring them. I want comprehensive combat data on both parties."

Keanid sprang up from under the ocean and opened fire on Blood Water with her rifles. As the mystical bullets bounced off his thick armor, he formed water into a fist and slammed her back beneath the waves.

Reiko charged toward him. He pivoted, directing his trident toward her and fired several gleaming bolts. She twirled, dodging the projectiles, and delivered a strong punch that knocked him off his wave. As he crashed into the sea, his tidal wave collapsed back into the ocean.

From the waves, a large water hand shot up to grab Reiko. She flew upward, just out of reach. "Valkyrie Flare!" she shouted as she scattered the hand into millions of droplets across the sea's surface. Not a moment later, large water tendrils flew from the surface and wrapped themselves around her, thrusting her under the waves.

As she fought against the bonds, Blood Water swam toward her with his trident. But Keanid blocked the attack with her twin swords.

With her opponent distracted, Reiko released an energy pulse from her body, which eliminated the tendrils. She shot through the water's surface, and as she hovered, she took in large gulps of air. She could make out Blood Water kicking Keanid away from him, but then he flew up. She readied herself for another attack as he shot out of the water and stood on its surface.

He engaged her with a series of swings and thrusts from his trident. She blocked his attacks, but another water fist attacked her side, causing her to drop back into the water. Keanid caught the sinking heroine and lifted her back to the surface.

Blood Water connected his trident to the back of his armor, grabbed both girls by their throats, and drew them toward him. Under his webbed feet, his tidal wave reformed, and he rode it to the beach.

Pedestrians fled as the triumphant warrior stepped onto the soft sand with his two captives. He slowly squeezed their necks, causing them both to choke for breath. But then he stopped and set their limp bodies down on the wet beach. He knelt before the hacking Keanid and lifted her necklace with his sharp nails to examine it more closely.

"You look just like your mother," he said with a voice as deep as the ocean itself.

Reiko's and Keanid's puzzled look mirrored each other. He stood and removed his trident from his armor. Holding it before him, the weapon radiated an ethereal glow, and Keanid's necklace responded in kind.

From her necklace, a holographic image of a woman with long blue hair appeared. Sadness tainted her beautiful face. "Love, our search for a new home in this world has failed. Only I and our daughter remain. As we feared, this world's waters are poisoned and incompatible with our physiology. I feel ill, but I will try to return to you as soon as I can. No matter what happens, my love will forever be with you, Varservious."

Tears welled in Keanid's eyes as the image faded.

"Her name was Naulla," Blood Water said with a gentle smile.

She stood and wiped her eyes. "I have so many questions."

"When you are ready, I will be waiting." He turned back to the sea and vanished under its tumbling waves.

She turned her tear-filled gaze toward her new friend. "That was my mom."

Reiko offered a reassuring smile and nodded.

From his helicopter, Mr. Nishimura watched the event in disgust.

"Bummer, boss." Johnny shook his head. "I didn't see that coming. He had them both on the ropes too."

"Pilot," he growled between gritted teeth, "get us out of here."

WARRIOR'S CODE

R EIKO WATCHED AS three armed robbers fled out of the bank's front glass doors and to their awaiting car. The driver barely waited for the last one to pile in before he slammed his foot on the gas pedal. The vehicle moved an inch forward before she swooped down and grasped the front bumper. With little effort, she flipped the car over onto its roof.

Its wheels still spun as one of the dazed robbers crawled out through the window and scrambled to his feet. He stammered to a female onlooker, who was more concerned about filming the whole affair than her safety, and yanked her in front of him. She screamed as he dug the pistol's barrel into her temple.

"Back off!" he shouted as Reiko approached. "I'll kill her. I swear!"

Reiko took another step but stopped. She could already hear the police filter onto the scene some distance behind her. "Killing in cold blood is something you're not capable of."

"Yeah? Take another step and find out!" He moved his weapon from the woman's head and pointed it at Reiko.

"Okay. I believe you," a familiar voice said behind him. A steellike grip ensnared the criminal's gun hand. He dropped to his knees.

Now free, the screaming hostage fled toward the police as they secured the perimeter.

Fighting back still, the robber cranked his neck back to find Reiko holding his hand. Looking forward again, the first Reiko still stood in front of him. "There's two of you?" he choked.

The first Reiko flickered and vanished in a splash of light.

"Energy projection decoy," she said from behind him. "Works every time." With that, she threw the man headfirst into one of the car's tires, knocking him out cold.

"Thank you for saving my life!" the former hostage yelled from behind the police.

"You're welcome!" She beamed as she waved. Deciding not to interfere any further, she launched into the world of wind above and left the police to their duties.

Maru's telepathic voice flooded her mind. *You seem very jovial today.*

It feels good to do good.

A productive morning then?

I had the honor of saving a life, Maru. What more could I ask for? Well, maybe some uninterrupted quality time with a certain detective.

Decorum, Reiko. Please practice it.

Sorry. I'll keep those thoughts to myself.

Speaking of interruptions, I'm registering two glaring energy signatures, and they're coming straight at you. From what I can make out, both are humanoid.

Reiko paused her airborne travels and levitated. *Anyone we know?*

Both are unknown quantities, I'm afraid. Prepare yourself just in case.

Right. Around this city, you never know what will show up. Reiko noticed the two figures in the distance. *I see them. An armored man and a woman with a beautiful blue cape. Another cape lover. That's a good sign.*

The man was garbed in silver and black armor, crafted from an unknown metal. A large cross emblem glowed soft white across his chest. "Hi." His disguised voice held an electronic tone. "You're a Justice Valkyrie from Volsogun, right?"

She nodded. "Yes. My name is Reiko."

Beside him was a beautiful woman with wavy black hair and brown skin. Her deep blue uniform was accented by gorgeous azure crystals. Her flowing cape complimented her uniform perfectly.

"Pleased to meet you," the man said. "I'm St. Guardian, and this is Azurite. We're from the Valiant Alliance. Ever heard of us?"

"Valiant Alliance is known throughout the known systems as a potent force for good," Reiko said. "I never knew you operated this far from galactic point zero."

"Then there's a lot you don't know about us." Azurite smiled. "Believe it or not, Valiant Alliance started its career on Earth years ago."

"Here?" Reiko widened her eyes. "This Class Two? I never would have guessed."

"We recently found out you were assigned here, and we came by to see if you would be interested in joining us."

"Me? Join Valiant Alliance?"

"Sure." Azurite shrugged. "Since you're here to protect the planet, you're stuck with us anyway. It wouldn't hurt if you joined a group of heroes who can help watch your back. Believe me, from a galactic viewpoint of Earth, it gets intense around—" She stopped. "That was weird."

"What is it?" St. Guardian asked.

"Energy fluctuation."

"I felt it too," Reiko said. "Like a warm sensation with a twinge of biting cold."

"Makes sense. You Valkyries are energy-based. So, what are we dealing with?"

"I don't know," Reiko admitted. "I've never felt anything like it."

"I've got a good guess." Azurite pointed toward a patch of multicolored light further in the sky. "The energy is being generated by whatever that is."

She tilted her head to the side. "Do you recognize it?"

"No, but it's definitely a portal of some kind. Its radiating energy is incredible. Whoever made it knew what they were doing."

St. Guardian turned toward the portal. "Sorry our meeting had to be interrupted, Reiko, but we can't ignore this."

"Neither can I." Reiko nodded. "How would you veterans normally deal with something like this?"

"Only one way," Azurite said with a confident smile. "We go in."

"Oh... Right." She concentrated on Maru. *Maru, a portal just opened above Driven. I'm going in. I may not be able to communicate with you once I'm through.*

One of those days, is it? Very well. Be careful.

I will. She turned to her new allies. "All right. No time to waste." Taking point, she sped toward the prism in the sky.

The two followed her.

They drifted into an unfamiliar part of space illuminated by distant gleaming stars. Their only landmarks around were a field of asteroids that floated aimlessly around them. Reiko flew and stood on the craggy surface of one, hoping to get a better view.

A ghostly chime sounded, and the chromatic portal shut behind them.

"Not really what I had in mind," St. Guardian said, not far from her. "I was thinking we would end up on some lush green planet with a fantasy look to it."

"Knights and dragons and all that? You'd fit in perfectly." Azurite smirked. "Where are we?"

"Let's see." He formed a holographic map of the galaxy in his left palm. "We're still in the known systems, and that's always a good sign. Give me one minute to pinpoint our location."

Reiko's eyes widened. "You have a galactic map?"

"One of the benefits of my armor."

"It must be very technologically advanced. Was it made on Earth?"

"It's not tech-based. It's crafted from Soul Tide. I'm a Soulvenger."

"I've never heard of a Soulvenger before." As she spoke, a whirring noise emanated from the asteroid close to her feet. To her surprise, a laser turret sprang from the asteroid's surface. "Where did that come from?"

Several more emerged from the other asteroids surrounding them. Once they had all been deployed, they turned their barrels to a particular part of space and opened fire.

"This is a fire line!"

They all turned toward the target area and witnessed a fleet of ships prepare to return fire.

"We better move before we get blasted in the crossfire!"

The three heroes soared away from the laser exchange, only to be riddled with laser fire from a spacecraft that raced by at high speed.

St. Guardian said, "That ship... That's Orbian architecture!"

"Damned cyborgs!" Azurite stabilized herself and stopped in place. "They never quit, do they?"

Reiko drifted to rejoin the other two. "I have not faced Orbians before, nor have I ever heard of them. Are they bad?"

"To the core!" Azurite's fists clenched. "That means those turrets belong to them."

"Why would they attack those ships?"

"The Achilles' heel of all cyborgs: parts. They're always in need of parts." St. Guardian dissipated the map in his palm. "They've been known to raid whole colonies for them. If you don't mind, see what you can do with that fighter. It's circling around for another attack."

"Right." Reiko shot through space and used her body like a bullet, flying through the ship. In a furious ball of rolling fire, the craft reduced to nothing more than scattered fragments of burnt debris.

St. Guardian was stunned. "Did you see that?"

Azurite laughed. "I sure did. My girl took out the whole thing by punching through it."

"I thought entry-level Justice Valkyries were supposed to have a power rating of six."

"She's more than that. A rookie couldn't do what she just did."

"Tell me about it."

Reiko returned to her two new friends, sporting a broad smile. "Taken care of." She spotted something beyond them and nodded toward it. "Is that an Orbian?"

The two turned as a humanoid garbed in an armored space suit flew toward them with the aid of a jetpack.

"No, it's not," Azurite confirmed. "Looks like he came from one of those ships."

"Thank you for the assistance, friends," the individual said as he reached them. "I'm Captain Galmore, commander of *Phantalis*, the third vessel of the fleet."

"St. Guardian." He pointed to himself. "Azurite and Reiko. It was our pleasure to help."

"Please, come on board. The general wants to personally thank you for your help in defeating the Orbian menace."

"What about the laser turrets?" Reiko asked. "Do you want us to do something about them as well?"

"Reiko?" Azurite asked.

"Yes?"

She pointed at the asteroids' remains, decimated by the ship fleet.

"Oh."

"Please," St. Guardian said to the captain, "lead the way."

Secured within the airlock, Galmore pressed his back to a metallic pad on the wall. In moments, his helmet and space suit removed themselves from his body in a modular fashion and stored themselves neatly on the wall. "It was fortuitous to run into you all out there. The Orbians have been hounding us ever since we had to evacuate our home planet." The airlock's door slid open. "Please, this way."

As the four coursed down a polished corridor, they passed the ship's inhabitants, who looked like humans and were clothed in color-coded jumpsuits.

"Where are you guys from?" Azurite inquired.

"Carthia. We're Carthians."

St. Guardian lowered his voice, sounding more professional. "Carthians? Yes, I've heard of your people. Though very little, I must admit. What prompted you to leave your home world?"

"A geological anomaly. At least that was what our scientists said. Corrosive clouds bellowed from under our planet's surface. Small pockets at first, but they expanded worldwide. The projected death toll put us on the brink of extinction, so we evacuated."

"If the crisis was that widespread, I'm surprised you had enough time to organize a mass exodus."

"We salvaged what we could with the time we had. We mortgaged our future on eight star-class vessels. Still, the price was too high."

"I counted six," Azurite stated.

"Yes." Galmore's tone turned somber as he stopped at the doors leading to the ship's bridge. "The general can elaborate on that."

He opened the bridge door, and the three followed closely behind. The bridge itself was technologically complex with humming terminals and colorful holographic displays. The personnel numbered around fifty, who went about their duties while paying little mind to the captain and his new guests.

In the bridge's center stood a towering chair with various tubes and hoses running to and from it. An old man with a trailing white beard sat at its helm. A variety of electrical nodes and lines ran from his body and connected to a terminal. He, without a doubt, was a cyborg himself. "Welcome to the *All-Journey*, my friends. I am General Norceran." A warm smile formed on his wrinkled face. "You three truly are the heroes of the hour."

"You are too kind, General," St. Guardian said with a brief bow. "It seems we both have issues with Orbians."

"Savages! Bane of the stars! Their attempt to best us has failed thanks to your efforts. Tell me, how much do you know about us Carthians?"

"I know that you are engineered human hybrids, immune to sickness and disease." He shrugged. "Captain Galmore informed us of your home world's fate. Allow me to offer my deepest sympathies for your loss."

"Thank you, St. Guardian."

His posture stiffened. "How do you know my name? I didn't mention it."

"I am the last first-generation Carthian. Therefore, I was made general, and, as tradition dictates, the general and his fleet become one. This chair not only connects me to every inch of my ships but to their personnel as well."

"Then losing two must have been like losing limbs," Azurite said as she folded her arms.

Galmore stepped forward. "How dare you!"

"Compose yourself, Captain. Leave her be." The general lifted his frail hand. "The Orbians have been chasing us ever since we left Carthia."

"There must be a reason," Reiko stated to ease the tension.

"Computer projections predict that the Orbians wish to capture us so that they may integrate our physiology with theirs, thus making them more resilient," Galmore explained. "We are, after all, one of the most successful genetic hybrids ever produced."

"What about extinction?" St. Guardian suggested. "Orbians will annihilate humans on sight, hybrid or not."

"But the simulations—"

The general nodded, stopping him. "That would explain a great deal, my friend. A possibility that seems truer than we are ready to accept. Orbus, their leader, personally saw to the destruction of *Alpha-Ranza*, the fourth vessel of the fleet. I can't begin to explain to you what a devastating loss it was."

"Indeed." Galmore nodded. "By the time we discovered they used shadow binding technology to hide in the fabric of space itself, it was too late to save the *Alpha-Ranza*. We could only evacuate as many as we could."

"Shadow binding?" St. Guardian tilted his head to the side. "I didn't realize they were capable."

"Neither did we. In response, we developed new scanning procedures, but we're still not certain of their accuracy."

"And what of the other vessel?" Reiko asked. "Did Orbus destroy it as well?"

"No." The general shook his head. "It wasn't destroyed."

"Then where is it?" Azurite asked.

"It vanished from time and space."

She put her hands on her hips. "How is that possible?"

"The seventh vessel, the *Endrastic*, carried an experimental warp drive system. During the Orbian attack, I gave the captain permission to use it, and so he did."

"I've never seen anything like it," Galmore recalled. "Space folded around the ship like a wave and swallowed it whole, leaving nothing behind."

Reiko raised her hand. "Speaking of space, which quadrant are we in?"

The general directed her to a large holographic galactic map. "There. The sixty-second quadrant."

"Oh, you use the number system. We Valkyries use the standard Terran Magnera nomenclature."

Galmore moved to the map and highlighted the precise quadrant. "We are here."

"Wow." Her eyes widened. "We traveled that far from galactic zero?"

"Is something wrong?"

"Captain, it seems our new friends are lost." The general grinned. "Delomaus, the planet we wish to colonize, is two quadrants away if you wish to travel with us."

"That might be best for now," St. Guardian said. "At least until we find out why we're this deep in space."

The bridge flashed red as an alarm echoed throughout the ship.

The captain turned to his leader. "General?"

"We are detecting a potential threat, but the visual scans indicate nothing."

Azurite turned toward the holographic screens. "Could it be another camouflaged firing line?"

"You could be right." St. Guardian examined the visual display. "There's a collection of asteroids up ahead. General, we'll go out there and have a look, if that's okay with you."

"Yes, of course. I thank you once again for your bravery."

He turned to Reiko. "Are you up for some more action?"

"Yes!" She smiled. "This team stuff is kind of exciting."

"Okay then, ladies. Let's move out."

In moments, the heroes exited out of the ship's airlock and flew into the gulf of space.

"Did you hear the old guy?" Azurite asked as they flew further away from the *All-Journey*. "Sixty-second quadrant?"

"Yeah," St. Guardian said. "We are very, very far from Earth."

"You two familiar with the quadrant numbering system?" Reiko asked.

"It is strongly suggested to commit all quadrants—names and numbers—to memory in the Valiant Alliance," Azurite said with a smirk. "Believe me, it's a real pain, but you never know where you'll end up. Kind of like today."

"Oh. I guess that's helpful. I don't think they knew anything about the portal that brought us here though."

St. Guardian nodded. "That's my read too. They had nothing to do with it."

"Yeah, but we still need to come up with some answers as to why that portal hung in the sky so close to us," Azurite said. "It was like an invitation."

"There was something odd about that whole interview," Reiko added. "Galmore was honest and upfront, but I feel that the general was holding back. If he's connected to all the ships as he claims, then he should still feel the *Endrastic*, right?"

Moving from a folding layer of dark space, a creature resembling a nine-foot gorilla with metallic skin and a giant robotic eye that encompassed the upper portion of its head lunged for Reiko. She barely escaped its grasp and flew backward to create some distance between her and the hulking creature.

"An Orbian warmonger!" St. Guardian declared. "It veiled itself by shadow binding!"

She dashed her fist into the cyborg's face and followed that with another painful punch.

"Keep him busy!" Azurite called as her hands charged with energy. Within seconds, her glowing hands fired a shimmering blue laser that sliced the warmonger's left arm away.

"Good shot!" St. Guardian's right shoulder formed a multi-tiered missile launcher.

"Reiko, fire in the hole!"

The Valkyrie raced away from the injured creature as St. Guardian's missiles screamed through the void and exploded into the cyborg. The cyborg was reduced to smoldering parts that floated into the infinite distance in an instant.

Reiko sighed. "I'm glad we took it out quick. If that thing had gotten its hands on me, it would have—"

An ion bomb, hidden within the cyborg's chest, exploded, sending an aura of burning light in all directions and tossing all three unconscious heroes through the void.

St. Guardian stirred. His eyes opened, and the world through his helmet looked like a metal cell saturated by bleak lighting. Azurite and Reiko rested near him on a wall. Their hands stretched over their heads, bound by energy-shielded clamps. His situation was no better.

The cell door slid open, and two Orbians entered, holding their auto laser rifles before them. They looked like the rest of their hybrid race: the same purple and green body armor and a single giant eye that encompassed the upper portion of their heads. The lower half of their faces resembled a metallic version of a human skull.

Entering behind the first two, an Orbian stood about seven feet tall with unique details on his armor. This was, no doubt, their leader. "Vanguard Alliance! It is a pleasure to see your numbers suffer by my superior Orbian technology."

"Not so loud, okay?" St. Guardian said. "My head's still ringing."

"You got a name, gruesome?" Azurite said as she opened her eyes.

"I am Orbus, Lord of the Orbian Cabal. While you are in my custody, you will be wise to answer my questions. If not, you will feel the wrath of my psychotronic power."

"Your minutes are numbered, Orbus." She pulled against her bonds. "Use them wisely."

"Let us begin by satisfying my curiosity. How did you defeat my warmonger? It was designed to decimate an army."

Reiko stirred. "If that is the height of your battle technology, the Carthians have little to fear from you," she said lazily.

St. Guardian chuckled. "Good one."

The towering foe gripped her face and blasted her with a warping beam from his giant eye. She closed her eyes, recoiling in agony.

"Mock me at your peril, little one!" Orbus barked after he ceased his attack. "Now, intelligence reports indicate that you were seen leaving the *All-Journey*. What did Norceran tell you? Did you make an alliance with him? Did he mention the *Endrastic*? Answer me!"

"You're wasting your breath, ugly," Azurite spat. "We're not telling you a thing!"

"Insolent wretch! Perhaps you will think differently after I reduce your ally's brain to paste!" Once again, he held Reiko's face.

"Not this time!" St. Guardian's shoulder armor formed into a missile launcher and fired projectiles into Orbus and his guards.

The multiple explosions sent the host flying across the cell. Azurite ramped up her energy output and melted the wall behind her with a burning blue glow. She then flew full force at Orbus, taking him through the wall behind him. St. Guardian moved to Reiko, who struggled to break her bonds.

"Those are energy inhibiting cuffs," he explained. "That's why you're having trouble. Just hold still. I'll get you out of there in a second."

Azurite punched through several walls with Orbus' body until the final wall ripped into a spaceship hangar. She stopped her flight midway through the room, allowing momentum to continue taking Orbus through the air.

A small army of cyborgs scrambled to arm themselves.

"No. We're not doing that." She pushed her glowing fists before her and fired twin beams into them. A satisfying chain explosion burst from the soldiers and spread across the ships docked in the hanger.

St. Guardian pried the clamps from Reiko's wrists. The vessel shook around them. "Let's find Azurite and get out of here before this whole place explodes!"

They flew through the series of holes that Azurite created until they reached the burning hanger.

"Azurite!" He could barely make out her floating figure due to the growing flames.

"Coming!"

As she turned, Orbus shot her with his notorious psychotronic power, causing her to collapse onto the burning hanger floor.

"Reiko, make a hole!" St. Guardian ordered as he flew to rescue his comrade.

"You got it!" Reiko punched through the wall, exposing the room to the vacuum of space. As items and various wreckage flew through the hole, she turned her sights to Orbus' menacing figure. "Try attacking me again, coward!" She shot toward him, avoiding the wave of his psychotronic beam. Her fist slammed into the skull portion of his face and tossed him back into a bellowing bed of fire.

"Insignificant maggot!" Orbus shrieked as his chest unit folded open. A wide concentrated beam shot from it, striking her. It punched her out of the ship and into space.

On *All-Journey*'s bridge, Captain Galmore watched the tremendous explosion via a holographic map. "Do you think they made it?" he asked his general with a somber tone.

"In this instance, like all others," the general responded, "we must embrace our core ethic. We must hope and believe."

On the verge of consciousness, Azurite rubbed her head and tried to focus on the fuzzy light drops that filled the endless backdrop around her.

"How are you feeling?" St. Guardian asked as he hovered by her side. "You took a pretty nasty blast back there."

"Is Orbus dead?"

"I can't tell." He looked toward the massive collection of drifting debris in the distance. "I'm sure we'll see him again someday. You know how that works."

She smiled. She was all too familiar with the many ironies of heroism. "Yeah, I do."

"Hey, Reiko." He waved as she flew toward him. "You still in one piece?"

"Yes. I suppose now I can say I'm familiar with Orbians. I don't like them much at all. But, on the bright side, I have learned a great deal, and learning is part of being a protector."

"Somebody's shooting for the top of the class." Azurite chuckled. "Watch out, St. Guardian. Looks like you've got competition for the teacher's pet department."

"Ha ha," he responded dryly.

"I am wondering..." Reiko pointed toward a tall palace, composed of gleaming light and perched on a floating bedrock of stone, that drifted some distance away. "What's that?"

St. Guardian's eyes widened. "That's an excellent question."

"It's one gorgeous pad," Azurite admitted.

"Let's have a look." Reiko flew toward the magnificent structure with the other two in tow. After a short glide, they landed on the rock foundation.

"I've never seen such architecture before," Azurite said with wonder in her voice. "Who could have built such a place?"

"Maybe she can tell us."

Reiko nodded toward a woman in a silvery flowing dress that hung from her hips and was held together by straps that crossed her chest. Her long hair glistened like the stars themselves. She stood in the palace entryway, smiled at them, and entered.

"She wants us to follow."

"What do you think?" Azurite asked her partner.

"It could be a trap, but I don't think so. Let's give her the benefit of the doubt."

"Okay," she said, not sounding too convinced. "I mean, what else could happen today?"

As they walked into the glowing castle, Reiko's mouth dropped. Its structure looked as though it was forged by a strange blend of science and dreams. "It's so beautiful."

St. Guardian saw the woman from a distance and approached with caution. "Hello. I'm St. Guard—"

"Guardian of Valiant Alliance. I know who you are," she said in a kind and authoritative voice. "I know all of you are champions, and you are welcome in my home. I am Kasara Tori, Keeper of the Solerex."

"The Solerex?!" His eyes widened, and his jaw dropped. "The Cosmos Shard?! If the legends are true, you must be the Vortex Witch."

"A name the eons have unfortunately branded me. I prefer Kasara. Please, follow me."

They followed her deeper into the vortex palace.

With each step, Reiko got more lost in examining the building's structure. "This place... It seems it was built by impossibilities."

"It is formed by, and contained within, the vortex of time and space," Kasara explained. "Think of it as a stream flowing under a bridge. Reality would represent the bridge, and time would be the stream. The Solerex would be a small stone that stands above the water."

"Such concepts are difficult to comprehend. All of this just seems so unreal."

"Unreal?" She repeated with a grin. "There's more." She led them into a vast chamber with a wall that glittered with pinpoints of starlight. A massive crystal carved by unknown hands revolved above a swirling pool that funneled into infinity. "There, champions! Witness its grandeur with your own eyes. There is Solerex, the Cosmos Shard!"

"Magnificent!" St. Guardian said. "And the pool beneath it? What is that?"

"The Pool to Another Forever."

"This day just gets weirder and weirder." Azurite took a step back. "Why do I have this funny feeling that we mere mortals shouldn't be allowed to see these things?"

St. Guardian nodded. "I'm feeling that way too."

Reiko stared into the Solerex. "It feels like home."

"Tell me, Kasara," he said plainly as he continued to examine the giant shard, "why did you allow us to come here?"

"I am in need of champions." She stepped closer to him with a warm smile. "Will you offer your aid?"

"If you know who he is, you know he's got a fiancée," Azurite blurted.

Reiko turned. "He's getting married?"

"Yeah, but she doesn't know about his superhero alter ego."

She put her hand over her mouth. "Ooo."

"I'll tell her," St. Guardian said in a stern voice.

"When?" Azurite pressed further.

"Later. I'm doing hero business right now." He returned his attention to Kasara. "What do you need help with?"

"When you entered into this part of space," Kasara said, "you were allowed to see the Carthians and learn of their plight."

Reiko thrust her finger into the air. "It was you who opened that portal on Earth?"

"Yes."

"But creating a portal from many quadrants away is unheard of."

"Not for someone like her, Reiko," St. Guardian interjected. "She's supposed to be from a race of powerful dimensional beings called celestials."

Azurite turned sharply toward him. "How did you know that?"

"Boss taught me everything he knows about cosmic and dimensional beings. You know how he is."

"Yeah, I do, teacher's pet," she said in a louder voice. "Just because you're his protégé, you get all the inside knowledge that the rest of us don't. I guess that's one of the perks of taking up the St. Guardian mantle."

Ignoring the others, Reiko walked closer to the mysterious hostess. "Is it true, Kasara? Are you a celestial?"

"St. Guardian is correct. I am."

"Why do I feel like I know you?"

"We've never met."

She paused for a moment and then got back on track. "We spoke to the general and heard his story. It is both tragic and hopeful."

"He told you of a ship that vanished."

"The *Endrastic*." She nodded.

"Hold up!" Azurite turned to the mysterious hostess. "It must have upset some kind of cosmic balance, and that's why we're here. Right?"

"That's right," Kasara confirmed. "Your mission is simple. Destroy the *Endrastic*'s experimental drive or disable its use."

"I hope you're going to point the way to the ship cause that thing could be anywhere."

"I created a portal for you before. I shall do so again." With a wave of her hand, another prismatic door opened in the empty air before them. "Please hurry. The experimental drive is creating a strain on the very fabric of this dimension."

"We'll do our best, Kasara. I promise." St. Guardian nodded to his teammates. "You ready, ladies?"

"Sure." Azurite smirked. "Let's do this."

The three entered through the portal. Afterward, it vanished from existence.

Shunen wiped the blood from his face as he withdrew his blade from an orc's body. He drew in the battlefield's stale air and surveyed the red-stained land. His men, twenty in all, had victoriously driven back the latest band of invading monsters.

He trotted away from his latest kill and looked for any one of his numbers who required aid. Relief washed over him when he was confident that, although tattered and fatigued, they were safe.

"The Lady was with us," he whispered as he gazed up at the blue sky. "All right, you lot!" he shouted as he sheathed his bloodstained blade. "On your feet! Come on!"

The weary soldiers stirred and formed together.

He witnessed nothing but exhaustion on their faces. "We held them back, lads. All it took was a morning!" he barked in a rousing voice. "Today, we showed the enemy that humans are not to be taken lightly! That will certainly give those green-skinned pigs something to think about the next time they try to advance their ranks on our sacred soil!" He unsheathed his blade and pointed it toward the earth. "You see what we did today, lads? We gave our ancestors a present, an offering. Today, we gave them the blood of their enemies! Today, we honored our ancestors with the Warrior's Code, and now our ancestors will honor us!"

The group lifted their weapons with an enthusiastic cheer.

The three heroes exited into a lush world with rolling emerald fields and strong trees that gently swayed with the cool breeze.

Azurite took in the sight with a smile. "Looks like you got your fantasy world after all."

But then her vision blurred. The world spun. "My head... It's spinning..."

"Yeah," St. Guardian agreed. "I'm not feeling so...hot."

Reiko helped the two sit down. "What's happening?"

"No idea." He slid off his helmet, exposing his youthful face and sandy blond hair. "This doesn't usually happen...when using unconventional means of travel."

"It could be a dimensional barrier thing." Azurite rubbed her head. "Hopefully, this passes soon."

"I've heard of this kind of thing happening...on occasion." He squinted his blue eyes toward the distance. "Reiko, could you take a look around? Make sure nothing dangerous is coming our way. We should only need a few minutes...to recover from this. I hope."

"Of course. I'll be back shortly." She took to the skies.

Shunen surveyed the battlefield and nodded. "Let's collect what we can before we return to camp. I can already see a good bit of scrap. We'll melt the orc's weapons and armor and hopefully make something respectable out of their shoddy craftsmanship." The smile escaped his face as the ground shook.

"What is that?" one of his soldiers asked.

He drew his blade from its resting place. "Forget the scrap, lads. I think we've got bigger concerns."

His eyes widened as a team of orcs rolled a portable ballista onto the battlefield. Behind them, a company of armed orcish warriors screamed.

"Tighten the formation!" he cried.

"There are too many of them!" one soldier shouted.

"No, lad." Shunen positioned his blade before himself. "It's just a bigger offering."

The ballista fired toward his concentration of soldiers, but a woman with a red whipping cape punched the bolt in flight, snapping it in two. She then darted for the wooden siege weapon, uppercutting it into the sky. It tumbled over the orcish soldiers and crashed into pieces onto the stained green earth. The orc commander ordered his soldiers to retreat, and they did, disappearing beneath the same hill they had once come. The woman then soared toward the baffled human soldiers and landed before them.

"Hello," she said with a kind smile.

The men cheered.

Shunen fell to one knee before her, and his fellow soldiers followed suit. "I don't believe it!" His eyes welled with joyful tears. "You've returned!"

"Returned? No, you are mistaken. I've only just arrived here with a couple of—"

"Do you see this, lads?" He stood and faced his men. "Our ancestors have accepted our offering and have smiled upon us! The Lady has returned! It is a good omen! We will be victorious against Dregart's legions!"

Reiko listened to a new chorus of cheers from the battered men. The celebration descended into fear though as St. Guardian and Azurite landed beside her.

"What's going on here?" St. Guardian, wearing his helmet again, asked.

Reiko shrugged. "I'm not so sure."

Shunen stepped forward. "You brought more champions with you, my Lady? This is truly a happy day! I am Shunen Brenhart, a humble company leader who serves in His Majesty's army." He gave a brief bow.

"Come. We must see Field Commander Aldevin at once and tell him that the tide of battle has changed!"

"Um... Okay," Reiko said with little confidence. "Lead the way."

The three followed Shunen and his men past a hill. There, a series of skiffs floated above the grass.

"Are those rowboats or something?" Azurite asked as she watched the soldiers pile into the curious vehicles with no oars or sails.

"Look at the bottom." St. Guardian pointed. "See those spheres sticking out?"

"Yeah."

"They contain Soul Tide. I can feel it."

"So, they're not using science?"

"No, they're using spirit power."

"Then you definitely got that fantasy world." Azurite tapped Reiko's shoulder. "Is there anything you want to tell us? Why do you have such a reputation with these people?"

"I have no idea. I find that tough guy's words unnerving."

"Excuse me, Brenhart." She waved her hand to capture his attention. "What do you call this world?"

"Orandica, of course." He beckoned them to join him in his skiff. "Come now. We must be off!"

Once they were seated, he took control of a wooden handle at the skiff's bow. He pulled it back, and the small vehicle lifted a few inches into the air. Moving the stick forward sent the skiff in motion at a surprising speed.

"That's so cool." St. Guardian chuckled. "The rowboat has a flight stick."

Azurite shook her head. "You know, you only get this kind of stuff from other worlds."

They hovered across the lush earth for some distance until they approached a large military camp's makeshift walls. The soldiers parked the skiffs, and the occupants exited.

Shunen jumped from his and raced toward the camp's entrance. "Commander! Come and see! Lady Reina has returned!"

"Reina?" Reiko echoed. She, along with the other two, followed behind.

Commander Aldevin, a clean-cut middle-aged soldier, exited the center tent and paused as his eyes met Reiko's. The rest of the camp around them fell into silence.

"This doesn't look good," Azurite whispered.

"If they attack, we'll just leave," St. Guardian responded. "No harm, no foul."

Aldevin's eruption of hardy laughter broke the silence. He walked toward Reiko with his arms above him. "Our ancestors shine upon us! Lady Reina, it is truly an honor to see you again! Shunen, where did you find her?"

"On the field of battle, Commander. Just where I would expect to find her."

"Of course!" The commander gathered her in his arms for a warm embrace. "The Lady has always been at home on the battlefield. My, how you have changed. But never mind that. Please, tell me, who are your companions?"

Free of the smothering hug, Reiko pointed to her new friends. "This is St. Guardian, and this is Azurite."

"Well met, my friends. Come. Let us dine in celebration." The commander turned to his quiet camp. "The Lady has returned! Victory is ours!"

As a round of cheers exploded from the camp, the trio followed both Aldevin and Shunen into the center tent.

"You certainly are popular." Azurite looked toward the rejoicing faces. "I'm getting kinda jealous."

Reiko averted her eyes and focused on the ground before her. "Don't be. They're not cheering for me. They're cheering for someone else."

Miles away in his castle's inner courtyard, Nalthean Dregart moved among the machinery labyrinth that surrounded him. Sorcerer robes draped over his muscular build. At least, that was what he had been called for many years. Only a sorcerer was brave or foolish enough to stab at the very fabric of existence, the threads that held the universe together.

"No. Not enough power," he said as he monitored his machine's readings. He contemplated his calculations. He then looked at the sizable glowing sphere near the center of the courtyard. The unstable energy mass was partially encased in a fractured metal shell. On the broken surface, the word *Endrastic* was stenciled in bold lettering. "If I reverse the polarity of the—"

"Master!" A hulking orc warrior barreled into the courtyard.

"What is it, Bone-Break?" He did not bother to hide his frustration. "If you are here to report another failure, you will discover how perilous life can be, even for your hardy species!"

"She has returned," the creature said with fear etched in his prominent, pig-like features.

"What?" His voice was a little more than a whisper as color drained from his bearded face. "What did you say?"

"Lady Reina has returned!"

The morning turned into the afternoon. A modest feast in Reina's honor stood before the trio. Shunen and Aldevin were seated on opposite sides of a table with the heroes situated between them. Shunen dug into the delicious lamb before him while his commander displayed a more refined eating etiquette.

St. Guardian, with his helmet on the table beside him, said, "Thank you for such a warm welcome."

"It is our pleasure, Lord Guardian." Aldevin nodded to the Soulvenger and then turned his attention to Reiko, who had hardly touched anything on her plate. "You remember Dregart, don't you, my Lady?"

"Dregart?" she responded blankly.

"That wizard who lives in the castle at the base of Saber Rock Mountain? He's the reason for all the attacks we have endured. About a year ago, after you disappeared, he allied himself with orcs from the Burning Valley Tribe. I suppose they were closest to his locale. Either way, he used them to raid mines all over the realm."

"Mines?" St. Guardian looked puzzled. "What kind of ore was he trying to get a hold of?"

"Silver at first. Then copper."

"He didn't want jewels?" Azurite asked.

"No." Shunen sucked marrow from a bone he had been gnawing on. "And that was the most peculiar. The mines are filled with them."

The commander nodded. "Dregart attacking anything is peculiar enough."

"Why do you say that?" Azurite asked.

"He never was a threat before. He stayed in his castle, living a quiet, solitary life. Then out of the blue, he began raiding mines. Needless to say, the king is most displeased."

She smirked. "There ain't no mystery here. Can't you see that he's doing this because of a woman?"

"A woman?" Shunen fought with a cloth in an attempt to clean his fingers. "Dregart had no woman."

"Don't kid yourself. There's a woman involved in this. He's either trying to impress her, get her attention, or doing what she told him to do."

"Dregart's love life is irrelevant," Aldevin assured. "It doesn't change the fact that he needs to be stopped."

A soldier in chain mail burst into the tent with wide eyes. "Sir, Dregart is here!"

He sprang from the table. "By the blood of my ancestors! Raise the alarm!"

St. Guardian stood and put on his helmet. "It's showtime."

The group of five exited the tent and saw the renegade sorcerer standing idle with a spear in his grasp. It had a white cloth neatly tied to its tip. Aldevin's men drew their weapons as they formed a circle around the lone intruder.

"He's alone, sir," Shunen assured.

Aldevin shook his head. "Have some men search the surrounding forest for his orcs. This could be an ambush."

"Right." He drew his blade and pointed to a few of the soldiers. "You, lads, with me!"

Dregart watched Shunen's party exit the camp. "Commander Aldevin, I trust you see that I possess a flag of truce. Under it, I am afforded temporary protection according to the Warrior's Code that was created by Lady Reina herself."

"I know the law, villain!" Aldevin snapped. "Why are you in my camp?"

"I heard Lady Reina has returned. I've come to welcome her back to our noble realm."

Reiko stepped into Dregart's view.

His calm demeanor gave way to fury. "Who is this?! Explain this impostor, Aldevin!"

"How dare you say such a thing! This is Lady Reina in the flesh!"

"Do you not have eyes?! Look at her garb... Her height." His voice hissed as his eyes burned. "You may know little about me, Aldevin, but you should know that I am not a fool! You will pay for this deception! I will tear away the very strands that hold this world together! Mark my words!" With a wave of an illuminated hand, he faded from their presence. His spear dropped to the earth.

"What was that all about?" St. Guardian asked the commander.

Aldevin's lip trembled. "I know not."

"Well, he looked tore up from the floor up." Azurite folded her arms. "Now we know who the woman is. You know, that dude's a lot younger than I thought he would be. Aren't all evil wizards supposed to be older than dirt?"

St. Guardian pressed on. "Commander, can he make good on his threat to destroy Orandica?"

"That I cannot answer," Aldevin said. "He is a powerful sorcerer, but to destroy all the realms, I just don't know."

"He can't do that with just a crystal ball," St. Guardian added. "He'll need an enormous source of power, and I don't think he'll get that from anything on this planet."

Azurite nodded. "I was thinking that too. He's got the experimental drive."

"The question is: does he know what to do with it?"

Aldevin turned to the silent Reiko. "Lady Reina, let us not delay. Lead us in an assault on his castle. Together, we can stop his wicked schemes."

"His face..." Her gaze was still fixed on where Dregart had once stood.

"What?"

"Did you see his face? He was in pain."

"My Lady, please. I must insist that we attack!"

"You're right." She snapped out of her trance. "How soon can you get to his castle?"

"Do you not recall where his castle is?"

"Just a little test, Commander."

"It is twenty miles northeast of here."

"Excellent," she said, continuing her bluff. "And now for another test. Where did I live? I mean, where do I live?"

Aldevin shrugged. "I know not. No one knew. You kept it a secret. But you were frequently seen in a field to the east." He pointed. "That way."

"This realm has no shortage of fields. Anything nearby I can use as a landmark? I need more, Commander."

"Shodran's Spring is there too. If you recall, it's a natural spring that shoots upward from a small lake."

"Thank you." She beamed. "You passed the test."

"What's with all the game show questions?" Azurite asked.

"Could you two please go with them?" Reiko asked. "I want to check out that field. I'll catch up with you all at the castle."

"Okay," St. Guardian agreed. "Sounds good. But don't be too long."

"Thank you. I'll meet up with you all shortly." She drifted up into the air and shot eastward.

In the sky, Reiko drew in the unpolluted air with a smile. She stopped her flight as soon as she noticed a gushing fountain in the center of a clear lake encircled by trees. She stretched out her open gloved hand and closed her eyes. In a few moments, she felt a faint energy pulse. "There you are." She floated, careful to follow the weak signal. Her short trek ended as her hand touched an invisible wall about three hundred feet from the ground. She generated the same energy signature she used to go into her own dimensional home and glided in.

The crystal home was familiar, like every Valkyrie home, but unlike others, the light was faint, and the air was stale. The atmosphere seemed dead. But she could still feel a slight energy trace from within. Like the last defiant flicker of a candle before it went out. She kept going further. "Your energy is still here, so where are you?" she whispered.

"Reina," a hushed voice echoed from the main chamber. "You've come back." A purple crystal shard slowly drifted toward her.

"I'm sorry, but I'm not her."

The servo-crystal paused. The light within it was fading as well. "I beg your pardon, Valkyrie. I thought you were Reina."

"You're Reina's servo-crystal, aren't you?"

"Yes, she gave me a name. I'm Remus."

"Hello, Remus." She gave it a pleasant smile. "I'm Reiko. Can you tell me where Reina went?"

"I wish I could. She left and has yet to return. The power drain on her home and myself has been substantial."

"What can you tell me about Reina?"

"This way, please."

Remus hovered down a corridor and into another room with dim lighting. This larger room was decorated with carved columns and sweeping arches that stretched across the ceiling, a style Reiko was not familiar with. An intricately carved statue that featured a broadsword with a matching shield stood in the center. Next to the weapons off to the side, a set of armor was placed on a rack.

"She was certainly much taller than me," Reiko noted.

"We came to this planet three hundred years ago, our second assignment world. She exemplified what it meant to be a true Valkyrie. Her bravery became an example to others."

"She sounds quite remarkable."

"She created the Warrior's Code, which was universally adopted by all the kingdoms in this realm. It encompassed not just battle but diplomacy as well. She helped shape a good, thriving world. But I warned her..."

"Warned her about what?"

"Falling in love with a native. It never works out."

"So, I've heard. Who did she fall in love with?"

"A man of great intelligence called Nalthean Dregart. They wed in secret some time ago. She always spoke about how much she loved him and how happy they were."

Reiko's brow furrowed. "Remus, I must know where she went."

"I wish I knew. She's out of range of my sensors, and our psychic link has been broken for a long time. She must be very far away."

"Did she say anything before she left?"

"She told me to wait for her."

Reiko took Remus into her hand, brought the servo-crystal back to its

145

docking pedestal, and inserted it into its resting slot. "You've done well in serving your Valkyrie. Rest now."

"You're leaving too?"

"Yes. Conserve your energy." She walked out of the home with a gentle smile and took back to the open blue skies.

Remus watched the door to the dimensional home seal itself once again. "It was an honor to serve with you. Reina."

Outside of Dregart's castle, Azurite pummeled from the air and smashed her energy-charged fist into the earth, scattering a horde of orcs into the air. St. Guardian followed the attack by blasting the massive opponents with a series of gleaming lasers from his gauntlets. Aldevin and his men held back as the two Valiant Alliance members made quick work of the castle's guards.

In his makeshift lab, Dregart stood by the dimensional drive sphere with his hands buried deep within. Its power coursed through him, and by some strange twist of fate, he absorbed it.

"Dregart!" Bone-Break rushed to his master's side. "The kingdom's soldiers have almost penetrated the castle. We need your monster. Now!"

"Aldevin's troops? Here?" The sorcerer's voice seemed distant as his mind was elsewhere.

"Yes! He brought champions with powers similar to Lady Reina. We need your creature to destroy them!"

"Very well." He turned toward the empty courtyard. "Pharon Vulmyr, come. I have need of you!"

From the courtyard's furthest recess, a wave of bandages snaked their way next to the sorcerer and wrapped themselves together to form a nine-foot humanoid figure with four arms protruding from its sides.

Dregart bowed. "Pharon Vulmyr, I have freed you from your dimensional prison, and now I ask you to make good on your promise to serve me. Go forth and destroy the intruders!"

The mummified creature offered a silent bow in return and exited the courtyard with unbelievable speed.

Bone-Break attempted to disguise his fear, but Dregart could see through it. He closed and locked the courtyard's thick oak door. "What manner of creature is that?"

"He was once a prisoner, trapped within this swirling sphere of vortex energy."

He pointed toward the sphere. "Is that what that thing is?"

Dregart smiled. "Was. To me, it has become so much more."

The fearsome Pharon Vulmyr leaped over the castle's front gate and landed on the ground before the heroes and the soldiers, reaching out with all four of its limbs. A piercing war cry echoed from beneath its wrappings. A few of Shunen's men from the back ranks fled while screaming.

Azurite threw an orc that she had been beating to the side. Her priorities just changed. "What do you call that?!"

"Trouble." St. Guardian hovered into the air. "Let's keep it away from the soldiers."

"Four arms. Figures." She shook her head. "You know, it's just like a man to—"

"Roshonda! We need to focus on the monster, not your dating problems!"

"All right." She flew next to her partner. "Let's get into this!"

The two engaged with the creature, who barely acknowledged several of their most potent hits. In response, it employed its vast speed to deliver an impressive offensive of its own, striking the heroes repeatedly with its massive fists.

Reiko burst from the sky and slammed into the ground before the green-skinned warriors, releasing a shockwave that sent them soaring in all directions. She saw the battle between the four-armed mummy and the heroes but ignored it. The vortex energy radiated not too far away. Following the energy trace, she flew into the castle and smashed through the inner courtyard's door.

As she landed, she was met by a hulking orc warrior's sword.

"I'll feast on your bones, little one!" he slobbered as he swung at his petite opponent.

With a flash of her fist, the monster sailed into the air and crashed into the ground, unconscious. She stepped toward Dregart, who was consumed by the crackling machinery. Energy radiated from the glowing sphere.

"What does your machine do?" she asked.

"So, the impostor graces me with her presence." He turned. "Their purpose is to take the sphere's energy and store it in various metals that I had those green brutes extrapolate from the mines. My machines are primitive, I know, but needs dictate my actions. I must harness the sphere's energy before it dissipates."

"I'm not an impostor," she admitted.

"Really? You came here to mock me?"

"I'm not Reina."

"Do you recognize what this is?" He pointed at the sphere. "It's a whole dimension I scavenged from a craft that fell from the stars. It served as a prison for a creature. But I will use its power to turn back time or destroy the world trying!"

Reiko took a step closer. "I'm not Reina."

"Then who are you?" he spat. "Why do you wear her face?!"

"I'm a Valkyrie from the planet Volsogun. So was she. She never told you who she was, did she?"

His face flushed, and the veins in his forehead bulged. "Volsogun? Who sent you to mock me?!" His hand sliced through the air. "She was everything to me! I will not suffer a world without her. I will have her back, or I will have nothing!"

She stepped closer. "I'm not Reina."

Tears formed in his eyes. He touched her cheek. "You have her eyes. Her face." His voice choked. "Why do you look like her? Where is my Reina?" He fell to his knees.

She placed her arms around him. He returned her embrace. He pressed his tear-stained cheek against her and wept.

"She loved you, Nalthean." Her eyes watered. "It would break her heart to see you harming the world you shared together."

"It hurts..." He shook. "I don't want to go on without her."

"Do it for her. Honor her memory. Carry on her vision of the Warrior's Code." Their eyes met. She held his sorrowful face in her hands. "Reina married an honorable man, a man whom she dearly loved. Be that man again. For her."

"You're right." He nodded. "She deserves so much more."

They both stood.

Dregart returned to his machinery and powered them down. "I will return Pharon Vulmyr to his prison." He flipped a few cumbersome switches, and the sphere hummed with power once again.

"That giant four-armed monster?"

"Yes. One of the dimension areas was his prison. I freed him to serve me. Foolish, I know. The energy that has been taken can also be restored."

During its battle, the wrappings on Pharon Vulmyr's arms shifted from fists into blades. It utilized the weapons with deadly precision as it continued its relentless attack.

"Stay back!" St. Guardian shouted to Azurite as one of the creature's blades raked across his chest plate.

She shot further into the air, well out of the monster's reach. "Keep him busy, so I can blast him!"

He formed a long sword of his own that solidified from spiritual light. He engaged Pharon's blades, making sure to keep it at a reasonable distance away from Aldevin's men.

"Okay, ugly." Azurite's hands charged with blue energy. "Open wide." She fired a searing laser beam that struck the creature in the center of its chest.

It screamed in agony from under its bandages.

"Good shot!" St. Guardian held his blade before him.

The creature took a few steps back. As it recovered from the burning attack, it roared in fury.

"I'll hit him again!" Azurite called as her hands charged up.

Pharon Vulmyr stomped toward St. Guardian but then stopped dead in its tracks. A shimmering light sheathed it, and it dissolved into the light that shot back into the castle.

Reiko and Dregart watched as a ray of light flew through the courtyard's broken door and absorbed into the glowing sphere.

"The creature is secure," he said. "Now. For the sphere." He flipped a few more switches in sequence, and, with a brief violent tremble, the dimensional orb shrunk in size, matching a golf ball. He stepped toward the ball of energy and picked it up.

"How were you able to collapse a whole dimension?" Reiko asked.

"It is composed of vortex energy. Size is irrelevant concerning dimensional spatiality."

"And how do you know such things?"

"Take it." He placed the shimmering sphere into her hand.

"Thank you," she said with a gentle smile.

"It is I who should thank you. I promise I will make amends for my actions, and I will honor the memory of my beloved."

"I wish you the best." She hugged the desperate man, and he returned her embrace.

"Oh man," St. Guardian muttered as he entered the courtyard. "This is an unexpected turn."

"What is going on here?" Azurite asked.

Reiko walked toward St. Guardian and placed the dimension in his hand. "Here is Kasara's dimensional problem. It's a prison for that four-armed creature."

Azurite placed her hands on her hips. "You stuffed that big mummy into that tiny little thing?"

"Thank you, Reiko," he said. "We'll take this back with us. I know of a place back on Earth that keeps things like this. What about Dregart?"

Reiko looked back at the quiet sorcerer. "He is no longer a threat to this world."

"Just like that?" Azurite said, sounding unconvinced.

"Just like that."

A prismatic portal manifested in the empty air beside the three.

"That's our cue," he said, relieved.

"Yeah." Azurite nodded. "It's been fun, but it's time to roll. I'm exhausted."

The two stepped through the door. Reiko smiled at Dregart, who nodded toward her.

After Reiko left, the sorcerer watched as the portal vanished. Armor clang through the stone corridor. Aldevin, accompanied by Shunen and his soldiers, flushed into the courtyard.

"Surrender, Dregart!" Aldevin pointed his blade at him. "There is no escape for you!"

"Very well," Dregart said. "I will come peacefully."

"That was too easy." Shunen examined the area. His eyes landed on the unconscious orc. "Do you think it's a trick?"

"We'll just have to see." Aldevin slowly approached Dregart. "Did the champions come here?"

"Yes."

"Where are they now?"

He looked to where they had vanished with a smirk. "Elsewhere."

Kasara greeted the three with a smile. "Welcome, champions. Your mission was a success. I thank you."

"We were happy to help," St. Guardian said.

"Now, I am sure you are eager to return to Terra." With a wave of her hand, the celestial created another dimensional portal. "Go in peace, champions. Do not concern yourself with the Carthians. I will inform them of *Endrastic*'s fate."

"Kasara," Reiko said with a melancholy voice. "Do you know if Dregart will be okay?"

"I am not allowed to share such things, young Reiko."

She nodded.

"I can tell you that you have taken your first step toward your greatest challenge."

She tilted her head to the side at the celestial being, but before she could get a word out, Azurite spoke.

"Come on, girl! Shake a leg!"

She bowed toward Kasara and exited the castle of impossibilities.

The new chromatic portal exited on top of a building within a bustling cityscape.

"Well, that was weird." Azurite shook her head. "Where are we anyway?"

"Driven," Reiko blurted. "I can tell by the smell."

"All in a day's work, I guess." St. Guardian noticed her looking down and away while rubbing her arm. "Reiko, you still with us?"

"Sorry. I just have a lot on my mind."

"I know you haven't had time to think it over, but I hope you'll consider joining our team."

"Thank you for the offer. I'll think about it."

Azurite smiled. "You take care of yourself, okay?"

"I will."

"I'm beat," she said and sighed, turning to St. Guardian. "Let's go back to Newtopia."

"Agreed. See you later, Reiko. Don't be a stranger."

With that, they took to the skies and soared into the distance.

Reiko watched them until they vanished. She then looked further into the distant blue. "Reina, wherever you are, your husband still loves you and is waiting for you. Please return to him."

EXTRA ARMOR

"THIS PLACE IS so beautiful." Reiko looked around in wonder at all the sights and sounds as she strolled down a sidewalk that stretched the length of an outdoor shopping center.

Keanid shot a curious gaze at her friend. "That's the seventh time you've said that."

"I really like how the lights hang from those pole things all the way down the street."

"Yeah, electricity is amazing." She glanced at her diving watch. "It's almost four. We've been here all afternoon and haven't hit a clothing store yet."

"Yes, we'll have to do that."

"Well, we have to do something to expand your wardrobe."

"I did." Reiko looked down at the jeans she had formed earlier in the day. "See. The last time I went out without my uniform, I wore shorts. Now, I have jeans."

Keanid pulled her blue hair back and tied it up. "As I said, we have to do something to expand your wardrobe." Her eyes glued to somewhere. "There we go! Come on."

Reiko followed her into a store called Marlee Trendz. Her eyes widened at its sheer collection of clothing aimed at young women. "This place is so big and offers a plentiful bounty of garments."

"You still sound artificial with your English sometimes. Watching TV will help with that, you know."

"I don't own a TV."

"We'll add it to the list. Now, if you don't mind, let's return our focus to the clothes." She led Reiko to a corner of the store. "This place is where I get all my surfer girl stuff."

"Surfer girl?"

"Yeah, you know, the surfer girl look."

Reiko gave her a blank stare.

"A girl who surfs. On a surfboard." She rolled her eyes. "The type of style that I normally wear. Like now."

"Oh." Reiko smiled. "Right. I heard the look was called beach bum."

"Bums don't shell out the kind of money it takes to buy these clothes. I'll warn you now that this place is pricey."

"You said that every store in this district is expensive," Reiko countered.

"Yes, they are, but unlike those other stores, I like to shop here. That makes it even more pricey."

"I suppose I do not understand what you're saying."

"Yeah, I guess not. The language barrier thing again. Let's just look around before a salesperson comes and bugs us." She led Reiko to a collection of colorful blouses, which Reiko enthusiastically sifted through.

"Have you visited him yet?" Reiko asked after a while.

"No." Keanid looked through the offerings on a separate rack. "I'm kind of scared to."

"He's your father."

"But what if he's not?"

"The only way to find out is to talk to him. If nothing else, you learn more about your mother." Reiko picked up a blouse off the rack and inspected it further.

"Yeah, you're right." Keanid glanced in her direction. "That's not your color."

She put it back and drew out another. "This?"

"Nope."

"You're going to say that about everything I choose, aren't you?"

"What can I say? You're not good at coordination. You know, sometimes I'm amazed at how alien you are."

She put the item back. "It takes one to know one."

"You don't know that."

"Neither do you. Talk to your father."

"Well played, girl from another world." Keanid couldn't help but smile. "I'll give you that one. But I'm curious. What's this whole need for clothes shopping anyway? You didn't care about this stuff a week ago, so why now?"

"I have been advised that I should only wear my uniform when I'm doing Valkyrie things."

"Why?"

"I can then blend into a crowd and hide from the Reikonoids."

"Oh, yeah. Your fan base." The mermaid chuckled. "I was meaning to ask you about them."

She winced. "It wasn't my idea."

"I bet. I've seen them looking for you on social media. That's just creepy."

"I don't like that kind of attention at all. I wish they would stop."

"Yeah, like that's going to happen. I read about several groups forming on the mainland."

"Oh no."

"Oh, I was meaning to ask you about Akeda. You're really crushing on him, aren't you?"

Reiko smiled. "Very much so."

"Didn't you say he's on the rebound? That's the worst time to get a guy cause rebound relationships never last."

"He said she left him."

"Why? Was it because of him or her?"

She looked away. "What about your detective?"

"Joe? We went out a couple of times. I'll admit that he's fun to be around. But I just wish he would stop asking me if I would consider wearing a seashell bikini."

Reiko plucked a shirt from another rack. "A what?"

"Apparently, in his mind, that's what mermaids should wear. That shirt isn't you either."

She defiantly placed it back. "What is me then?"

"Something cute and sassy or colorful and fun. Just sit back. I'll find something." Keanid thumbed through another couple of racks and returned with a crop top shirt with full-length sleeves. "Here we go. Check this out."

She barely looked up. "That looks almost the same as the one I chose."

"Yeah, but this one would look better on you. Come here." Keanid hovered her new find over Reiko's torso to see how it would look on her.

Reiko's eyes widened as she noticed CupCake Kitty emblazoned on it through the nearby full-length mirror. Her mouth fell open.

"So, you like it?"

She pointed. "That's CupCake Kitty!"

Keanid took another look. "Oh, yeah. It is."

"That's CupCake Kitty!" she shouted again.

"Maybe you should keep that up. I don't think they heard you clearly across the street."

"Sorry." Reiko regained her composure. "But that's CupCake Kitty."

"I guess you're a fan."

"To put it lightly, yes."

"Here." Keanid handed the shirt over. "Do that copy thing, and we'll see if it works."

"Okay." Reiko got closer to the mirror and reshaped the shirt she wore to mimic the one she held in her hands.

"That's wicked," Keanid said with a bewildering smile. "I wish I could do that. How does that work exactly?"

"It is a benefit of being a Valkyrie. The energy we are gifted also contains sub-matter. That's what our uniforms are made of. It also makes them almost invulnerable to any form of attack."

"So those new jeans you're wearing..."

"Is made of sub-matter as well. All my clothes are. How does CupCake Kitty look on me?"

"You two were made for each other. Have you ever considered wearing real clothes made from real materials?"

"I suppose." Reiko looked down at her copied shirt with a smile.

"Looks like we got ourselves a winner. Now, let's put that back and..." Keanid paused and turned away. Her voice lowered a bit. "Fine. I'm shopping with Reiko, just like I said. I'll be home soon. Love you, Dad."

"Was that human father?" Reiko asked after she turned around again.

"Ever since the attack on the house, he's been paranoid," Keanid muttered. "He really hasn't been himself."

"Understandable. His home was blown up. How's the reconstruction going?"

"Ahead of schedule, actually." Her face lifted. "Dad's now wanting to install some high-tech security system and some other junk that's supposed to keep us safe. It's a good thing we can afford all that."

"I don't mean to pry, but how *do* you two afford all those expensive things? I thought Abe retired years ago."

"He did, but he also raised a mermaid who travels the ocean floor and picks up sunken treasures. We've been auctioning those things off for years."

"Ooo. Sunken treasures. That sounds exciting."

"Let's just say money is not an issue. Ever since the attack, I've tried to get dad interested in something like going into the restaurant business to keep him occupied, but he's fixated on rebuilding the house. Maybe when it's done." She wandered to a rack of jeans and picked out a pair. "Try these. This shade of blue will look good with that shirt."

Reiko touched the jeans, and hers changed to match.

"Perfect fashionable street camouflage." Keanid smiled as she put the jeans back. "Those fanatics will never find you."

"I guess." She returned to the mirror and looked herself over. "Maybe I should wear a mask or helmet to hide my face from now on."

"I wouldn't bother. They've already got your number." Keanid glanced at her watch.

"And on that note, I'd better head back to Dad before he worries himself sick. Did you ever find out who that green-haired punk was?"

"No," she admitted. "After that ocean lab exploded, Akeda said the police had no leads, so they're looking into the people who built it."

"Well, keep your eyes open. You can bet those guys are still out there, and they still want you dead for whatever reason."

"I'll be careful. Thanks for hanging out with me."

"No problem! Give me time, and I'll teach you everything you need to know about your new home planet. Later." With a brief wave, Keanid left the clothing store.

"Bye." Reiko took another look at herself before leaving. She wandered down the sidewalk, viewing other merchandise through their expansive windows.

"Hey, Reiko!" A voice echoed some distance away. "Hold up!"

She turned to face the familiar voice and found Detective Appulo walking toward her. She smiled. "Detective Appulo! It's so nice to see you. What are you doing here?"

"There's a little gourmet shop that sells a type of maraschino cherries that my wife loves, so I was instructed to get some on my way home from work." He lifted the plastic bag in his hand. "As you can see, mission accomplished. You know it's weird seeing you in street clothes. I almost didn't recognize you without the cape."

She shrugged, not really knowing what to say. "Sometimes I like to put on other clothes."

"Between you and me," he said with a wink, "the real reason why I stopped by was to give my wife more time to set up my surprise birthday party."

"Today is your birthday?"

"It sure is! Another trip around the sun. Hey, why don't you come to the party?"

"Are you sure? I've never been to a birthday party before."

He chuckled. "Then come on. I'm parked over here."

Captain Tower navigated through rows of cars in the Driven Police Department parking garage until he arrived at his reserved space. His car chirped, letting him know his doors were unlocked.

A black sedan pulled behind his car. Its window slid down, exposing Johnny Run-Time's smile. "Get in."

Appulo and Reiko arrived at their destination: a large home with a generous yard on the outskirts of town.

"Here we are," he said as he rolled into the garage. "Home sweet home."

"You have a wonderful domicile."

"Thanks. It's been in my family for three generations, just perfect for a big family like ours." He got out of the car. "Man, my wife will be beside herself. She has heard all about you."

Reiko exited and closed the passenger side door. "I guess I'm in the news a lot."

"I'll say. Don't you watch yourself on TV?"

"I don't own a TV."

"Then how do you know who the bad guy of the week is?"

"That's never a problem. Trouble has a way of finding me."

"Speaking of trouble, don't you have a huge group of admirers?"

"Yes," she said with zero enthusiasm.

"Not cool, huh? Forget about them. Well, tonight, you're here to have fun." He entered the house with her in tow. "Hey, honey. I'm home. You'll never believe who I ran into."

"Now, this is a surprise!" Leilani exited the kitchen and greeted her guest. "It's a pleasure to finally meet you. I'm Leilani. Welcome to our home."

"Thank you." Reiko smiled. "I'm Reiko."

"You certainly need no introduction." She turned to her husband. "Kainoa, I know you said she looked young, but I had no idea she looked this young."

"Yeah, I wasn't kidding. Oh, here are those cherries as requested." He handed the bag to his wife and then turned to Reiko. "Come on in here and meet the kids."

As they stepped further into the living room, Reiko saw two chubby kids playing on a colorful rug that encompassed half the room. A third child sat in a wheelchair, consumed by a portable video game.

She gasped as she covered her mouth. "They're adorable."

One of the two, a little girl, raised from the rug and pointed at her. "Who's that?"

"This is a friend who helps Daddy fight crime," Appulo explained. "Her name is Reiko. Reiko, the man with the plan on the rug is Alika, our oldest. The man with the video game over there is Keona, and this little ray of sunshine is our youngest, Malie."

"Hi." Reiko waved. "It's nice to meet all of you."

"That CupCake Kitty." Malie pointed at Reiko's shirt.

"It sure is."

"Where the rest?"

"Rest of what?"

"Your shirt!"

Reiko's face flushed. "I'm... Um... I'm picking it up later."

Alika stood with toy cars clutched in both fists. "When are we going to eat? I'm hungry."

"Okay, okay." Leilani swayed back into the living room. "Everybody come and sit down."

After getting the kids situated at the table, the doorbell chimed.

"I got it." Detective Appulo left to the front door.

From the table, Reiko heard someone wish Appulo a happy birthday.

"I was hoping you would make it. Come on in." The door closed. "Oh! Look who I ran into on the way home from work."

She froze with wide eyes as Detective Akeda turned the corner. He froze as well for a moment. But then they both smiled.

Captain Tower sat on the sedan's plush leather. He watched Johnny and a few henchmen in suits scroll on their phones. They traveled on the highway that orbited downtown with no particular destination to go to.

Tower rapidly tapped his foot. "You mind telling me what this is all about?"

Johnny faced his phone toward him. On it was a picture of Detective Akeda. "You know this cat, right?"

He nodded. "He's one of my best."

"Then this is going to sting," Johnny said cheekily. "In our efforts to spy on everybody's favorite space cadet, we happened to notice that she spends quite a lot of time talking to your boy. They got something going on?"

"Akeda's personal life is his business."

Johnny tucked his phone away. "The boss suspects they're close, so if something happens to him, glory girl should come running, and that's where you come in."

Anger cut through the captain. "I have done a lot for your boss over the years, and I have made a lot of compromises, but I will not jeopardize one of my detectives' lives!"

"My boss?" Johnny addressed his fellow henchmen. "Did you hear what this guy just said?" He shook his head. "Tower, did you forget who gave you your high and mighty position? Mr. Nishimura has been more than generous with you. Now listen up. A drug deal is going down at nine a.m. tomorrow at the Pinnacle Height Financial construction site. All you have to do is make sure your boy is there. Got it?"

Tower said nothing.

"What? You got a conscience now? It's too late to play hero." Johnny turned to the driver. "Let this dude out somewhere. He's got some things to think about."

The car screamed off the highway and stopped in front of a convenience store. Tower exited the car.

"You know," Johnny said, "if you're a little tense, I could prescribe something for you. Free of charge for cops on the payroll."

He slammed the door and watched as the car sped away into the night.

Under a canopy of shimmering stars, Reiko, Akeda, and Appulo relaxed on the back patio.

"I don't know about you guys, but I'm stuffed." Appulo rubbed his belly with a satisfied grin.

"The food was amazing and flavorful," Reiko said. "I haven't had anything like that before."

"Thanks, Reiko. I'm happy you both were here for dinner. We gotta do this more often."

Akeda leaned against the patio's wooden railing. "So, why do you always eat ramen when your wife is such an excellent cook?"

"Because she doesn't do it often, but when she does, my taste buds better look out."

Reiko watched a wind chime sway to the will of a light breeze. "That sounds so beautiful."

"Oh, that old thing?" Appulo smiled. "That wind chime has been hanging up there for as long as I can remember."

She smiled. "Its sound reminds me of home. We have a style of music called Ildeklatik. It's kind of similar."

"Speaking of your home,"—Appulo looked up to the night sky— "where is it up there?"

"I can't point to it. It's too far away."

"Yeah... Man, there sure are a lot of stars up there."

"I used to count the stars. I don't anymore."

"Why not?" Akeda asked.

She shrugged. "There are too many."

Leilani appeared in the sliding doorway. "Kainoa, could you give me a hand inside?"

"Sure. I'll be back, you two." He entered the house and closed the door behind him.

Reiko fidgeted with her hands. "Detective Appulo has such a beautiful family."

"You don't have to be so formal, Reiko. His name is Kainoa."

"Right. It will take some getting used to." She moved closer to the detective. "It may seem silly, but I don't know your first name."

"It's Daniel."

"Daniel. That's the most gorgeous name I—" She paused, catching herself. "I mean, it's nice."

"Do you have a last name?"

"No. It's just Reiko. I'm sorry."

"Why are you apologizing?"

"For all the bad things that have happened to you because of your association with me."

"Hey, it's not your fault." He placed a hand over hers.

"I just don't want to see you hurt." Her nervousness bled through her attempt to steady her composure. She looked up into his eyes. "And I don't know what I'm doing right now."

"Neither do I." He pulled her into his arms and kissed her.

Once they ended their embrace, she took a step back in an attempt to understand what had just happened. "I... Um... I should get going," she stammered. "Please tell Kainoa and Leilani that I had a wonderful time." She flew into the night sky and disappeared into the distance.

Reiko entered her dimensional home and shifted her street clothes into her robe. She wandered into her room in a dreamlike state and collapsed onto her bed.

Maru floated in behind her. "Is there something wrong, Reiko?"

She lay on her back and placed both hands over her heart. She stared at the ceiling. "I'm in love."

"Oh, no." The servo-crystal groaned.

The following day, Detective Akeda entered Captain Tower's office. "You wanted to see me, sir?"

He nodded. "Have a seat."

Akeda slid into the chair stationed before the captain's desk.

"I got something for you to look into." He took a quick glance at his watch. "I received a tip that in approximately one hour, a drug transaction is going down at the Pinnacle Height Financial construction site. I want you to go there and see what you can find."

The detective tilted his head. "Doesn't Maretti normally handle that kind of thing?"

"I want you there because I think the transaction is a cover for something bigger."

"Do you trust your source?"

"I know they aren't lying if that's what you mean."

"All right." The detective stood. "I'll head over there now."

Reiko paced back and forth. "I can't believe it, Maru! We kissed!"

"Please, Reiko, calm yourself. Display some decorum." Maru drifted faster in an attempt to keep up with her frantic pace.

"I'm so excited! I don't know what to do next!"

"You could always go on patrol like a good Justice Valkyrie."

"Don't be so grouchy, Maru." She stopped. "Why can't you just be happy for me?"

"I told you, these types of relationships rarely work out. Remember what you told me about Valkyrie Reina and her husband? He went mad with grief."

"Because he loved her with everything he was. He was willing to sacrifice everything for her."

"Not to mention destroy the world."

"That won't happen to us."

"And why not?"

"I'm not Reina."

Akeda parked his car a block away from the construction site and strode down the sidewalk, paying close attention to the people who dotted his surroundings. Tower's instructions were too vague for his liking. He followed the chain-link fence that separated the construction site from the public. Nothing seemed out of the ordinary.

Noticing a wide alley on the opposite side of the street, he made his way in that direction. Before entering, he surveyed the urban pathway. Other than pieces of trash propelled by the wind, the alley was void of any activity. He decided to take a more in-depth look. Afterward, he would walk the construction perimeter one more time. Tower must've been misinformed either about the transaction or the time.

Akeda pressed further into another alley. He paused when he heard a car block the entrance behind him. It approached slowly at first but then sped up, racing toward him.

He barely escaped the vehicle's path by jumping to the side at the last moment. As he rose to his feet, the car screeched to a halt, and several men in suits piled out, each armed. He fled toward a junction in the alley as they opened fire. He ducked behind a dumpster as shots whizzed by him. Behind the trash bin, he heard their footsteps getting closer. Staying put was not an option.

He composed himself and unholstered his pistol. He raised it up, fired several shots that dispersed the group, and bolted further down the alley. His strategy seemed effective until a bullet snagged his right shoulder, forcing him to drop his pistol. Ignoring the pain, he carried on with his escape.

Within the vast maintenance bay, Tynoval, a Turexian doctor, stood before the condemned medi-suit with a holographic pad in hand. His task was to identify and understand how a Volsogun servo-crystal hijacked the suit made from superior Turexian technology. The suit remained as it was when it was returned, battle damaged with its weapon package still installed.

Hemnari, Tynoval's assistant, watched as the doctor followed the list of established diagnostic procedures.

"As you can see," Tynoval continued, "this is a unique case. Never has a medi-suit, or any of our technology for that matter, been appropriated by an unauthorized intelligence. Hence, the lengthy diagnostic procedure."

"The unauthorized intelligence used a psychic link, did it not?"

"Yes, and therein lies a most perplexing problem. How can we protect our technology from future psychic intrusions?"

Hemnari nodded. "It is a fascinating problem. Master Tynoval, if I may?"

"Please."

"Is this mobile unit considered safe?"

"Yes." Tynoval looked up from his readings. "Of course. Though for testing purposes, it has been condemned from service."

"Is it wise to keep its power core charged to full capacity?"

"We must. It is part of the diagnostic protocol." He chuckled and looked back down at his readings. "Ease your mind, my young apprentice. This unit is no longer under alien influences."

The medi-suit's exterior lights flashed as it stood upright on its own.

"Master Tynoval?" Hemnari sputtered.

The unit abandoned all external connections and hoses from its frame.

"Master Tynoval?" Hemnari said louder.

The suit locked and loaded its weapon payloads, assessing its wartime capability.

"Master Tynoval!" Hemnari shouted. "It's happening again!"

Tynoval looked back at his pad for some answer to this unit's sudden animation. "The bio-imprint of the last occupant, the human known as Akeda, has not been wiped. The human must have sustained significant damage, enough to initiate activation."

The two watched in amazement as the suit marched toward the ship's hangar.

Akeda continued to run, attempting to ignore the growing bloodstain covering his shoulder. The pain slowed him down some. He knew he had to make it to the street, where his survival chances would improve.

From out of nowhere, a henchman tackled the detective, and both tumbled onto the concrete. Akeda sent his elbow into the guy's nose, which made the henchmen recoil and gave him just enough room to escape. Both scrambled to their feet. Fortunately for Akeda, he was faster. He kicked the inside of the guy's right knee. As the henchman buckled, Akeda grabbed the back of his head and shot his knee into his nose. With a spray of red, the henchman fell, clutching his face while screaming.

Akeda noticed a few more henchmen running his way, so he continued his trek out of the alley. Twenty feet later, he stumbled, feeling adrenaline leaving him. He had to stand his ground. He sighed, glanced at the blue sky tucked between the buildings, and turned to face his opponents, who reloaded their guns as they closed in on him.

"Chill out, man," one said with an artificial smile. "We're not here to kill you. We're here to take you to your appointment."

Akeda counted four in front of him. Who knew where the others went? Nothing about the situation was in his favor. He gritted his teeth.

He flew toward the first henchman and punched him down to the pavement. Seeing an opening between the others, he attempted to make a break for it. But the largest of the three caught him. The henchman grabbed him and spun him around toward another henchman, who punched the detective in the gut and followed that with a punch to the face. His glasses shot into the air as he dropped.

The henchman who Akeda first punched returned to his feet and kicked him in the side, making the detective roll over in agony. "You think you're all that, copper?!" He kicked him again. "I'm sure the boss wouldn't mind if you got roughed up before we handed you over. Whaddya say, copper?!" He kicked him again. "Wanna play for a bit?" He swung his foot again.

This time, Akeda blocked the attack with his own foot and punched the henchman in the kneecap. He lifted himself up, grabbed the henchman by the hair, and used his weight to drop his forehead down onto the pavement. "Not really," he said as he spat fresh blood from his mouth.

The remaining henchmen watched as the detective slowly rose to his feet.

One of them aimed his gun at the injured cop. "You're tougher than you look. We can't have that."

Before he could pull the trigger, an imposing humanoid-shaped machine adorned with heavy guns and missile launchers descended from above. As it approached Akeda, its chest, arms, and legs folded open. In a fluid swooping motion, it encased the detective within it. The suit folded closed once he was secured and made its battle assessment.

"Open fire!" one of the henchmen shouted.

A hail of gunfire struck the medi-suit and ricocheted off its armor. The suit responded by launching itself into each of its opponents and hitting them with its large fists. The impact of the punches sent their broken bodies flying into the graffiti-stained walls.

From over neighboring roofs, several animots with jetpacks opened fire on the suit. The medi-suit launched several missiles from its payload, destroying the airborne assailants in a chain of violent explosions.

Reiko stood in front of her full-length mirror, shifting through her limited clothing inventory. "Do you think shorts or jeans look better on me?" she asked Maru, who observed the strange ritual in silence. "Keanid was right about the clothes. You can never have enough. I should go shopping with her more often."

"Reiko!" the servo-crystal said with concern. "Multiple explosions have been set off in downtown Driven."

"Downtown? Lead me to it." She formed her uniform and shot out of her home.

Akeda looked at his hands covered by the medi-suit. "It's like this thing is a part of me...like an extension of...me." He shook his head. "Where is all this energy coming from? I feel so alive...and powerful." His attention turned to the motionless henchmen, who were scattered about the alley. "I didn't kill them, did I?"

Within the suit's helmet, a scan appeared on the internal visor and confirmed the physical being of his attackers. All suffered from broken bones, but none were life-threatening.

"You can read my thoughts, huh?" Akeda said to the suit. "That's convenient. Scary but convenient."

"You look familiar," Reiko said as she landed by the medi-suit. "It looks like you've been busy."

He turned to her. "You think?" he said sarcastically.

"Follow me up to the roof. We don't want the human authorities getting the wrong impression about you." She flew to the top of a nearby building.

The medi-suit followed.

Inside a parked van two blocks away, Johnny Run-Time ripped his headphones off and threw them against the monitor before him. "Are you kidding me? A Turexian medi-suit?!" He rubbed his eyes and turned to his henchmen in the van. "When did he get imprinted?"

The van stayed silent.

"The suit has to have your imprint before it can protect you! So, when did this guy get imprinted? Anybody?" He stomped on the van's floor. "The Turexians are neutral. Why would they give this fool a suit?! The boss isn't going to like this!"

"Are we done here?" one of the braver henchmen asked his infuriated boss.

"Yeah. We're done. That cop's got more surprises up his sleeve than a genie. Let's go."

Reiko looked over the roof and at the busy city street below. "I saw pieces of robots scattered down there. Why were you fighting robots?"

Akeda lifted the palms of his hands. "How do I get this thing off me?"

The question seemed odd to her. "The same way you got in, I would expect."

"But I don't know how I got in it. It just sort of did it for me."

She furrowed her eyebrows and lowered her eyes. "You're not a Turexian?"

"Can't you recognize my voice?"

"No. It sounds like a machine is speaking. Do I know you?"

"You can't see my face?"

"No. The blast shield is down, and I don't have X-ray vision."

"It's me! Daniel Akeda!"

She gasped. "I thought I recognized that suit! That's the same suit Maru hijacked with you in it. It's not supposed to be here."

"You think?"

"I was told that it was condemned because Maru compromised the crystal imprint interface."

"This thing is supposed to be condemned? Well, it works just fine."

"I'm still curious... Why were you fighting robots?"

"One thing at a time. I just want to get out of this. Do you know how?"

"I don't, but Maru might."

"Who's Maru?"

"How comfortable are you with the suit's controls?"

"Surprisingly well. The movement is pretty fluid too. Why?"

"Because we have to fly to get to where we're going."

"As long as this thing doesn't run out of gas, I should be fine."

"It shouldn't." She nodded with an assuring smile. "Follow me." Once again, she drifted up into the sky, followed by the medi-suit.

"Being weightless feels weird, but I got this." Akeda looked down at the shrinking city below. "We're not going far, are we?"

"Afraid so. Don't worry. I'll go slow." She soared at a moderate pace while he clumsily navigated the air behind her. She watched him as his arms and legs rolled with the air stream.

"This feels amazing!" he shouted. "Look at the city down there!"

She giggled at his excitement. Focusing forward, she extended out her hand, and a shimmering door opened in the sky. "We're almost there."

The two coasted into Reiko's home and landed.

His mouth dropped. "What is this place?" He took in his beautiful crystal-crafted surroundings.

"Welcome to my home. It's in a pocket dimension separated from the rest of Earth."

"You live here?"

She nodded.

"This place is amazing. You people have a thing for crystals, don't you?"

"Yeah, I guess we do. Never really thought about it before."

He walked toward the crystal shard floating in the middle of the room.

"Reiko, who is this?" it bellowed.

"Maru, this is Detective Daniel Akeda. You should remember him. Daniel, this is my best friend, Maru."

"Yes, but he shouldn't be..." the servo-crystal's voice trailed off. "The medi-suit! What's it doing here?"

"Well, I was hoping you could tell me," Akeda said with firm resolve. "One minute, I was fighting for my life, and the next thing I know, this suit swallowed me up."

"I see. Did you sustain an injury during your conflict?"

"Yeah. I took a bullet to the shoulder."

Reiko gasped. "You're hurt? Why didn't you say so?"

"Reiko, one moment, please," it said. "The situation is rather simple, really. The Turexians must've not wiped your bio-imprint from the suit. When it detected your injury, it activated and did what it was programmed to do: protect and heal the wearer in a battlefield scenario."

"So, what you're saying is," Akeda said, "this thing worked as advertised."

"I'm not sure what you're implying. Advertising to do what?"

"I mean, it's functioning like it's supposed to."

"Undoubtedly."

"That's some comfort. Can you tell me how to get out of this thing?"

"The medi-suit follows your mental commands."

"Mental commands, huh? Okay..." He went still for a moment. The combat shield then lifted, and the front of the medi-suit folded open. He stepped out. "That's amazing!"

"Your arm." Reiko took his injured arm into her hands, alarmed by the circular splotch of blood that soaked through his jacket.

"Reiko, it's fine. I don't feel any pain."

"Easy to see why." Maru floated by his arm. "The wound has been sealed and healed. With a few hours of rest, you should be back to peak efficiency."

"Unbelievable," she whispered as she inspected Akeda's arm.

"You're telling me," he said. "This alien tech is nothing short of a miracle."

"Where are your glasses?"

"I lost them in the fight. It's not a big deal though. I have another pair at home."

"I've just…" She couldn't stop staring at the constellations that shined in the detective's eyes. "I've just never seen you without them."

"Ahem," Maru stated loudly. "I believe we have a more pressing issue at the moment."

"We do?" she asked with a dreamy voice as she continued to gaze at the detective.

"The medi-suit."

"Oh, yeah." She snapped out of her trance. "I'll return it to the Turexians. We already violated the Terran Magnera Agreement once, and I certainly don't want to do that again."

"There is a small problem with that, I'm afraid."

"What do you mean? You know I'm on probation."

"When I borrowed Detective Akeda's body to operate the medi-suit, it imprinted with him. It will return every time the detective sustains a substantial amount of damage."

Reiko's eyes widened. "Why didn't you tell me this before?"

"I apologize. I thought it was a mere theoretical possibility. I didn't think it would actually happen."

"So, we have stolen alien technology?" Akeda asked.

"No, we didn't." She shook her head. "I'm giving it back. And once I do, the Turexians can figure out how to fix the encoding issue."

"Reiko, I'm registering an incoming holo-message," Maru said. "Its point of origin is the Turexian medi-craft.

"Uh-oh. That can't be good." Her voice filled with dread. "Okay, Maru. Let it through."

A shimmering blue image of a Turexian with a pleasant smile materialized before them. "Greetings, Justice Valkyrie Reiko. I am Lead Technician Roldama of Medi-craft *Tor-Dal-Zah* of the Turexian Empire."

She bowed. "It is an honor to speak to you, sir."

"We seem to have a bit of an issue that I hope you can help us with."

"I'll help in any way I can."

"A mobile medical unit has responded to its imprinted user, a human by the name of Akeda. Have you seen it?"

"I'm afraid we haven't seen a properly functioning exo-suit, but we will let you know if we encounter it," Maru blurted.

"I see. Thank you for your cooperation."

As the holographic image faded, Reiko looked at her servo-crystal with wide eyes and her mouth agape. "Maru, I can't believe you just did that! Why did you lie to him?"

"I said I haven't seen a properly functioning exo-suit, and I haven't. This is a fortuitous situation in which we find ourselves in, and I feel it would be best if the suit stayed close to Detective Akeda."

Akeda crossed his arms. "And why is that?"

"You have fallen prey to otherworldly threats before, and there is a high probability that it will happen again. Having the medi-suit at your disposal will be beneficial in such circumstances."

"You have a point." Reiko tilted her head. "I didn't think about that."

"Now, let's focus on customization."

"How in the world do you do that?" he asked. "This thing isn't a car."

"I assume you're referring to an Earth vehicle."

"Yeah... A car?" He shrugged. "The thing that drives on the roads?"

"Yes, of course."

"You're still learning about this planet you're supposed to protect, aren't you?"

Reiko shrugged with an uneasy grin. "Yes, we are."

"Enough about that," Maru said. "Let's not forget that this medi-suit was built with the battlefield in mind. Therefore, it has been adapted to many combat situations and terrains. Since it's coded to you, you can alter its appearance and external configuration with a thought."

"It does look a bit bulky. All right. I'll give it a shot." He closed his eyes.

The suit's front opening slid shut. Its exterior slimmed down and reshaped into more of a humanoid contour. Its exterior weapons folded inward, holstering themselves to the suit's new frame. The exterior was recolored red and blue with a yellow trim on its chrome base. Once he was done, he opened his eyes. A smile formed on his lips.

"Red and blue?" Reiko asked with a smile.

"Your uniform has made quite an impression."

She beamed with a muted clap. "That's flattering."

"One thing left to do." Maru floated close to the detective. "Allow me to observe the relay crystal that Reiko gave you."

Akeda slid it out of his pocket and presented it to the servo-crystal. "Here you go."

A glow of light encompassed its form. The small shard responded in kind. Its light pulsed. The small shard pulsed in a similar pattern. A few seconds passed, and then the pulsating lights ceased.

"There," Maru said. "Not only will the medi-suit respond to your injuries, but you can summon it to your aid whenever needed. I synced your mental commands to its distress response protocol."

"So, I can call this thing?"

"With a mental command, yes."

"This is incredible. It's not every day you inherit confiscated alien armor. Are you guys able to keep it here though? I don't want this thing anywhere near my home in case somebody accidentally sees it."

"Not a problem," Reiko said. "Your mental commands to the medi-suit will not be impeded by this dimension."

He paused. "How secure is this home of yours?"

"Unless permitted by myself or Maru, nothing can enter save for other Valkyries and psionic wavelengths."

"That's some security. Listen, I need to get back to Driven. There's something I need to take care of."

"All right," she said. "Where do you wish for me to take you?"

"Just to my car."

She smiled. "Let's go."

Racked with frustration and guilt, Captain Tower arrived at the Driven Police Department parking garage and exited his car.

As he did, Akeda stepped out from behind a concrete support beam that stood close to the captain's designated space. "Captain."

He noticed blood caked Akeda's torn suit jacket. "I'm glad you're in one piece. You okay?"

"No. I'm pretty far from okay."

"What did you find out?"

"You set me up." Akeda's fists tightened. "How could you?! I thought you were a man of integrity! I looked up to you and so does the whole department! So, who is it, Captain? Who has you in their pocket?"

"Tengu Raid," Tower muttered. "They got to me when I was climbing the ladder. You don't make rank in this town unless they pick you."

"It's that bad?"

He nodded. "Over the years I tried to protect the department from the raid's influence. I thought that if I did their bidding, I could protect my people. But I was wrong."

"Why set me up?"

"They wanted you because of your relationship with Ms. Reiko."

Akeda shook his head. "And what are you going to do now? Have me killed?"

"No. I'm going to do the right thing. I've been looking forward to this for a long time." He extended his wrists.

He hesitated for a moment before he produced his cuffs and fastened them to Tower's wrists.

"Their leader is Ryuhei Nishimura."

"The business tycoon?"

"Tengu Raid is bigger than you think. We'll have to get the feds involved."

"Is there anyone else in the department that I should look out for?"

"I have plenty of evidence to offer the prosecution plus plenty of names. Be ready, though. Once they hear that I've been arrested, things will get real ugly real fast."

"Yeah."

"You're a good cop, Daniel. I'm proud to have served with you."

Akeda paused and closed his eyes. It took him a moment to form words. "You have the right to remain silent."

BALANCE OF POWER

K EANID WALKED AWAY from her lighthouse's noisy reconstruction. She traveled along the coast until she found a large boulder that provided a gorgeous view of the sea. Climbing to the top, she removed her shirt, shorts, and sandals and placed them in a pile beside her feet. As she stood in her bikini, a foreboding sense of fear and apprehension gripped her.

She drew in the salty morning air. "You can do this," she told herself with shaking confidence. "This is what you've been searching for."

She dove into the welcoming sea waves. Under its layers, her body shifted, forming her mermaid tail, and she used its strength to thrust herself toward the ocean floor. Coasting through the water was always a welcoming sensation to her. It eased her anxiety.

Until she saw the exterior of the Kryodon temple. Her stomach churned as she swam through its entrance.

With her hands, she climbed up the stairs until her head broke the water's surface. She changed her form once again and stepped out of the ocean. Intricate designs and carvings covered the floor and walls. The temple's interior, illuminated by an eerie bluish light from the walls, looked so alien yet so familiar.

She continued down a corridor that led to a central chamber. Small pods lined every multi-sided wall, and embryos thrived within them. Blood Water sat on a throne in the center of the room. Though he didn't move, she felt his eyes watch her every movement. She stepped toward one of the pods and took a closer look at the young life floating within a protective membrane of embryonic fluid.

"This is a spaceship, isn't it?" she asked as the thought drifted in her.

"Yes." His deep voice resonated. "We originate from Kryodon. But we came to this planet seeking sanctuary. Shortly after this craft landed, several scout ships were sent to seek a new home. None returned."

"Are you alone here?"

"No. As you can see, the future of our race waits to be awakened. A process that will begin once a new home is found."

"You don't look like them, do you? Kryodons, I mean."

"I was genetically modified to be their ultimate warrior and protector."

"A human, Abraham Medalious, found my mother while she was very ill. He tried to help her but couldn't. She asked him to look after me, and he did. He loves me as his own. He takes care of me."

"A surfacer accepted you?"

"He did more than that. Even though he knew I wasn't human, he still raised me like his own daughter. But that's not why I'm telling you this. I'm telling you this because that was forty years ago. Why do I still look so young?"

"Kryodons age at a much slower rate than most species. In a thriving environment, our average life expectancy is a thousand years."

Her mouth dropped. "Whoa..."

"Are you all right?" he asked.

She nodded as she attempted to gain her composure. "Yeah, yeah. Great." She focused on her next burning question. "What was she like? My mother?"

By partly closing his webbed hand, Blood Water drew drops of water from the atmosphere. The drops formed into a life-sized figure of Naulla before them. "Beautiful and enchanting. The day we were pair-bonded was the happiest I had ever been. When she left to lead one of the scouting expeditions, I had no idea she was with a child. If I did, I would have kept her here with me, and fate would have been much brighter for us all." As he opened his hand, the figure fell away into a shower of seawater. "What name did Naulla give you?"

"Keanid."

He smiled. "In our tongue, it means blessed one. She must have given you that name because you are the first of our kind born on this world. I am Varservious. To my people, I am the Tide Protector. To my enemies, I am Blood Water."

"I saw. You scared the surfacers, and you scared me. What you're capable of doing scares me."

"This craft was under attack. I acted accordingly." He rose from his throne.

Keanid took a step back.

"There is so much you need to learn about your people and our home world. There is so much of our history I wish to show you. Let us start anew."

She pushed aside her fear. "I'd like that. I want to get to know you. Our history. Everything."

"Good. In turn, teach me about this world. My dream is that one day our people will awaken in a new home under the waves, and as they do, we will be there to greet them, as father and daughter."

Two dark, unmarked vans screeched to a halt outside Nishimura's building. Armed individuals in riot gear piled out from the back and rushed toward the front lobby. Their automatic rifles spat hot lead onto unsuspecting security personnel and civilians, killing all in sight. After the bodies dropped, and the floor flushed red, the invaders continued up the stairwell.

Nishimura sat at his desk, watching the invaders make their way further up the stairs via his monitor. Johnny and Dr. Denoda watched the invader's blatant disregard of human life with him. Nishimura's security team, wearing their tengu masks, burst into his office.

"Sir!" one of the masked henchmen shouted. "The police are here. It's a raid!"

Nishimura stood. "Dr. Denoda, fetch The Omni-Wing."

With a respectful nod, Dr. Denoda exited the room.

"You know"—Johnny drew a revolver from his pants—"we should have had Tower killed as soon as he was arrested. He spilled his guts. Now this happens."

Nishimura observed as his security team attacked the invaders. He noted the combat techniques used in their struggle against his people. He stood and accepted his blade from Dr. Denoda. "Those aren't the police. This is an invasion."

"You're right." Johnny turned his gun toward Nishimura. "It is!" With that, he shot his boss in the left leg.

Nishimura grabbed the side of his desk for support as searing pain throbbed through his bleeding limb. Fighting through the agony, he noticed several fake police officers kick down his office door and enter. "Kill them!"

On his command, his henchmen drew knives from their sheaths and attacked the intruders. He unleashed his sacred blade and cut down three opponents who were foolish enough to challenge him.

"Sorry it had to be this way, but you were always a liability!" Johnny yelled from a safe distance across the room. "The real boss is here now."

A waving light washed over Dr. Denoda. As it faded, he took on a different form. He wore a glaring red military uniform encased with a personalized exoskeleton.

"Who are you?" Nishimura hissed.

"I am Colonel Denoda of the Blood Dire Army. We have been infiltrating your organization for over a year now, Nishimura, and you played right into our hands. When our psychic wave projector placed the suggestion about the Valkyrie in your head, it set our gears in motion. All the money you invested into killing that alien was used to further my agenda. There is only one last objective I have to secure."

Nishimura seethed with rage. "And that is?"

"No one but you could release The Omni-Wing from its sheath. It's the only weapon that can pierce the skin of a Justice Valkyrie."

"You want my ancestral blade? You'll need an army."

"We are an army!" Denoda raised his hand, which glowed with violet light. The Omni-Wing flew from Nishimura's hand and landed in the colonel's grip. "For the blood that was spilled!" A gravitational blast from his opposite hand launched Nishimura through the bay window and over the streets of Driven.

As Nishimura fell, he stretched out his arms. Artificial raven wings extended from under his suit jacket. He sailed to a sidewalk and retracted his wings so that they would be hidden from view. Moving with a slight limp, he ducked down an alley and disappeared.

"He's resourceful. I'll give him that," Johnny said as he watched his former boss vanish. "We should send a patrol to look for him before he hides away in one of his safe houses."

Denoda's sight was transfixed by the stunning spectacle of the mystical blade. "Nishimura is irrelevant now. Lieutenant, I want you to go to the lab and ensure everything is prepared for our Valkyrie guest. Then release the prisoner. Let Operation Balance of Power commence!"

"Sir, yes, sir." Lieutenant Run-Time nodded.

Ultra Valkyrie Rei entered the Tower of Observation on Volsogun and bowed. "Grand Valkyrie. I received your summons." Her eyes caught the swarm of creatures on a holographic map in front of Misa. Tiny dots fanned around Volsogun's atmosphere at an alarming rate. "What are those?"

"We can't place the species," Misa said in a grave tone.

Rei took a few steps forward to get a better look. "I recognize them. I destroyed three on Crondorone. Honestly, they look like manufactured hybrids to me."

Another Valkyrie entered the room. Her voice shook as she spoke. "Grand Valkyrie, we have verified that when the insectoids consume any material, they multiply."

"Incinerate on sight without hesitation!" Misa commanded. "Not one of those creatures can be allowed to make planetfall."

"Where did they come from?" one of the two Valkyries who stood beside Misa's side asked.

"Isn't it obvious?" Rei asked dryly. "They were delivered to us."

"But why?"

"The Valkyries of Volsogun have made many enemies over our long history. With your permission Grand Valkyrie, I'll face them head-on."

Misa nodded. "Do what you do best."

"By your command!" Utilizing her teleportation ability, Rei transported herself into the gulf of space above Volsogun. Her eyes widened at the sheer number of insectoids that littered the vast expanse around her. She had clearly underestimated their numbers. To make matters worse, she noticed a small collection of asteroids in the distance: a perfect place for those creatures to feed and breed.

Out of her peripheral vision, she noticed a squad of Valkyries fly toward her. "All of you, with me!" she snapped. "No one returns home until the enemy is dead!"

"Yes, Ultra Valkyrie!" they shouted.

"Let's engage!"

Nishimura entered an underground parking garage. He opened a hidden panel on one of the concrete walls and inputted a secret code. The adjacent wall slid open before him. He traveled down a long corridor that opened into a large room that resembled a ceremonial chamber. Within were many vehicles, a generous cache of weapons, and a small army of ninjas garbed in ceremonial tengu uniforms.

One of his ninjas rushed to his aid and performed a spell steeped in tengu mythology, which healed his injured leg.

He nodded with a sharp grunt and walked up to a dais located before a ceremonial altar. "My subjects, the Tengu Raid has been betrayed, and our vengeance will not go unseen. The enemy has stolen the sacred Omni-Wing and has attempted to take my life. They have failed. A failure that will cost them dearly. Today, we strike, we show no mercy, and we shall have our revenge!"

He raised his arms to his masked followers, who responded with a war chant.

In his military uniform, Johnny arrived at the secret lab utilized for Blood Dire Army research. He grinned from ear to ear and nodded to the ample number of armed soldiers posted around. "That's always a good sight: an armed killer posted in every corner. That's what I like to see! It's like a little piece of home on this Class Two."

An overweight scientist approached the lieutenant with a smile. "Lieutenant Run-Time. What a pleasant surprise."

"How ya doing"—he read the nameplate on his lab coat—"Finnley. The colonel asked me to come down and make sure everything is tip-top with the power relay."

"Yes, sir. We conducted a routine check this morning, and she's as steady as ever."

"Today has been full of nothing but good news. That's what I like to hear."

"Lieutenant, we're still lacking an adequate power source to open the—"

"Don't you worry about that." Johnny gave him a confident grin. "I'll worry about that."

"Yes, sir."

"She'll have enough juice to do her job and then some. I promise. Now, let's move on to item number two. How's our guest?"

"This way, sir." Finnley led him to a widescreen monitor mounted on the wall above a series of computer terminals. Once activated, the screen's image showed Devaston bound with high-grade steel chains. A sheath of magnetic energy encased him within a metal cell. Froth collected on the sides of the dimensional creature's mouth as it breathed heavily in a controlled rage.

Johnny noted a thin device, laced with wires, surgically attached to Devaston's head. "Man, that is one scary dude. He looks absolutely upset."

Even through a monitor, Finnley avoided making eye contact with the enraged beast. "I still don't understand how you found such a creature."

"Wasn't hard, really. The tough part was convincing Nishimura that I opened a portal to an abandoned dimension by accident. We let him loose as an operational test, and this guy didn't disappoint."

"I remember. The news coverage was quite extensive."

"The destruction was great until the space girl showed up and ruined everything."

"How exactly did she beat him? There's no report on the matter."

"That's just the thing, Finnley. She didn't. She built somewhat of a rapport with him and convinced him to stop."

"Convinced him? Just like that?"

"Yeah. But that's okay because we're going to need that special little bond they have."

"If she didn't beat him, then how was he captured?"

"After dealing with the space chick, he didn't return to his dimension. He was spotted in South America, so we sent a team down. It took us a while to find him, but when we did, we proceeded with the capture. We just couldn't let an asset like that run amok, could we?"

"But how did you do it? I mean...look at him."

"I'll admit that it wasn't easy. We couldn't match his raw power, but we had Blood Dire technology at our disposal. A few solid blasts from a psionic wave dampener, and he was as aggressive as a newborn. But enough about that. How's his behavioral modulator functioning?"

"The impulses are functioning at peak proficiency."

"Good. I want him in a blind berserker rage when he's released to the public."

"Although we attached the unit to his head, there's no guarantee that he won't rip it off once freed."

"At that point, it won't matter, as long as he attracts the space girl's attention." Johnny grinned. "You ready to do this?"

"Yes, sir."

"Then, my man, release the beast."

Finnley imputed a series of numbers into the terminal keyboard. Accepting the code, the computer illuminated a large red button beside the keyboard.

"Ain't making history fun?" Johnny chuckled.

The scientist pushed the button, which released Devaston's chains and opened the cage door. The creature unfurled his wings with a piercing scream and soared into the blue skies above. After gaining some distance from the lab, he looked beneath him and saw the congested city of Driven. He let out another horrific roar and dove downward.

Shooting from the sky, Reiko caught a truck before it struck a car and thrust it toward Devaston. She lanced forward, punching both Devaston and his multi-wheeled car weapon through a building. Letting momentum finish the attack, she stopped on the opposite side of the building. As he struck the pavement, his massive weapon landed on top of him. Screaming, he tossed the vehicle to the side and returned to his feet.

You were right about there being a familiar energy signature, Maru, Reiko reported to her servo-crystal. *It's Devaston!*

Why is he attacking the city? I thought he was your ally.

There's something attached to his head. She landed on a pile of rubble. "Devaston! Stop! It's me, Reiko!"

He grabbed a truck. With one fluid swing, he swatted at her, punching her back through the damaged building. She flew back onto the street where she had first encountered him and crashed onto a bed of parked cars. As she hit it, the metal buckled, and glass exploded from the windows.

She sat up and wiped glass fragments from her hair. *He doesn't recognize me, Maru. You should see his eyes... They're pure rage. That means I'll have to—*

Devaston drove his feet into her from above, sending her through a car. With a roar, he grabbed her by the leg and slammed her into the ground on both sides of himself like a doll. He tossed her limp body into the upper floor of an office building. She crashed through a window and landed on the center of the large table. The office workers scrambled away from her and fled. A few stayed to capture the moment on their phones.

She took a moment to stand. "Run!"

Devaston vaulted himself through the shattered remains of the bay window and landed with a sneer. With an incredible burst of speed, Reiko drove both of her fists into his chest and sent him into the side of another building. Amid dust and debris, he punched her. While she was momentarily stunned from the devastating blow, he grabbed her by the cape and threw her back into the street. She struck the pavement, sending fractures through it. He jumped from the damaged building and landed on her, pushing her further into the street. She didn't move. He threw his head back and released a thundering victory roar.

However, several missiles tore over the street and struck him, exploding on impact. He flew off the heroine and into a group of abandoned cars.

Reiko slowly gathered herself to her feet as a medi-suit landed beside her, stabilizing her wobbly stance.

"Daniel?" she weakly asked as her blurred vision returned to normal.

"I'm here," he said. "We've got to get you to safety before he gets back up."

"No." She shook her head. "He's a friend."

He looked toward where the creature still lays on the ground. "Are you crazy? You can barely stand!"

"He's hurting. I have to help him."

Devaston stood and released another ferocious roar.

"Time's up," Akeda said.

The creature ran toward the two, but a glowing laser struck him from above. The blast knocked him back into the same group of cars from which he came.

They looked up to see a large helicopter similar to the one that had dropped the robot soldiers months ago.

"Now, who are these guys?" Akeda asked.

The aerial vehicle then shot a series of different colored laser blasts. This time, they hit Akeda and Reiko, who both collapsed unconscious on the street.

Swirls of nonsensical figures and images plagued Reiko's field of vision. She blinked and shook her head until the blurs solidified. A smiling, green-haired man wore bulky white glasses and a scarlet uniform. Two other figures—a nervous man in a scarlet lab coat and a tall figure in a red military uniform trimmed with an exoskeleton—stood near him. The scientist left to adjust the sophisticated clamps that held her arms and legs in an X frame.

"What's going on?" she asked with a groggy voice.

The nervous man jumped. "Colonel Denoda. The subject is awake." He then scampered off like the coward he was.

"Justice Valkyrie Reiko." The colonel approached her with a smug grin.

Anger flushed her face as she recognized the uniform. "Blood Dire Army! Are we still on Earth?"

"Yes."

"Then what are you doing here?"

"Conquering Earth for General Gore's noble cause. I led an infiltration unit here to this quadrant roughly two years ago. Your assignment to this planet was key to that decision."

"I don't understand. How could you have known I was going to be assigned here?"

"The Valkyr Sisterhood's procedures are laughably predictable. Over the years, we have calculated how often a Valkyrie is dispatched and what planet she is assigned to. This Class Two had been vacant for years, so we knew a novice Valkyrie would be assigned. Your arrival was clockwork. It is now time to reap the rewards of my careful planning." He pointed to a large monitor. "One quadrant away, my *Doom Sake* carrier awaits. We have been lacking power to bring it here on schedule." He looked at her with a wide smile. "Until now. We'll project your natural energy source into space, creating a portal for my warship. Once opened, the glorious invasion of this planet will begin."

"Bleed me of my energy?" She huffed. "That seems to be the goal of every lunatic I run across."

"It is a task that should have already been accomplished. Some time ago, we hired an alien named Magdaglia to harness your energy, but he failed."

"Magdaglia?! You hired that butcher?"

"Yes. It was because of his failure that we had to construct all this. It set our timetable back, but I am pleased to report that we are now back on schedule."

"You sound like the last Blood Dire colonel I encountered."

"Oh?" He turned toward her. "And what happened to him?"

"He was killed by a monster he thought he could control."

On the damaged street, Akeda stirred. "What kind of laser weapon was that?" he groaned as he rose to his feet.

"Hey, man." A citizen moved closer to him. "You okay?"

Before he could answer, the monster stirred.

"Get out of here!" He waved his hand at the civilian. "Everybody, get back!" He activated the medi-suit's guns and missiles, ready for an oncoming fight. Even with an impressive alien arsenal at his disposal, he still had no idea how he would defeat this monster. If Reiko lost, what chance did he have?

The monster groaned and rubbed his head. As he did, the strange device on his head crumbled between his fingers. He stood and looked over at his armed opponent within the medi-suit. "What happened?"

"You can talk?" Akeda asked, baffled.

"You understood me, so I guess I can. What happened?"

"You don't remember?"

"Robots are annoying. I wouldn't ask if I knew."

185

"I'm not a robot. I'm a guy in a suit. You tore up the city fighting Reiko."

"Tasty cakes?" His eyes widened. "I fought my schnookums?!" His attention went to the broken metal pieces in his massive hand. "Wait... Humans told me to hate her... Manipulated me to kill her." He clenched his fists. "Where is she?!"

"A helicopter attacked us. They blasted us with some laser weapon thing. I assume they grabbed her while we were down."

"Are you her ally?"

"Yeah, I am."

"You have a name, guy in a suit?"

"Um... Call me... Extra Armor. You?"

"Devaston. You will have a chance to make good use of your weapons, Extra Armor. I will find her, and I will make her captors pay! You will be given the honor of sharing my revenge!"

Akeda sighed. "Lucky me."

Colonel Denoda paced back and forth behind Reiko like a caged animal.

Johnny's voice broke the deafening silence as he entered the room. "Colonel, we've just received contact from the carrier. It's in position and waiting for the portal to open."

Denoda lifted The Omni-Wing with a smile. "Then let us not delay any further. For the blood that was spilled!" He thrust the mystical blade into Reiko's back, driving it through her heart.

As she released an agonizing scream, the energy endowed by The Guiding Source shot out of her chest and into the machine before her. Her eyes closed as The Omni-Wing absorbed the last of her power.

Denoda, Finnley, and Johnny watched in amazement as the Valkyrie's energy collected within the machine grew. A lab wall slid open, allowing the device to fire a beam of radiant light into the atmosphere above the Pacific Ocean. The laser ripped a gigantic hole in space, creating a portal wide enough for the colonel's carrier to cross through.

"Look at that, boss!" Johnny exploded as the tip of *Doom Sake* glided through the portal. "You did it! This planet is ours!"

Denoda grinned. "Operation Balance of Power has been a success!"

From downtown, Akeda, along with other curious civilians, watched in horror as a large warship entered the clear skies. "What's happening?" he asked.

"The origin of the light beam!" Devaston barked. "That is where we'll go! Hopefully, there will be someone to kill!"

Denoda watched as his ship made it through the portal. After it passed, the portal faded. He handed The Omni-Wing to Johnny and turned to Finnley. "Why did it close so soon? I had support ships in tow."

"I'm sorry, Colonel." The scientist checked his readings. "The power is exhausted. The Valkyrie's energy burned up much faster than predicted."

"I see. Powerful but fast burning. Not to worry. My carrier still has enough firepower to support a successful offensive. Lieutenant Run-Time, gather our ground forces and then await my command."

"Yes, sir," Johnny said. "What do you want done with the Valkyrie?"

Denoda glanced at Reiko's motionless body. "It's of no further use. Dispose of it." He pushed a button on his exo-suit and teleported out of the room with a bright flare of energy.

The lab's far wall exploded with a thunderous fury, sending debris and Blood Dire soldiers flying. Nishimura's tengu ninjas filtered into the lab within a cloud of smoke and engaged.

Nishimura himself, now garbed in the dark attire of a shadow warrior, severed Finnley's head from his neck with one fluid slice of his katana. The dead scientist collapsed onto the floor. Johnny whipped out his pistol and attempted to shoot him, but his blade was faster. He sliced off the hand that held the gun. As Johnny shrieked in agony, he dropped The Omni-Wing, which Nishimura retrieved.

Nishimura noticed machinery implanted within Johnny's arm, the telltale sign of cyborg enhancements. He paid it no mind as vengeance guided him to strike again. This time, he sliced open Johnny's bowels, which gushed out onto the floor before him.

Johnny fell back against some computer equipment and slid onto the floor, clutching his open stomach with his remaining hand. "I knew you'd take...personally. You never had a...sense of humor. Later, boss." He exposed a small spherical bomb within his free hand and pushed its scarlet button.

The lab exploded in a massive dome of plasma energy.

Maru sailed back and forth in the dimensional home, confused by the sudden cancellation of Reiko's mental link. "This isn't like her at all..." It paused. "Perhaps something— Wait."

A faint surge of power grew with intensity. Its energy signature wasn't familiar.

"Where is this power coming from?"

Within the lab's ruins, a wall of debris exploded off Reiko's standing figure. Her eyes opened as she drew in a deep breath of musty air. She gripped her fists as fear and rage coursed through her. A red gash crossed over her heart. She placed her hand over the wound, and it sealed with a soft glow. Her anger subsided as a faint voice spoke in her head.

Reiko, is that you?

Yes, Maru. It's me.

Is it really you?

Of course.

This power you're emanating... You shouldn't be able to do that. What happened?

Reiko looked up into the sky and saw a massive military vessel hanging in the air. *Maru, I have to go. Earth is under threat, and I must get to work.*

In the sewers that ran under the lab, Nishimura lifted himself out of a blanket of twisted metal and rubble. Bloodied but standing, the yakuza boss looked at The Omni-Wing, which he clutched in his grasp. He laughed as a drop of blood ran off his chin and fell into the water at his feet.

"Blood. Blood means life. I am alive. To thrive in the shadows. This world must believe I am dead." He burst into a fit of echoing maniacal laughter. "Ryuhei Nishimura is dead, and the Tengu Raid with him! But I shall start anew. I will resurrect my Tengu Raid as an army, and they will hail me as their king!

"The shadows are my territory! Blood is my currency! Dread this day, world, for a new era has begun! The Tengu King is born!"

As Reiko prepared to leave for the spacecraft, Akeda and Devaston landed in the destroyed lab.

Once Akeda's feet touched down, he scooped Reiko up in his arms and held her. "You're okay! I thought the worst had happened."

She closed her eyes and enjoyed the embrace, even though it was delivered through a cold metallic shell. "I'm okay."

"Hey, guy in a suit, hands off my schnookums!" Devaston barked.

"Devaston." She moved away from Akeda and held the jealous creature's hand. "Are you okay?"

"Don't worry about me. Sorry if I attacked you. Humans made me do it. Honest!"

She smiled. "I know you wouldn't do anything to hurt me."

"I hope the apologies are over because we have huge problems," Akeda interjected. "It looks like smaller ships are detaching from the main one."

She watched the smaller vessels filter into the sky. "They're called the Blood Dire Army."

"What do they want?"

"They're a military force here to conquer Earth. That large craft is one of their flagships, and I'm guessing the smaller ones are troop transports."

"Great." The detective sighed. "So, what's the plan?"

"See if you can stop the transports. I'll attack the main ship."

"By yourself?! Reiko, forgive me for saying this, but you look like you're about to collapse at any second."

"There's no time to argue, Daniel. Stop those transports."

"Sounds like fun to me!" Devaston shouted. "Come on, guy in a suit. Let's grab some sky!"

Reiko lifted herself onto her tiptoes and kissed Akeda's helmet on its cheek. "I'll see you soon." Not delaying another moment, she burst into the endless blue.

Keanid turned away from Varservious.

Abe's voice continued to ring through her communicator. "Keanid, can you hear me? Keanid!"

"Yeah, I hear you. What's up?"

"Where are you?"

"I'm underwater. But I'm in a pocket of air, so I can talk. What's going on? Is this about the house?"

"The house? No! That's all under control. Listen. A freakin' spaceship came out of nowhere, and it's dropping smaller ships. Your caped friend and that demon from hell that showed up a few months back duked it out downtown, tearing everything apart in the process. Driven is in complete chaos right now."

She shuddered. "That demon showed back up? Is Reiko in trouble?"

"Honey, right now, it looks like we're all in trouble. If you're safe where you are, stay there! I love you, kiddo."

"Love you, too," she faintly said. With a face wrought with concern, she turned to her birth father. "I don't know what's going on up there, but could you help me?"

"What happens with the surfacers is of no concern to me. My loyalty is to our people."

"That's where you're wrong!" she snapped. "You want to find a peaceful place for our people? This is how you do it. On this planet, the sea and the land go hand in hand. The sea will know no peace if the land knows chaos."

"You have compassion for the surfacers. I can see it in your eyes."

"I have compassion for all life, land or sea."

"You are the bridge I could never be." Varservious stood from his throne, taking his trident in his clawed grasp. "Take me to this chaos."

Akeda spun in the air as he dodged several missiles fired from one of the transport ships. He returned a hail of laser fire while targeting the engines, which exploded with a direct hit. He smiled. "This targeting system is no joke!"

Devaston circled behind a transport, which he grabbed and sent it slamming into another. He laughed as he relished an almost deafening yet satisfying explosion.

Colonel Denoda paced, wearing a displeased expression.

On the flagship's bridge, one operator turned from his scanner to address the colonel. "Sir, the transports are under attack. Three have already been destroyed."

"Visual!"

A three-dimensional holographic image opened before the angered colonel. A figure in a medi-suit and Devaston made quick work of his unprepared transports.

"All in vain," he growled through clenched teeth. "Relieve the sky of their presence! Open fire!"

The laser turrets along the ship's exterior burst forth a curtain of searing fire at the airborne heroes. In response, the two flew away, dodging the hail of laser fire. Several shots struck the populated streets of Driven.

"Sir, we have incoming!" the controller said. "South! Southwest!"

Denoda looked out of one of the bridge's windows to see Reiko flying straight for the ship. "Impossible! She's dead! I killed her!" He stared in disbelief. "Destroy that Valkyrie!"

Several of the ship's turrets pivoted, now aiming at the approaching heroine. They spewed their deadly projectiles, which all missed their fast-moving target.

Reiko smashed through the main bridge's window and slammed her clenched fists into Denoda, driving him into a wall. She punched her enemy several times before launching him into a terminal display. The terminal exploded in a cloud of smoke and flames.

As she turned, the colonel reappeared behind her and gripped her by her throat, using his augmented strength to choke her. She grabbed his arms and shot upward, slamming him into the ceiling. Once his grip loosened, she turned and drove her fist into his face, sending him out of the bridge's broken window and tumbling onto the ship's exterior. His boots magnetized, allowing him to get a stable footing as he faced her. She hovered out of the bridge and landed in front of her foe.

The wind whipped around them. The sky overhead flashed with lightning and cracked with thunder. Ominous clouds formed a canopy of darkness. Reiko noticed several waterspouts forming below, grabbing a few troop transports and slamming them into the violent waters. She could barely make out a tall figure holding a trident while riding the unpredictable waves.

"He's helping us," Reiko whispered. "Good job, Keanid."

"You're just as resilient as the rest of your damned species!" Denoda shouted. "A quality I underestimated. Do you think you can stop me? What chance does a novice Valkyrie have against a Blood Dire officer?!"

She lifted her fists before her. "I've done it before."

She bolted toward her enemy, and the two traded blows. His speed matched hers as he punched her, sending her stumbling back. He tackled her, shooting them both back into the bridge and out of the slamming rain. With the bridge evacuated, both combatants continued their fight unimpeded.

Denoda grabbed her fist mid-strike and punched her into several terminals. He jumped by her side and yanked her from the floor. "Time to die!" Once again, he gripped her neck and squeezed.

With her face turning red, she grabbed both of his wrists and, drawing upon the last of her strength, twisted his arms until both echoed a loud snap.

He dropped the gasping heroine as he stumbled back, screaming. Both of his arms dangled at the elbows. The exoskeleton that supported his arms was broken as well. "How?!" he shouted. "How could you be this strong?!"

She coughed as she rubbed her aching neck. His question echoed through her head, a question she had no answer for. All she had now was a purpose: protect Earth. She straightened herself, glaring at her opponent. "I'm a Justice Valkyrie, and this world is under my protection!"

She flew into him, knocking him out of the bridge. His body tumbled into the distance over the black waters as she sailed up further into the heavens.

As lightning flashed around her, the Valkyrie turned to *Doom Sake* and laced her gloved fingers together. She channeled her energy into her hands, which burned. Fighting through an almost unbearable strain, she shot a wide scarlet beam from her joined hands and guided it to slice through the entire carrier, first vertically and then horizontally. The ship exploded on all sides as it broke up in the air. Each severed fragment collapsed from the sky and plummeted into the turbulent sea below.

Reiko remained still. Her arms dangled by her sides. Exhaustion overtook her, but she knew she had to continue to fight. The possibility of Blood Dire soldiers making landfall was all too real.

In the space surrounding Volsogun, Rei and the other Valkyries were close to ending their campaign of decimating the insectoid threat before they reached the planet's atmosphere.

Rei, Misa said telepathically, *I hear you and the Valkyries are having great success.*

Affirmative. It shouldn't be long now before the threat is contained.

Good. I have another mission for you.

Go ahead.

We have received a distress signal from Dev-Sravan. Ships have been attacked by the same insectoid creatures that attacked us. They have set up a defensive perimeter around their planet, but it looks like it's only a matter of time before it's breached. I need you to go there and stop the threat.

Rei released a burning bolt of energy across the void, incinerating hundreds of insectoid creatures. A sharp pain stabbed her right arm as a shaft of light broke forth from a fissure that opened in her arm. She paused and looked at the fresh injury with horror.

Rei, can you hear me? Are you okay?

I'm fine. She placed her other hand over the fissure and sealed it shut. *Dev-Sravan. I'll be there soon.*

I will join you as soon as we liberate Volsogun.

Right. She looked at her arm and clenched her teeth as anger swelled within her.

Reiko watched as the last flaming remains of the *Doom Sake* disappeared beneath the ocean's waves. Satisfied that the threat of the carrier had been destroyed, she flew toward the land. There, from a distance, she saw Daniel, Devaston, and Keanid fighting the last of the Blood Dire troops. Blood Water, still standing on the waves, made sure no other crafts could threaten the land.

She smiled. If such a strange group of heroes could band together for the common good, she is only one of many protectors. The thought gave her much comfort. Though her assignment of protecting the world was a monumental task, she didn't have to do it alone.

As she drew closer to the heroes, another figure caught her eye. The figure, clad in black body armor, stood on top of a smoldering rain-soaked building. She soared toward the figure.

"Ultra Valkyrie Rei." Reiko attempted to sound more confident than she felt. "What brings you here?"

Rei grasped both sides of her helmet and removed it. As the Ultra Valkyrie's silver locks fell to her shoulders, Reiko's mouth dropped. Her face was identical to Reiko's, save for a scar that ran across the bridge of her nose.

She held her helmet at her side and gazed at Reiko with a grave expression. "It's time."

CENTER OF THE STORM

T HE PERFECT DAY stretched around Reina and Nalthean Dregart, her new husband. Blinding sunrays cradled the blue sky. The meadow relinquished a sweet fragrance of budding new life. Reina, traveling on horseback, drew in the air with a smile. Nalthean rode his horse bedside hers. He glanced over at his statuesque bride sporting her braided black locks. Their horses climbed a vista and paused, giving the two a chance to take in the breathtaking valley that sprawled beneath the hill.

"And there it is." He grinned. "The Valley of Ecera. As beautiful as its name."

"I've never seen it before. It's gorgeous."

"It's gorgeous? That's all you can say? Look at the unspoiled lands and the crystal-clear waters and smell that clean scent of morning."

"It looks like the whole valley was painted by a master's hand." She sighed. "I'd say it's almost as beautiful as Deeta-Toada. It's a small planet with pink skies and purple oceans located just outside the Nodrestin Cluster."

"More tales of distant stars? I have married an odd one indeed."

Within Reina's mind, Remus' voice emerged. *Excuse me. I know now is not the best time, but I have detected a threat near Cove Falls.*

Any allies in the vicinity?

None, I'm afraid.

Very well. I'll be there shortly. Reina turned to her husband, who was still captivated by the scenery. "I have to adhere to the Warrior's Code. I shall return shortly, my love."

Nalthean simply nodded. "I'll be waiting."

She soared off the back of her horse and into the blue. She shot over the green realm and flew for her destination. Flying closer to the small town of Cove Falls, she witnessed an army of orcs advancing from the south. Unfortunately, their champion, a ten-foot troll, rallied them forth with the wave of an enormous spiked club and guttural commands.

"This must be that new group from Tralor Marsh that I've heard about," she said. "I suppose it's time I introduced myself."

She burst downward, planting her fists into the champion's chest and sending the massive monster into a stone wall that surrounded the town. As the orcish archers nocked their arrows, she removed her shield from her back. The orc's arrows snapped against her shield as she leaped into the air and slammed her fist into the earth before them. A major shockwave created by the impact carried the orcish warriors through the air. She unsheathed her sword and engaged the few still standing. Her skillful maneuvers proved deadly as she hacked down her clumsy opponents. Back on his large, clawed feet, the champion attempted to slam her with his club, but she dodged the cumbersome attack. She sheathed her blade and flew upward, delivering a devastating uppercut to her giant opponent. The monster landed somewhere in the ocean.

Behind her, the townspeople cheered her victory. She rested her feet on the green earth and waved at the cheering crowd. "You're safe now," she assured with a warm smile. "They won't attempt to expand their territory in this direction anytime soon."

I'm sorry to intrude again, Reina, Remus said in her mind, *but an Ultra Valkyrie is here to see you.*

Her smile dissolved. *I'll be there.* Closing her eyes, she used her teleportation powers and vanished from Cove Falls in a flash of light. A second later, she appeared in her dimensional home.

Standing before her was Rei with her helmet in her hand. She looked upon the Ultra Valkyrie's face, which matched her own. "It's time," she said, devoid of emotion.

Reina nodded as she moved to a statue. "It's funny." She removed her shield and sword and placed them on the figure. "I've been thinking a lot about you and me recently. There are so many stars out there, so much life. I know you used to spend a lot of time counting them."

"I don't count the stars anymore. They're too many."

Reina turned to her and looked into her blue eyes. "Maybe you should start again, and when you do, count a few for me." She looked over to her servo-crystal. "Remus, when I leave, lock the house and wait for me."

"I will, Reina."

She wiped away a single tear that ran from her eye. "Okay. I'm ready."

Reiko trailed behind Rei as they walked into her dimensional home.

"Reiko, I didn't know we were having guests." Maru drifted toward the visitor. It stopped when it recognized the guest's identity. "Oh my. It's Ultra Valkyrie Rei." Its voice dropped. "Wait. Why does she look like you, only taller?"

"I'm confused too, Maru," Reiko said.

"Quiet," the Ultra Valkyrie barked. "A millennia ago, it was decided that because of the increasing threats across the galaxy, prolonging the lives of the Ultra Valkyries and the Grand Valkyrie herself would be beneficial. To do that, the creation of genetic clones was authorized using Turexian technology. While allowed to live their own lives, they could generate energy independent of their host, which could be absorbed, if needed, to prolong her own life. Usually, a maximum of five clones were made from a single host. My case was different. There were six: Reign, Reiley, Reiona, Reisha, Reina, and you, Reiko."

"That explains why you can tap into a power that exceeds that of a normal Justice Valkyrie," Maru stated. "A small portion of Ultra Valkyrie Rei lies dormant within you."

Color drained from Reiko's face. "I didn't pass the trials, did I?"

"No. Of course, you didn't. Your peers outperformed you in every way. Nevertheless, Misa granted you the power of a Justice Valkyrie and sent you into the field in case I needed you as a power reserve."

"That's why you saved me from Solesta. Saving me was saving yourself." She paused, reading Rei's face. "You're dying, aren't you? And it's time to recharge."

"I must protest!" Maru exploded. "Reiko is a Justice Valkyrie of Volsogun, not a battery for you to restore yourself!"

"Be silent, servo-crystal! You don't have a say in the arrangement with my clone. You don't have a life."

"Maybe not, but I have a name. It's Maru! A name Reiko gave me. That's more than you ever gave her!"

"They were right," Reiko muttered as a tear trickled down her cheek. "We are vampires."

"Only to each other," Rei said. "Dev-Sravan is under attack, and I must aid them. To do that—"

"You have to recharge. Was this the Grand Matriarch's idea for us from the very beginning?"

"No, it wasn't. She was better than any of us. I know this revelation comes as a shock, but now you know why I'm the last Ultra Valkyrie."

"The others ran out of clones to absorb, and they passed away. I'm your last energy reserve, and I'm going to die. Just like my clone sisters before me."

Rei slapped her. "Wake up! Do you realize how many lives I've saved?!"

"No." Tears welled up in Reiko's eyes as she touched her red cheek. "Only those you took. All my clone sisters had lives of their own! We had our own experiences! Reina was married!"

Rei looked away. "You don't understand!"

"Yes, I do! The time I have been here on this planet—all my successes and failures—is mine! I have friends! I'm in love! This isn't some clone talking. This is who I am! You took that from them, and you're going to take it from me."

Silent, Rei paused and then put on her helmet. "Look after Earth," she whispered as she walked to the door.

"You're not going to survive, are you? This is a battle you can't win, and you know it."

Refusing to look back, the Ultra Valkyrie left her dimensional home.

A sickly quiet fell.

"I don't know what to say," Maru said after a while. "I... Reiko, we're getting a message."

A life-sized holographic image of Grand Valkyrie Misa appeared in the center of the room. "Reiko, is Rei there?"

"No," she said, repulsed by the sight of her leader. "She left for Dev-Sravan."

"I fear she may need your help."

She nodded without making eye contact.

"You are a good Justice Valkyrie, Reiko. Compassionate and loyal. Now, do your duty to Volsogun and go assist Ultra Valkyrie Rei."

The betrayal cut through her. As the image faded, Reiko cried with a rush of painful tears.

"You know what she means, Reiko," Maru said. "Don't go."

"Don't you see, Maru? I have to. A whole planet is at stake! Millions of lives are counting on her. I can't be selfish. I may have failed the trials, but I am still a Justice Valkyrie." She wiped fresh tears from her face and walked toward the door. "To the end."

"Reiko?"

Standing in the doorway, she turned toward her friend and offered a weak smile. "Maru, when I leave, lock the house and wait for me." With that, she soared out of the house and through sheets of rain, no doubt caused by Blood Water's weather interference. In flight, she homed in on the communication crystal she gave Akeda and flew to its location.

Within minutes, her feet landed on the rain-soaked side street outside his small house. It wasn't large enough for a family but perfect for a single or a couple.

The door flung open, and Daniel stepped out. "Reiko! Everyone has been worried about you! Where have you been?" His questions ceased when he saw the sorrow weighing on her face. His voice dropped. "Reiko?"

She rushed up to him and hugged him tightly. "I love you!" she said, trying her best to fight back her oncoming tears.

He wrapped his arms around her. She broke the embrace and took a few steps back, putting space between them. Forcing a smile on her rain-soaked face, she looked at him one last time before bolting into the gray sky.

She tore through the atmosphere and into the open vacuum of space. As she flew away from her assignment world, she released an agonizing scream and left a trail of crystallized tears in her wake.

Torlon, the noble commander of the *Hyratha*, assessed the vast cloud of insectoids that drifted closer to Dev-Sravan. He glanced over at the other military crafts in orbit, which were battling the mysterious invaders. A multitude of laser cannon shots lit up the black void. "Status report!"

Gernath, the vice commander, approached his superior with haste. "Sir, we were just informed that two warships have been consumed, and the enemies are multiplying!"

"Are all armaments ready to concentrate their fire on the main body?"

"Yes, sir!

"Then fire!"

The *Hyratha* aimed her exterior cannons and fired a magnificent barrage of destructive lasers into a massive grouping of insectoids. Other than incinerating several pockets, the attack had little effect on the enemy's advancement.

"Sir," Gernath cried. "Seven percent success! We're getting an incoming message from the commander of the *Kledma*."

"Patch it through!"

Appearing as a holographic image, the commander's face was wrought with worry. "To all active ships, this is Commander Jyrek of the *Kledma*. Our hull has been compromised, and the enemy has boarded our vessel. We won't last much longer. We believe they have breached our engines and—"

In the distance, the *Kledma* exploded into a giant ball of fire, releasing a shockwave that rocked all other war vessels in the vicinity.

"Damn it!" Torlon spat. "Prepare all cannons to fire again!" He moved back to the window and saw several swaths of insectoids burn and vanish from existence. "Gernath! Something is happening outside."

The vice commander rushed to the window to witness a multitude of searing beams fan through the insectoid army, incinerating all they touched. "Is that another fleet?"

"No," Torlon whispered as he watched a glowing warrior in sleek black armor stand on a large fragment from the *Kledma*. "The Valkyries have arrived."

Rei charged her hands and blasted several bolts that equaled the same devastating power as a fleet of starfighters through the oncoming insectoid army. She winced as a fissure opened on her leg and bled light. Ignoring it, she continued to pour out a series of destructive laser attacks.

Following the Ultra Valkyrie's lead, the other fleet warships followed suit to create a strong perimeter, unleashing their arsenal at the insectoid threat.

A few more minor fissures opened on Rei's skin. She sent another series of blasts into a massive cloud of enemies. The attack's strain made her recoil as her helmet cracked over her right eye and broke into pieces, freeing her silver hair. With many enemies remaining, she knew it was time for her last stand. A conclusion she had no time to lament.

She postured herself for a final maneuver stance she named The Final Valhalla, a technique designed as a last effort, a dying move to utterly destroy her opponent. Such a time had arrived.

She engulfed herself with a sphere of blinding, searing energy. She fought back the pain as several cracks broke her skin. Attracted by the engrossing light, the sea of insectoids flew toward her. Knowing she only had seconds left, she raised her hands and screamed at the oncoming army. Before she released her final blow, she noticed Reiko tearing through space to reach her. Once close, the novice Valkyrie reached out and laced her fingers together with hers.

Now an extension of the Ultra Valkyrie's massive power, Reiko screamed as raw energy tore through her.

A gigantic explosion erupted where the two Valkyries once were, unleashing a massive wave of energy. It incinerated all the insectoids in the sector. The warships rocked once again as the power sent a shockwave above Dev-Sravan.

In a moment, it was all over. The space was calm above the planet.

Appearing in a burst of light, Grand Valkyrie Misa, with two Valkyrie escorts, appeared over the planet. She noticed the charred remains of the destroyed battleship hovering within view. But no Rei. "Secure the ships and make sure the planet is safe," she commanded her subjects.

As the two flew off, she soared toward the drifting wreckage. Moving through the debris and drifting bodies, she saw a woman crouched on a floating part of a warship. Energy crackled across the figure's form. Her long silver hair draped across her flowing black cape.

Washed with relief, Misa flew and landed behind her. "Rei, you survived!" She smiled as the woman raised to her feet and clenched her fists. "I'm relieved to see your mission was a success."

Much shorter than Rei, the woman turned to Misa and glared at her with piercing blue eyes. No scar trailed across the bridge of her nose. "Call me Reiko."

With an explosion of speed, Reiko slammed her fists into Misa. She struck her with mighty blows that produced a shockwave with each devastating impact. While Misa tumbled through the void, she continued her onslaught by projecting three other versions of herself. Each blasted Misa with burning lasers from their closed fists. The four joined back together and struck Misa with both fists, sending her shooting like a falling star. She crashed onto the lush surface of a green planet.

Misa's impact punched a crater into the surface. Slowly, she crawled from the hole only to see Reiko flying at her at a blinding speed. With a fist blazing with power, Reiko punched her through one of the mountains that stood several miles away. Misa skipped across the surface, along with a collection of boulders and other debris until they all eventually stopped on a bed of grass.

Reiko landed before her, slamming her glowing fist into the earth. The impact shook the ground, along with the trees. The sediment, along with the mountain fragments, lifted and floated around her. "You knew!" Reiko screamed. "You knew the whole time!"

"Rei..." Misa stumbled to her feet. "What happened to you?"

"My name is Reiko! Instead of consuming me, she gave me her power!"

Disbelief struck the Grand Valkyrie. "Why would she do something so stupid?"

"She didn't kill them. She kept them alive in her, never to be forgotten. That's why she spared me. She couldn't do it anymore. She hated what she had become! She hated you!"

"All of Rei's power cannot be contained in a clone body. It's simply too much. It will kill you."

"That's my problem then, isn't it?" Reiko stared into Misa's hazel eyes. "Listen carefully. I'm going back to Earth. My new home. If I ever see you or any of your Valkyries anywhere near it, I'll kill you!"

Misa stayed silent as Reiko shot off at the speed of light. She cast her gaze from the sky to the torn ground around her. "Rei's...gone. Now I am truly alone."

Once Reiko reached Earth's atmosphere, a sharp pain stabbed through her chest. She paused her flight as she buckled. When the pain subsided, she regained her composure. She flew over the planet's blue surface and coasted through Driven's light drizzle. Reaching Akeda's home again, the exhausted Valkyrie landed, surprised to see him still standing outside on the front porch.

"Reiko?" He rushed to her as she fell.

The strength to stay awake had left her. He scooped her up and carried her inside.

Reiko stirred on a couch. Her blue eyes fluttered open. While not recognizing where she was, she struggled to stand. "Ow." Every muscle in her body ached, but she managed.

She examined the modest living room, noting a full bookcase on one wall and sparse decorations. As she took in her surroundings, she noticed long black hair that reached the center of her back. She also wore her white robe once again. "This can't be right." She ran her hand through her hair. "Shoulder length. I like shoulder length." She attempted to shift the sub-matter, but that ability did not respond. "Why can't I change?" Through her confusion, she noticed a few pieces of luggage standing by the main door. "Was I coming or going?"

Akeda entered from a hallway and smiled when he saw her. He embraced her and kissed her forehead. "Last night, it was silver, and now it's black. And it's long. Can't you make up your mind?"

Saying nothing, she held him with all her strength as tears formed in her eyes.

"It's okay," he said gently. "You're safe now."

She nodded with her face pressed tight into his chest. "I know."

"Listen, I don't know exactly what's been going on with you, but things are getting too crazy here. I think we need to take a vacation for a while. I already called into work and told them that I'm taking a leave of absence."

She looked up at him, confused. "Where are we going?"

"Anywhere. Come on."

"I can't change my clothes, and I don't think I can walk. I don't know what's happening to me."

"It's okay. We'll figure it out. Let me help you into the car."

He wrapped his arm around her and helped her walk outside. Under the light drizzle, he got her into his car and reclined the seat, so she could rest. She watched the rain collect on the windows as he toiled to place all his luggage in the vehicle. Once accomplished, he got in, started the car, and drove toward Driven.

She placed her hand on the passenger window and traced several trails that streaked across its exterior surface with her finger. "I don't count the stars anymore. There are too many."

"Yeah. I remember you saying that at Kainoa's house," he said as he turned the radio to his favorite jazz station.

Reiko, seemingly in another world, watched the city as it scrolled past the window. "Rei died. She died, but she spared me. Just like she spared my sisters within herself. She gave them to me. Because she trusted me. She knew what I would do."

"Who died?" He merged onto the highway. "And what sisters? What do you mean?"

She smiled as she looked at the gray sky above. "She knew I would bring them back."

www.ingramcontent.com/pod-product-compliance
Lightning Source LLC
Chambersburg PA
CBHW072056170626
46813CB00004B/1372